Heroes of the Middle Ages

Natalie Segal

Library of Congress Control Number: 2026912140

Contents

Dedication

For the Stone Coast Sisters, who were the first to tell me I could write.

For Uncle Hy, whose gift of a book started it all.

Acknowledgment

Nothing happens without help and encouragement. So many teachers like Suzanne Strempek Shea, who saw something in my writing, and C. Flanagan Flynn, who read many drafts of this book and always had an incisive critique, kept me writing when I would have stopped.

The Stone Coast sisters, especially Darlene, pushed one another, laughed and cried together, and we got through.

And my writers group, Carmen, Aubrey, Roberta, and Anita—they listened to the first draft, commented on the second draft—I'm surprised they kept listening, there were so many drafts.

My daughters had such wells of patience when I was learning to tell stories. Thanks to Julia and Dayva, who let me learn, and thanks to everyone else who helped me and encouraged me along the way. I could not have done this without them.

About the Author

Natalie Segal is a late-blooming writer who used to work as a technical writer and college teacher of first-year composition and technical writing. She's helped to raise two daughters and a couple of cats, gone to school a lot, and now she writes contemporary fantasy (with haiku and other poetry on the side). She loves to dance (rumba, foxtrot, East Coast swing), watch birds, and write. She's published short stories and haiku. This book is her first novel.

Chapter 1
Saturday

No murder scene is easy to look at, but this one, this impossibly inside-out body, was as bad as the worst Miriam had ever seen. Worse than the boy whose uncle had used a machete to teach him not to lie, as bad as the other inside-out body six years ago.

As she scanned the room, Miriam had to hold her breath despite the mask covering her nose and mouth and the Noxzema smeared under her nose. At least the walls were free of spatter, and the large panes of the floor-to-ceiling windows were clear, letting sunlight stream into the room unimpeded. The floor offered an entirely different picture.

Highly polished narrow oak boards provided a fine background for the large pentagram inside the circle, both painted in what looked like white enamel, with black candles at the points where the star met the circle. Just like the last one.

The body, the anatomy lesson, sprawled across the center of the circle. One outflung arm had knocked over a candle. Blood and black wax congealed in a small splotch on the floor outside the circle.

Thank God she didn't have to take samples or photographs or get closer to that *thing*. She knew, she *knew* that it had been a human being, but it no longer resembled anything living. In just her quick scan, she had seen the heart and maybe the stomach and some intestine. She knew.

She couldn't hold her breath anymore, so she turned away to gasp, caught the sharp tang of blood, shit, and sulfur, and felt the heat rush up her neck and over her face and ears, because of strong emotion, she knew, before she stalked down the hall to the kitchen where everyone else had taken refuge. Lieutenant Winewski, a couple of young guys in sports jackets she didn't know, several guys in uniform she did know, and Downie, her former partner, *current partner?* —her colleague in Cold Case.

The tallest man in the room, in great shape despite being 56 years old, looked good with that buzz cut, *and why the hell did she care how he looked?* Here came the heat again; every guy in the room would attribute the red face to the mask, which had to come off *now*.

After her first gasp for air, she breathed deeply and accepted a tissue from one of the uniforms, Ahern, to wipe the Noxzema from under her nose. She kept the blue vinyl gloves on.

"Nothing stops that stink," she said, dropping mask and tissue into the bag Ahern held out for her. "Thanks."

"Miriam Fine," Winewski said. "Meet John Prentice and Allan Garber. They caught the call."

They were the two suits she didn't know. Prentice looked like a young Bruce Willis with a lot more hair, and Garber looked like the stereotypical Aryan youth, tall, blond, crew cut, brilliant blue eyes, broad shoulders. "That explains why *they're* here. But why am I here, Mike? This isn't a cold case."

Winewski shrugged. "But the one from six years ago is."

Downie snorted. "The Feds took that one."

"And got nowhere," Miriam finished for him. "No DNA other than the dead guy's, and no matches for him. No trace of the killer, none."

"And yet, here we are again," Winewski said. "Do me a favor: Compare and contrast."

Miriam eyed Downie, who raised one shoulder and let it drop, the go-ahead.

"Okay," Miriam said. "Last time it was a house, this time it's an apartment. Both are high-end residences, both vacant, both recently painted, cleaned, and ready for sale. The body. The bodies," she corrected, "are both literally inside out, not simply flayed?" Had she seriously just said "simply flayed"? She had. It was that kind of case.

"The skin is on the inside, organs and so on are on the outside. Assuming the autopsy on this one confirms that." And it would. She knew it would. She'd looked long enough to know that. "The last one, six years ago, the fingertips had been burned off, so no prints, and the teeth and jaw had been smashed."

"Thorough," someone said.

"Very." She breathed. "That guy was never identified, by the way. There is one big difference: This scene is,"—she looked at Downie—"would you say clean?"

He nodded.

She repeated the word. "Last time, there was blood everywhere. I mean, on the walls, the ceiling, in pools on the floor." She swept an arm from floor to wall to ceiling. "Everywhere. Button figured it was most of the guy's blood.

Exsanguinated, he said. If the vic hadn't died from the trauma of being turned inside out, he would have died from loss of blood."

Grimacing, she turned to Winewski. "The Feds will take this one, too."

"We'll work it till they do."

She wouldn't say so out loud, but she couldn't wait for the Feds to take over. She'd hated the damned impossible body last time, and she hated this one and all the signs of witchcraft. Magic—"I forgot to say. The family that owned the house where the other body was found? They brought in a priest to, I don't know, cleanse the place? He said it was black magic." Which she did *not* want to believe in, but how could you argue with an inside-out body?

"You don't believe in that shit," Garber said.

Shrugging, Miriam let her eyes wander to calm herself down. The kitchen, like Cousin Hannah's, was all dark cabinetry, stainless steel appliances, granite countertops, recessed lighting —the one room probably worth more than all of Miriam's possessions, she suspected, also like Cousin Hannah's kitchen.

Speaking of Hannah, "You know," she said to Downie, "Hannah's husband, David, remember? Before they were married, he lived in this building. Third floor." One floor down from the murder scene. "The engagement party was held in his apartment." She'd enjoyed that party, appreciating the luxury without wanting it. Too cold for her.

As if no one else were in the room, Downie squinted at her. "The house where the other body was found, that was next door to the one you lived in just after you graduated from UConn, wasn't it?"

Oh, but he had a good memory, and why did he remember that about her? "Coincidence?" She didn't believe in coincidence, and neither did he, but she could hope out loud.

"Unlikely," he said.

"But then, if the locations are related to me and at least one of my cousins…"

"And they're not current locations, Mir," Downie said. "They're older." Someone else started to say something, but Downie stopped whoever it was with a raised finger. "So, it could be someone with an old grudge."

"But if it involves one of my cousins, too, then it's not a case. *Probably* not a case."

"We should check the old cases anyway."

They nodded at the same time. That's why she loved working with him: They thought together.

Another question came to mind. "Whether it's a grudge or an old case, why not come at us directly?" Miriam squinted at him. "You get more bang for the buck that way, no?"

Downie squinted back. "I think we need to talk to Cal Jones."

"Who the hell is that?" Garber snarled.

Miriam smiled at Downie before turning toward Garber, who was going to develop a reputation as a pain in the ass if he wasn't careful. He'd already made a good start in that direction here. "A professor in Religion and Folklore at UHart. She studies—"She waved a hand toward the back room—"this kind of thing, advises people. She helped us clear a couple of cases."

Winewski nodded. "She's discreet and knowledgeable."

"You didn't bring her in on the last one?" Prentice asked.

"We didn't know her then, and anyway, the Feds came in pretty quickly on that one," Miriam responded. She could hear Forensics people walking into the apartment. An excuse to leave.

Winewski nodded. "Okay. I think you two are done here for now, Mir. Talk to Jones and let us know what you get."

Miriam nodded and turned to leave, knowing Downie would follow. "It's Saturday." Her father would have been furious at her working at all. He'd have been especially furious because she was working on the Sabbath. She'd never told him. "Jones probably won't be at the university," she said over her shoulder.

In the wide foyer, Button and his team were putting on overalls with hoods, booties, gloves, masks, the whole deal.

"Hey, Mir, Downie," Button said.

"Hey yourself, John," Miriam said. "How are you?"

"I hear it's a beaut, this one." Button and his four men and one woman, suited up almost like astronauts, picked up their tool boxes from the beautiful wood floor.

A beaut? More like a horror show. Terrifying. Miriam could only shake her head.

It was Downie who spoke. "Remember that inside-out body six years ago up on Prospect?"

"Oh." Button's eyebrows rose. "Shit. Well, maybe this time we'll get ID and solve it."

"Looks like the perp's been practicing," Downie said.

"So have we." Button chuckled. "So have we."

Did the guy sound excited? Not quite. But Miriam had had enough. She stepped around people, used her arms to push the door open, and stood in the hall to breathe. In a way, she understood Button's enthusiasm. He was the best criminalist in Connecticut, probably in New England. The Feds regularly tried to poach him. But he stayed in Hartford for whatever reason. He didn't share reasons with her.

And she definitely didn't share his enthusiasm for weird cases. She knew why she and Downie got the other weird one, not to mention the levitating minister, the goat sacrificed in Bushnell Park on the summer solstice, followed by the chickens killed on the grave of a reputed witch in the Tower Ave cemetery. The brass, using a thought process she unfortunately could follow, had decided that Downie's two years at St. Thomas Seminary and her Orthodox Jewish upbringing qualified them as experts in religion and therefore capable of handling what everyone in Robbery-Homicide and Cold Case called the *X Files*. *So original.*

It wasn't worth arguing over.

Especially since they'd retired and gone their separate ways until they came back for the Cold Case Squad, and now she stood here on the black-and-gray Berber carpeting, surrounded by gray flocked wallpaper, waiting for her partner so they could decide how to proceed on yet another weird case.

She wasn't supposed to swear anymore, making the effort for her grandchildren, but only one word would do, and she said it.

"Fuck." She decided to expand on the thought. "Holy fucking shit."

Exactly then, of course, the elevator opposite her opened and another uniform, this one young, smirking, stepped out. "Ma'am," he said.

She smirked right back. *Ma'am* knew a few words worse than that and in a couple of languages other than English, which she would gladly teach him. And if they let him see that body, he'd probably exercise his vocabulary, too.

Downie stepped into the hall at that point, letting the uniform into the apartment.

"Sorry," he said. "Prentice thought of some questions for Doctor Jones."

"Let's just go, please."

Despite still being gloved, Downie used an elbow to push the down button on the elevator. Very discreet, that button, black on a black panel. *Mustn't let the paying customers see how things work.*

Even the bell, when the elevator car arrived, was a soft chime, not the usual bright *bing*, and the car itself was covered by the same wallpaper and Berber carpeting as the hall.

All very spiffy. But somehow, a person had gotten into this building and into an empty, locked apartment, murdered a human being using a method no one could explain logically, and got out of the building, too, without setting off any alarms, and, as far as anyone knew so far, without starring in security camera footage.

Somehow, the spiffiness didn't impress quite so much.

Downie elbowed the button for the lobby. "You okay?"

She wasn't about to tell him why she wasn't okay. Other than the obvious. "The last time? When Izzy wasn't home, I slept with the lights on for weeks."

And now, since Izzy had left home for good, the lights would be on every night. *God.* "You okay?"

He shrugged as the door opened on the granite and glass lobby.

Bravado or just not sharing?

The security man at the curved stone desk didn't have to say a word to share *his* feelings. His pallor made them obvious. If she had discovered that body—well, she'd known what to expect, and she didn't feel especially rosy.

"Come on, Mir," Downie said, peeling off his vinyl gloves. "Let's go track down Jones."

As she started on her gloves, he smiled at her. "And then we can get something to eat."

She snorted at him. "One: I don't think I'll be eating for a week after that. And two: I'm going to babysit for Sadie and Mark. I'll try calling Jones from Maddy's and let you know when she'll be available for the consult."

They walked to the front door together, dropped the gloves into the bag held out by a uniform, and provided their names so he could check them out of the scene. Other people would be questioning tenants, examining hallways, stairways, elevators, garbage cans, the parking garage, the cars in the parking garage. She could go to her daughter's house and play with her beautiful grandchildren.

"How about a movie, then?" Downie asked.

The man was hitting on her. "Seriously?"

"Mir. We're both free. There's no reason not to enjoy ourselves."

She *had* noticed that he was aging well, hadn't she? No pot belly on George Downs. And he didn't have to be protected from the job the way she'd protected Izzy and the kids.

But did she want to get tangled up with a man again? Granted, he was handsome, but he was a non-Jew, and she just wasn't sure. She'd have to think about it. A lot. "After the case is finished," which, given the circumstances, was never going to happen.

"I'll hold you to that."

She smiled for him as she pushed through the heavy doors, then smiled to herself as she stepped around one of the saw horses holding a small crowd of people back. It would take some real magic to ever get this case closed. And how likely was *that?*

Chapter 2
Saturday

eter realized he had been staring at the computer screen for at least 20 minutes without actually reading a single line of the spreadsheet. He pushed himself away from the desk and spat, "*Skata.*"

The word had been his father's favorite response when a line fouled, a net tore, a knife slipped. There lay the problem. His father had not cursed for almost a thousand years. Peter had not fished with his father for almost a thousand years.

He turned away from the computer on the antique desk, antique but far younger than he was, and the flat screens on the wall across the room with their stock quote and news chirons and faced the windows that ran from the dark wainscoting to the white crown moldings of the wall behind him.

The trees separating the house from the neighbors had budded. A couple of maples had actually flowered, all thanks to the odd warm spell they were experiencing this March. No leaves provided privacy yet, but that did not matter. The windows were glamoured to appear dark, opaque to anyone looking in while admitting light and scenery to anyone looking out.

So Peter could sit and stare at the trees and consider his situation. On his next Saint's Day, he would be one thousand and five years old, assuming his father's reckoning had been correct. His oldest son was born, he had reported, in the third year of the papacy of Ioannes, John the Eighteenth. In the current manner of counting years, that meant he had been born in ten oh six.

"A thousand and five years," Peter said out loud. "That is a long time to live."

The trees, of course, made no comment.

He thought he must have been about twenty, perhaps twenty-one, when the monster turned him. Before that, his father had been talking to Junia's father about a betrothal he had been more than willing to accept. A pretty girl with a modest smile and wide hips, Junia would have made a fine wife and mother. He would have had a family, he would have taught his sons to fish as his father had taught him, they would have worked hard, and they would have been long dead, but they would have had love. *He* would have had love.

Instead, he had a lot of money, a pretty house, an occasional sex partner, and a thousand and almost five years of life.

He had the *phyle*, of course, a fancy Greek word for a tribe. They were, when they were honest with themselves, a gang, the pack of wolves, three spell-casters, and one vampire, him, Peter Smith, so-called. The wolves had the pack, the casters had families. He had his money, his house, the *phyle's* protection, and too many years.

"Too long," he said quietly. "Too long alone."

Peter grimaced and stood up. He was turning broody like that fool of a vampire on television. Apparently, human females found that brooding presence attractive. He found it annoying, to say the least, and incorrect about many things.

Foolish of him to allow an imaginary creature such as that one to irritate him, but he definitely felt irritation.

He picked up his cell phone, slid it into the back pocket of his jeans, and knew suddenly and certainly that he had lived too long. "I have had enough."

The words should have shocked him. He had been born Catholic, after all, in a Catholic village, in a Catholic world. Suicide was a mortal sin.

When the monster turned him, Peter left Catholicism behind because he thought he was possessed by a demon and without a soul. He eventually came to understand that the Church was wrong about the demon and his soul and began to wonder what else the Church was wrong about. He decided not to bother with the priests anymore.

But he had behaved like a monster, not out of choice, of course, but still, he had ravened and ravished and killed. And he had tried to kill himself. Isaac ha-Levy had rescued him from that attempt.

Peter saw much to admire in Isaac's religion, but the consumption of blood, animal or human, is forbidden to Jews. And Jews also forbid suicide except to avoid profaning God's name.

Nevertheless, Peter had had enough. He was ready to die.

The problem was how. The only sure way—well, the only way magicals thought worked to kill a vampire was beheading. The humans' method, the stake through the heart, caused a great deal of pain, not to say agony, as he knew from personal experience. He had taken months to recover, but he *had* recovered, so he knew the stake would not work.

Garlic, silver, crosses, none of that worked. Only the sword had even a chance of success.

It was the way he had stopped William Lowell when that vampire decided drinking humans dry was his right. The *phyle* had sent Peter and his *katana* to deal with William two years ago. That William had not turned to dust after the beheading as the greater magicals did when they died, that he had required burying, left a question as to whether beheading actually worked. However, William had not left his grave in the two years since, so Peter felt some hope.

He would ask Martin to use the sword on him.

Before he did so, he had to take care of his personal assets. The Trust and the Fund would take care of themselves, though Martin and Gerard could step in as needed. It was the house, the cars, the books, particularly the incunabula and the first editions, the Dante, the Quarto, the Folio, the Kyd, the Marlowe, the page of Shakespeare in the writer's hand, his real treasures, that required care and legal disposition. His will and related documents required review, perhaps alteration.

He would talk to Phillipe—No, Phillipe would not be available till Monday for unspecified reasons so his business had to wait until then. Still, he felt better for having decided. He could have dinner with Martin and relax as much as he could there.

Martin's house was not to Peter's liking. All glass and metal, wall-to-wall carpeting, modern art on the walls, Peter found it cold and unfriendly. But then, he did not have to live there, only sit on the leather chair in the dining room and eat the filet of beef, warmed so the blood and juices oozed from the raw meat as he touched it with his fork.

Instead of eating his own filet, Martin seemed to study Peter as he ate.

"Do I have blood running down my chin?" Peter asked once he decided to be annoyed by his friend's stare.

The Alpha wolf huffed, then frowned. "You stink of despair." He cocked his head to one side. "I understand you can't smell yourself, but you do know you're thinking dark thoughts."

Of course, the wolf could smell Peter's mood. Even in their human form, the wolves' sense of smell exceeded that of ghouls, vultures, and bears.

Peter laid his fork and knife carefully on his plate. "Your staring does not help."

Martin huffed again. "I will stop staring then, but I will *not* use the sword on you, my friend."

Peter smiled. He knew Martin's true name, therefore could compel Martin's cooperation in his suicide. Now he picked up his fork and knife and cut a piece of nearly raw meat. "I will not go rogue to force you."

He saw awareness in the wolf's eyes before he ate the meat. Peter also knew that Martin would suffer if he were compelled to kill his friend.

Could Peter do that, force his friend to kill him? They had helped each other so often in the two hundred years since the wolves and the vampire had met. But he wanted to die.

"After a thousand years, things begin to feel...the same. A different language, different scenery, but the same careful hiding, Martin. And I have no lover with whom I can share my true nature."

The occasional human bedmate was no substitute for a true lover, someone he did not have to hide himself from.

Martin shrugged. "Find a *conocedora*, then."

As if *conocedoras* were thick on the ground. The ones who know, who can see the auras of both magicals and humans and know whom they are looking at, were far more common than vampires, but *conocedores* were more likely than their female counterparts. Peter had had male lovers, of course, but he felt inclined lately toward women. "You understand Vampires do not work like a wolf pack, yes? I do not get my pick of the females simply because I am the Alpha male."

Martin actually laughed. "It's not so simple as that. It requires agreement on both sides. And Jeanne took some convincing, believe me. But there must be a caster, someone magical who would have you, Peter."

Peter swallowed the last of his filet. "We know all the magicals in the Hartford area, do we not? Do you see someone suitable?" The *phyle*, three unaffiliated vampires and six *conocedores*, along with various fairies, brownies, two *voduisantes*, and a court of elves constituted the entire magical population of Hartford County. *C'est tout,* as Martin would say.

Suddenly sober, Martin shook his head. "I will think of something, Peter. Please be patient and let me try to help you."

"It will take me time to take care of my things, Martin." But the likelihood of Martin's finding a magical who would even consider taking the vampire as a lover was just…Peter could not use the word "impossible" because he knew the impossible existed. The wolves were impossible. He himself was impossible. But Martin's success as a matchmaker was…call it unlikely.

No. Peter was alone, and he had had enough. No mistake. Peter the Vampire was done.

Chapter 3
Saturday Night

Magic had nothing to do with it. Hannah Levine didn't chant spells or mix potions or create charms or amulets, nothing like that. She simply pointed and thought, and things moved. Ergo, she wasn't a witch.

Hannah was *not* a witch.

But David—David would think she *was* a witch. A dangerous, bad woman.

And he would leave her.

As a young woman, she had assumed she'd never meet a man who would love her and so lived her life as if the consequences didn't matter, but then she met David, found a good teaching job, and married him. Now, in 2011, she had a man and other things she did *not* want to lose.

If he knew what she could do, she would lose *everything*. Her father had left her mother. David would leave her. Now, when she felt almost calm and settled, she didn't want to have to go back to hotel rooms and the exhausting work of charming people.

So why had she shown Cousin Rose what she could do?

The easy answer was that Rose had looked just this side of panic there in Barnes & Noble. Because she'd known her phone was going to ring, who was calling, and possibly why. Big mistake Rose had made there, swearing about Ellen Lipman before the cell had even rung. She looked like a rabbit who'd seen a hawk when she checked Hannah across the table.

So Hannah had pulled Rose into a corner and rearranged a few books on the shelves without actually touching the books. Rose calmed down after that.

But Hannah knew it was a mistake the moment she did it. A secret is a secret only when just one person knows it. She'd kept a lot of secrets for a long time simply by never sharing them with anyone else.

Of course, Rose was no gossip. In fact, she was a joke in the family because she didn't even talk about her girls unless asked point-blank, and even then, she only answered questions. So she wasn't going to run to anybody and reveal anything. Not good old safe Rosie.

Hannah swept her eyes around the den in the one-story wrap-around she and David had bought just after they got married. They'd agreed on the pale gray walls on which hung photos of both their previous lives and families and David's flat-screen television.

Along the walls ran short bookshelves they'd picked out together, filled with books they'd each read and loved. They'd chosen the brown leather love seat and sofa together, too. She ran a hand in a caress along the top of the cherry desk, where she corrected papers, where she'd drawn plans for the courtyard garden that she would plant later in the spring.

She was 52 years old, and she loved this new life of hers. The one problem, the next-door neighbor's abusive husband, would be taken care of by the police. That's what the police are for.

But the most recent secret wasn't a secret anymore.

She had to protect herself, her marriage, her job, and her things. She would never use the ability in front of anyone ever again. That was number one. She wouldn't practice anymore, either, as she had since she discovered the ability a year or so ago. Hot flashes and telekinesis. Who would have even imagined it could happen?

Maybe, if she didn't use it, it would go away, the way her piano-playing skills had faded. Not totally gone, but clumsy and unenjoyable, not good enough for public consumption.

But now there was Rose. She'd have to cut Rose off. Of course, if she cut Rose off, she'd have to cut Miriam off, too. She couldn't talk to Miriam without talking to Rose, and vice versa. If she invited Rose to supper, she had to invite Miriam. That's the way the three of them had worked since they were little girls. Cousins who happened to be good friends.

That was then; this is now. No Rose, no Miriam. A decision had been made.

Now she could turn her attention to the pile of quizzes in front of her. Not the way she used to spend Saturday night, but David was doing a double shift in the emergency department, and the quizzes had to be corrected so she could give them back to the kids on Monday. Therefore, she would sit and read and grade.

The phone rang.

Saved from the quizzes, however briefly, Hannah was glad to pick up the cell phone next to the pile of papers without looking at the caller ID.

"Hannah Levine," she chirped.

"Hannah, it's Rose. Your neigh—"

Speak of the devil. "Rose, I can't talk now. You—"

"Hannah," Rose spoke firmly and loudly. "Your neighbor is coming home with a *gun*. He's drunk, and he has a gun. We have to do some—"

"What are you talking about? How do you know?" Really, it didn't make any sense.

"What d'you mean, how do I know? I *know*, that's how. The same way you...do what you do. But that's not impor—"

"Rose." This call was exactly why secrets should never be shared. She'd shown Rose what she could do, and now Rose thought she should save the world. *Ridiculous.* "I can't do anything. I *won't*. It's too—someone would see and—"

"Hannah, we have to help that woman. We can't just sit and do nothing."

"I'm not talking about this anymore." Hannah tapped the phone to end the call and discovered that her hands were shaking. Not tremors, just little quivers. Anger. Because Rose dared to presume—she expected—

That sealed the decision. *No more Rose. Absolutely no more.*

The quizzes had to be corrected, preferably tonight, preferably before David came home. And if the bastard next door showed up and shot his wife, the cops would take care of it.

Good. Hannah brought her attention to the first quiz on the pile. A problem arose almost immediately, of course. She habitually sorted papers from best to worst and corrected in the other direction, like saving the icing on the cake for last. It meant, unfortunately, that she slogged through the awful stuff first. It wasn't quite like eating the rich chocolate cake to get to that smooth, creamy, sugary icing.

The first paper, Macky James's quiz, was a paragraph of gibberish, maybe an attempt at poetry. Maybe. Every word, an exaggeration, she admitted with a sigh, was misspelled. Not *a* or *the*, but otherwise...

The driveway chime sounded on the alarm panel.

It was far too early for David to be home. So who was pulling into the driveway at 8:30 at night?

She'd have to turn off the alarm to open the door to the courtyard so she could go out and look.

On the other hand, no one was knocking or ringing the bell. Maybe someone who needed to turn around had seen the well-lit drive and decided it was a good spot.

Back to Mr. James and his attempt to distract her from the fact that he hadn't read *Animal Farm*, couldn't answer the most basic questions about the book, not that he could have answered a question even if he had read the book. His parents refused to have him tested—

Hannah jumped when her phone rang. After swearing softly, she checked the caller ID. Rose again.

She ignored the phone, and it stopped, then started again.

Rose used to be so unsure of herself, always hanging back, following where Miriam or Hannah led her. Now?

"Rose," she snarled into the phone. "I—"

"I'm out front watching the bastard trying to get out of his car. He's drunk. But I can see the gun. He's going to kill her. Please, Hanny."

"Oh, God," Hannah moaned. She could *not* allow anyone to see what she could do, so why in God's name was she already trotting down the hall toward the front door? Why did she punch in the code to disarm the alarm, stride across the empty courtyard, and step through the door onto the driveway?

"I called the police," Rose went on. "But they won't get here in time."

Hannah turned her phone off and stalked further up her driveway. Rose pushed her car door open and jogged over to her.

"There." She pointed.

Unnecessary. The drunken bastard was shouting his wife's name as he staggered toward his front door. "Elizabeth!" he kept shouting.

Hannah stared at the man. She didn't see a gun, and it would be simpler just to wait for the cops.

Then he stopped, straightened up, and faced her, and Rose. Hannah saw the gun then. He slowly raised it in their direction.

"Bitches," he shouted. "I'll—"

"Hannah," Rose whispered. "Do you see?"

Hannah saw. She pointed at the bastard and he fell face down on the grass. She pointed at the gun that he dropped when he fell, and it slid a few feet away from him.

Then she grabbed Rose's arm. Rose winced.

Too damn bad. "Never ask me to do this again, Rose." Cop cars screeched to a stop in front of the neighbor's house. "I don't care if the world is ending, I don't care, you hear me? Don't call, either. Leave me alone."

"For God's sake, Han. You just saved the woman's life. You can't—"

"No more. We're done."

Except, of course, the cops saw them standing in the driveway and, while most of them took care of the bastard and the gun, one of them came walking down the lawn toward them.

"Ladies," he said.

"Officer."

"Detective Alsop, ma'am. You shouldn't be out here, you know that. You could have been hurt."

"We didn't think." Rose sounded subdued.

Hannah nodded. "But we can go, right?"

The detective sighed. "We need to take your statements. I'll send someone down."

Rose turned to her. "You want me to stay till David gets home?"

Breathing deeply to make sure her voice was steady, Hannah turned away. "No. I want you to go home, Rose. I'm fine."

Rose didn't argue with her. Instead, Rose spoke to Detective Alsop. "Can I come down to the station in the morning? To make the statement? Although you know everything. We heard the noise. We came out. He fell."

Detective Alsop nodded. "Are you okay to drive, ma'am?"

Rose nodded. "I'm fine," she said and walked away.

Hannah didn't watch Rose go; instead nodded at the detective. "You'll have to ring the bell, okay? I'm going to set my alarm."

"That's fine," he said and walked off toward a group of officers watching a man photographing the gun where it lay on the lawn. "Someone will be in to talk to you in a few minutes," he called over his shoulder.

Hannah walked through the courtyard and into the house, all the while breathing deeply and praying that none of the neighbors had seen what she'd done. By the time she got to the kitchen, she understood that in the dark, even with the lights over the driveway, no one could have connected what she had done, pointing her hand, to the drunken bastard's fall.

She was safe for now.

The witch was safe.

Chapter 4
Sunday

Rose had been upset when she discovered she was precognitive. But the business with Cousin Hannah and the drunken neighbor had seriously unsettled her.

Let's not get carried away here, Rose. You're safe.

She had thought she was losing her mind—*Thank you, menopause*—when the knowing first started six months or so ago, along with the hot flashes, the tingling in her belly that signaled phone calls on any phone she habitually answered. She *hated* phones but had to use them, didn't she, and she had started knowing when they were going to ring before they rang. Lately, she also knew who was calling, and sometimes she knew why.

And then Hannah's neighbor—Rose had been meditating when an elephant started stomping in her belly, and the knowing just came to her.

Oddly, she didn't feel frightened of her ability. Frightened as usual about losing her job, her house, her friends. Not as frightened as she'd been before she started meditating, but frightened—though not so anxious, either, since she'd given up the caffeine, the cessation of which had also helped ease the hot flashes.

On the other hand, last night, she and Hannah had saved a life. They were *heroes*. Not that anyone knew, not that she would ever tell anyone, but they had been heroes. Saving a life was a *mitzvah*, a commandment, a blessing, a good deed.

Now, Hannah was more frightened than she was. Hannah the Brave, Rose used to call her. It was Hannah who had moved to France the minute she finished college, Hannah whose work used to take her to England, Italy, Hong Kong, Germany, and Japan all by herself, Hannah who had taken wealthy lovers and had gone on safari in Africa once and diving off Australia. All the while, safe little Rosie stayed safe in Connecticut and taught high school English and married the first man who asked her to marry him and gave birth to two daughters and raised them in safe and historic Wethersfield, the oldest town in Connecticut. Safe all around.

Now, it felt to Rose that she and Hannah had switched positions. Oh, Rose still lived in the safe little ranch, colonial blue on the outside, needing paint on the inside, and she still worried about ending up in a cardboard box under the Putnam Bridge, alone and unwanted. But she'd managed to earn a Ph.D. in composition and move from high school to college teaching, and she hadn't fought Harry when he announced he was divorcing her so he could marry another—younger—woman, and she wrote essays about the mystery genre that were quoted and discussed in other people's journal articles. Safe little Rosie had managed that.

While Hannah—what to think about Hannah? She'd gotten scared and selfish.

No, Hannah had gotten selfish *because* she was scared.

And there was a dark splotch on the ceiling where Rose had managed to kill the most recent spider. Rose could see the mark even lying there in bed without her glasses.

She had two choices: She could shut her eyes—it was Sunday morning, after all—or she could get up and get herself going. She had to go down to the police station to make her statement. If it wasn't too cold, she could walk a couple of miles outside first. Otherwise, she could use the treadmill. *Boring treadmill.*

Better than chewing on the problem of Hannah.

After pulling on gray sweats, socks and sneakers—New Balance, she was smug about buying American-made sneakers—she drifted to the kitchen and stopped for orange juice, which would give her a little energy to do the walk.

Sighing, Rose stood in front of the kitchen sink staring out the window at the back yard. The sun was coming up and there was no frost on the ground. March was being unusually warm, deceptively warm, but at least she could walk outside.

Goody.

Maybe later, she would call Miriam—*Oh, right, Rose. Call Cousin Miriam, invite her to lunch, and tell her all about Hannah, telekinesis, and precognition. Sure.*

Cool, logical Miriam, the cop. She wouldn't run. No. She'd walk politely but quickly away. Probably after calling the men with heavy-duty tranquilizers to take her funny little Cousin Rosie away.

If only Nana Pearl were still here. She always listened calmly and hugged her comforting love. But Nana had been dead a long time. Those hugs were long gone.

"Damn," Rose said out loud. "Damn."

"Swearing, Sweetheart?"

Rose froze. It wasn't just the voice. It was the aroma of lavender, the impossibility of that voice and that scent together. On top of hot flashes and Hannah's neighbor and Hannah and six months of precognition centered on phone calls, of all things. *Why not the stock market?*

She would start giggling if she wasn't careful. "No," she said. "I am *not* crazy."

"You aren't," the impossible voice agreed.

"O God, O God, O God," Rose groaned and rubbed a hand across her forehead, knocking her glasses sideways. "No, no, no."

"Look, Sweetheart. Please look at me."

"But Nana Pearl is dead."

"Yes, I am. For a while now. But I am also here now."

One breath, just one.

One breath, just one.

Rose straightened her glasses and turned slowly around. There, four or five feet away stood Nana Pearl, looking better than healthy. She was her usual—usual meaning almost 40 years ago before she'd *died* usual—lovely dumpling self, gorgeous white curly hair framing her round, smiling face. She wore the silk navy blue dress and jacket and matching high-heeled sandals she had worn to somebody's bar mitzvah or maybe it was someone's wedding? a year or so before she died, *for God's sake. 1970? 1971? A long time ago.*

"Oh," Rose gasped.

"You're not crazy," Nana repeated.

"Nana," Rose whispered, stunned by an overwhelming sense of loss, the need to hug and be hugged by the woman now leaning against her stove. Tears welled up and the urge to sob rose from her belly, all caused by a...a ghost, a memory of the woman who had died too soon, leaving a young girl unloved and unwanted.

Good to know all those years of therapy helped you deal with that.

Nana smiled tenderly. "I've missed you, Sweetheart. I'm sorry I left so early. I would have stayed if I could have, you know."

Not trusting her voice, Rose could only stand there, staring and working her breath. She or it was so perfectly a re-creation of Nana Pearl, right down to the over-precise pronunciation of English Nana had worked so hard to achieve. Almost no trace of Yiddish was left in her voice, just too much breath on the precisely pronounced *S*'s and *T*'s and sometimes the continental vowels.

And the scent of lavender, delicate because Nana had always kept sachets of lavender in drawers and closets rather than using perfume, filled the kitchen.

Lavender and Nana. Like bagels and cream cheese.

Smiling at the bad analogy, Rose shook her head once. "Nana," she said, her voice firmer.

"Rosie, my darling, listen to me. Tell Hannah to tell the truth."

"Hannah?" Hannah didn't lie. *Did she?*

"Also, it's okay for you to go to *schul*. But you and Miriam must be careful, Sweetheart. Very careful."

"What?" Rose started to argue. "Be careful about what? Nana—"

The land line rang. She hadn't realized it was going to ring, probably because she had been distracted—*there was an understatement*. She did know it was David Levine calling, though why he would call rather than Hannah—well, the only way to know was to pick up the phone.

And Nana Pearl disappeared. Just disappeared. *Soundlessly gone.*

"No." Rose heard herself whimper and straightened herself up. Rose Sherman did *not* whimper, not even alone in her own kitchen. She never cried in public and she did not whimper. Never, not anywhere, not anytime.

The phone rang again. She lifted it off its base on the little bookcase next to the refrigerator that held her cookbooks and turned so she could stare at the spot where her Nana had just been standing. "Hello?" It was easy to play ignorant when she was so shaken, and heat rose from her neck to the tips of her ears.

"Good morning, Rose. David here. Am I calling too early?"

She walked around 6:30 almost every morning, everyone knew, so he was just being polite. "Hi, David. I was going to walk. But is Hannah okay?"

"Well, she's pretty shaken about last night. It was…dangerous, Rose. For both of you."

Oh, yes, the foolish women who heard noise and ran out to see what was happening. "It turned out fine—It was a good thing we called the police."

"You could have been hurt, Rose. Or worse."

The only way to end the conversation was to agree with him. "You're right. We just...got caught up in the moment, you know? We didn't think."

"But you're okay? Did you sleep? Do you need—?"

"I seem to be fine. I slept." Surprisingly well, actually, once she'd gotten around the whole hero business. "I don't need anything." Rose smiled. "Thanks for asking, Doctor."

"Just making sure." No chuckle, just a soft sigh.

The man sounded unhappy. Though, according to Hannah, he wasn't nearly as unhappy as he would have been had he known what Hannah could do. "I'm fine, David. Really. Is Hannah there?"

"She's lying down. And I'd rather not disturb her. You understand."

Not really. Hannah wasn't a delicate little flower, nor had she actually been in any danger. Although, according to Nana—the ghost, the whatever that was—Hannah lied. So maybe there was a problem. But she saw no point in arguing. "Sure. Tell her I'll call. And thank you for checking." Harry would never have checked. He'd have sighed one of his put-upon sighs and walked away.

"You're welcome, Rosie. We'll see you soon."

Somehow, Rose doubted that. But she said good-bye, set the phone down on the base, and breathed deeply, wishing Nana Pearl were still standing there.

Wishing for a ghost? Really, Rose?

She straightened herself again. Whatever the *hell* was going on, she had to perform her life. Walk, make her police report, read a few more essays for the Junior narratology class, maybe read, do a little crocheting, call the girls—a privileged to-do list, wasn't it?

She had nothing to be careful of. And Miriam sat in an office reviewing Cold Case files. No worries there either. So...

So Rose would just ignore what wasn't supposed to be happening. She'd done it as a child; she could certainly do it now.

Easy-peasy, right?

Chapter 5
Sunday

S ara Berman chuckled to herself as she studied her target. Not a ward around the house, nothing to protect or even to alert the spell-caster living there. Nothing. As if the owner were an ordinary human being. All Sara could see was a short sidewalk up to one concrete step leading to a red door in a white house smaller than the gardener's house on the parental estate. There was a detached one-car garage off to the side at the end of a driveway with cracks in the pavement. The only landscaping was a few bushes Sara couldn't name and a large tree, still bare in a prematurely warm March. No herbs, no charms or amulets or anything to indicate that a knowledgeable and practiced spell-caster lived here.

The house did fit into the neighborhood, which would be labeled working-class, typical Hartford South End, Sara realized. It was easy to hope that maybe the old woman would be like her house, eager to fit in, glad to help.

But no. The small, frail-looking old woman who opened the door smiled at her visitor but lost the smile as she stared at Sara. She slammed the door shut before Sara could say her name or even hello. She would have to pay the old lady back for her rudeness. No question.

Ignoring the chill of magic that washed over her scalp and down her back—after the fact is *not* the best time to ward yourself—Sara whispered to the doorknob to unlock itself. It resisted until she repeated the words aloud, and then she simply pushed the door open and stepped into a dim, narrow hallway. On her right was an opening into a living room, on her left, a doorway to a dining room. She had an impression of well-polished furniture, well-tended plants, no old lady, no books. A staircase along the wall past the dining room door led up to a second story, and beyond the stairway, the hall ended in the kitchen.

And the old lady. There she stood, holding a vial of something watery and green, her back to a small stove.

"Please leave," she said firmly. "I have nothing you want." Her voice didn't quiver; her hands didn't shake.

"You don't know what I want," Sara said. "You don't know who I am or—"

The other woman laughed. "I may not know your name, but I see the blood on your aura. Anything you want will be foul." And she began to chant in Latin.

Sara didn't recognize the particular spell, but that didn't matter. The woman obviously wasn't wishing her a pleasant day. Shaking her head, Sara silenced the woman with a wave of her hand and let a satisfied laugh loose when the old woman's eyes widened in shock.

"I'm no amateur," she said. Self-taught though she was— because the one teacher she'd found had turned on her—she was a practiced spell-caster whose charms were the envy of any caster she met.

The old woman threw the vial at her, but without her voice to invoke the spell, it simply smashed uselessly near Sara's feet. The scent of pine with an undertone of something acrid quickly filled the small room.

"You should have thrown that when you opened the door," Sara said. "Now you'll come with me." She stepped over the puddle and grabbed the old lady by the arm. The old lady fought her or tried to, but she really was a skinny little thing, so Sara easily dragged her the short distance down the hall to the dining room. With her free hand, she pulled a chair away from the table—nice walnut, well-cared-for—and then used both hands to force the old lady to sit.

The old lady rubbed her arm where Sara had held her.

"I'm sorry to be so rough, but I need information that I've been told you have. So I'm going to let you speak to answer this question: How do you perform a blood curse?" A reasonable request delivered in a reasonable tone of voice.

The old lady's eyes widened again, and her mouth moved without sound until Sara waved her voice back.

"—tell you nothing."

Sara shook her head. "It's obvious I'm physically stronger than you and my charms are unstoppable. I'm certainly better prepared. You don't even have wards on the front—"

"I never needed them before," the old lady said. "It's—"

"I just need the steps for the blood curse and then I'll be gone."

"I don't know how to do a blood curse."

"Now you're lying." Sara made a cutting motion with her right index finger, stopping the old lady's breath. "You shouldn't tell lies, you know. It's rude, and you're wasting my time. I know you've performed it at least once, I heard people talk about you, and they said you were successful, so I'll ask you again. How do you perform a blood curse?"

She released the old woman's breath, but all she got for her trouble was a gasp for air and an attempt to rise from the chair.

"Really." Sara stopped the old lady's breath again as she pushed her back onto the chair. "You can't think you're going to get away. My request is not a difficult one. Tell me how to perform the blood curse. I've tried twice now, followed the instructions I have precisely. To the letter. But all I've gotten for my efforts is dead sacrifices. My enemies are alive and well and going about their business without so much as a sniffle. So you can see I really do need your expertise."

This time, when she let the old lady breathe again, the woman sobbed.

"You don't understand," she cried. "You don't understand. Everyone died. Everyone, even the babies, people I didn't know, people I had no quarrel with. It was awful, awful—"

"I don't care. I need to know."

But the old lady just kept crying on about so many dead, she hadn't meant to kill so many people, it was the one thing she was ashamed of in her life.

Sara ran out of patience. "Stop," she snarled and snapped her fingers.

The whining stopped, but the old woman grabbed her chest, her eyes frantic. "Help me," she whispered. And then—

Nothing.

She slid from the chair onto the rug and lay there, inert. Dead.

"Damn it." Sara knew she'd put too much power into her voice and stopped the old woman's heart. "Damn it," she said again and felt herself begin to shake.

She'd used a lot of energy since she'd come into the house. Of course, she had chocolate in her backpack. She set the fine black leather bag down on the chair the old lady had just vacated, fished a chocolate bar out, unwrapped it, and chewed while she considered.

A spell-caster who successfully threw a blood curse had power, real power. And knowledge, even if she chose not to use it. Her book of shadows would be a valuable resource by itself. If she also had other books, grimoires, even herbals, Sara could add to her own power.

After tucking the candy wrapper into the backpack, she took another candy bar and decided to start at the top. Attic to basement, she would search the house.

The attic was empty, however. Not even dust on the floor. Thinking that a spell might be hiding something, she waved a hand to reveal—

Nothing. If anything had been stored up here, it wasn't there now. So Sara moved to the upper story of the house, two small bedrooms and a bathroom, quite old, though the bedroom the old lady had obviously used, with hairbrush and cologne bottle on the dresser and slippers by the side of the bed, was furnished with a beautiful deco bedroom set, all polished and clean, if crowded in the small room.

The only books were a novel by Anne Rice, *The Witching Hour* of all things, and a notebook. Sara pounced on the notebook, one of those composition books with the marbled black and white cover and space for name and subject, and opened it to a list of expenses. "Electric bill–$68.00; light bulbs for front hall fixture–$7.00; lunch with Cal–zero. A treat!" and on and on, page after page.

"Damn it." Sara set the book down, opened the closet to rifle through the clothing, not housecoats and other old lady things, but nice trousers and shirts and simple but expensive looking flats with shoe trees in them, then checked the space behind those things. Again, she performed a spell to reveal anything hidden. Nothing.

Every room was like that one, clean, well-tended, small, containing nothing to indicate the presence of a powerful caster. Even the kitchen held nothing special. The herbs and spices were the same ones the parents' cook used: garlic, turmeric, nutmeg, and so on. Nothing a spell-caster needed. But the vial the old lady had thrown could not be bought at a grocery store. The ingredients had to have come from an herbal specialist, and then the old lady would have put them together herself. So where would she do that?

The basement door was locked. Smiling, Sara ordered it open and the light switch on, and she walked slowly down the stairs. Sure enough, to the right of the stairs stood a long workbench. Bottles and jars of leaves, stems and roots stood along the back of the bench. Sara knew them all, the wolfsbane, the hemlock, all of them. On a shelf above the table sat a collection of candles. No black, of course, but still, ritual candles, nothing just to make a pretty light or a pleasant scent. So the book had to be down here.

Except it wasn't. The furnace, the water heater, a couple of lamps, no secret doors, no secret safes. No book of shadows, no grimoire, no anything that could tell Sara where her blood curse kept going wrong.

And the old lady was dead.

There were spells for bringing the dead back and forcing them to speak, but those things required extensive preparation involving careful protection rituals and more time than Sara wanted to spend, not to mention more energy than she could afford to use just then.

Disappointed, Sara wandered back up to her backpack and stared at the old lady's body while she ate another candy bar. This visit had been a waste of time and energy.

Maybe she should just kill the women the way she'd killed this one and be done. Why spend the time—No. Her birth mother and the two bitches who had turned their backs on her mother had to *suffer*. They had to sicken and die slowly, not knowing why they suffered. They had to provide justice for Sara, who'd suffered through years of her so-called mother and father and lies, so many lies about who she was and how everyone loved her—

She would simply find a way to the make the curse work. "Third time's the charm" was the saying, right? Still, she had to find someone or a book, *something* that could tell her why the damned thing wasn't working. She was strong, and her charms saved her a lot of energy, but at some point, she was going to run herself down too far. She did know the dangers in the kind of spells she was running. She'd been eating a lot of chocolate the last few days, as if replenishing her strength was becoming a problem.

Sara shook her head. Obviously, she wasn't going to learn anything here. The old lady had given up practicing any powerful spells for simple charms, and that was that.

The *curandera* on Park Road would not help her, and Sara certainly wouldn't risk trying to learn anything from her. That woman was at least as powerful and skilled as Sara. Too dangerous to attempt to force her. In fact, Sara only went to the *botanica* when the woman wasn't there if she could help it.

There was one possibility, or so she'd heard, a person who studied folklore and collected books of shadows and grimoires. Sara couldn't remember the name, but she could go back to the neighborhood around the *curandera's botanica* and listen. The name would come up quickly as these things did among practitioners and their customers. That neighborhood was a tight community. And there was a terrific Cuban restaurant a few doors down from the *botanica* where she could replenish herself.

Good. She had a plan.

Sara swung her backpack over her shoulder and walked into the hall, where she saw a small round wooden table on elaborately carved legs. The old lady had left her keys and mail there. Without thinking, Sara picked up the mail, just looking at return addresses of bills and what appeared to be a card of some sort in an oversized square envelope, sent by C. L. Jones, with an address in Simsbury, Connecticut.

"Ha!" Sara shouted. Finally, a little luck. Cal Jones, she remembered, was the name of the book collector. Definitely. "Well, Mr. Jones. I'll be paying you a visit. Oh, I will."

With a word, Sara invoked a charm on her bracelet to gather any little bits of herself, skin cells, strands of hair, that sort of thing, and waited to a count of twenty for them to come back to her open hand. No one would know she'd been there.

With that, she left the little house and the dead body behind. She would visit the Cuban restaurant just to celebrate her lucky find.

Chapter 6
Sunday Evening

Hannah had not had a magical Sunday. Even hiding in bed, her imagination kept painting awful pictures, and she didn't feel safe.

She knew no one could possibly have seen her point at the bastard next door, and if they did see her, no one could possibly think that her pointing had anything to do with his falling down, but she kept picturing someone telling David what she'd done. Mrs. Kopetski across the street, Abel Miller diagonally across, one of them would whisper in David's ear. She could see the look of horror, then disgust, play across his face. In every single vision, he turned away from her, refusing her promise to never do it again.

Not a happy picture.

The worst part of it was that she had stopped the bastard without much thought. She'd said no, but she'd done it. She hadn't meant to intervene, but she had.

So how could she possibly promise not to do it again? *Dear God.*

And now, David was worried about her as if she were— her mother who played weak and stupid so her husband, Hannah's Daddy, wouldn't leave.

Hannah sat straight up in bed.

That was exactly what *she* was doing: playing helpless and frightened, so David wouldn't leave.

Holy—Yes, she'd done something risky, even dangerous, but no one, *no one,* could have seen. And if she didn't talk to Rose, she wouldn't be in any position to do anything so dangerous, so revealing, again.

She would *not* behave like her silly, paranoid mother. Ever.

She needed to shower and dress and do something about David, explain the upset without explaining, at least not honestly. It came to her in the shower, with the hot water beating on her back, that she could protect the secret by sharing another one. Destroy one secret to save another. She had enough of them that she could pick something minor—relatively speaking, of course—and allay his worries.

Once she got herself into jeans and a nice sweater, she went looking for her husband and found him in the kitchen, staring into the open refrigerator. Watching him from the doorway, she could only smile. He was a lovely man, 55 but in terrific shape with a high, tight ass, so good to hold—

"I'll cook," she offered from the doorway.

He turned halfway around so she saw the surprised look on his face. "Are you okay? You feel up to it?"

Padding into the room, she smiled. "I was being silly, David, really. He was drunk and it was dark and I don't think he even saw us. He was fixated on his wife, you know."

David's half-smile, half-grimace introduced his own apology. "I have an overactive imagination. From the emergency department, you know? I could see you and Rose..."

Hannah chuckled. "I did the same thing. Let my imagination run away with me. But it's okay." Maybe she wouldn't have to say anything more. Maybe this could all just blow over.

"Let me cook, David. Veggies and chicken. And there's a nice bottle of white wine, a Graves, I think." She walked to the fridge and shut the door, kissed his ear. "Keep me company.""

David ran a hand through his hair as he turned around to face her. "God, Hannah." His arms enveloped her. "I saw the cop cars and thought—"

Hannah made no effort to free herself from the safety of his embrace, just turned her head to the side so she could talk. "I know. We didn't think. But it's okay. We're okay."

"I know Rose is okay, too. I talked to her this morning."

Hannah carefully did not stiffen at the mention of her cousin. "You did?"

"I wanted to make sure she was all right, that she'd slept. She was there, too."

"And?" He'd already said Rose was fine, but she needed to know whether Rose had said something that needed explaining or explaining away.

"She even slept well, she said." David chuckled. "I know you've told me stories about her being afraid of doing things, but Rose has turned into a tough broad, you know that, right?"

Rose, as a tough broad, was definitely not an idea that Hannah had ever thought about. Ever. "Really? I have to think about that." Time to turn the subject away from Rose. "And what am I?"

David squeezed her a little closer. "God, Hannah, you're my treasure, my beautiful, amazing treasure. And I don't want to even imagine something like that bastard of a drunk coming after you with a gun."

"Me, either." She nestled close and relaxed into his embrace.

They would have variants on this conversation for a few days, and then life would move them on to whatever happened next. She knew. It had happened before. It would happen again. Maybe nothing so dramatic, but shit happened.

And all her secrets were safe.

Chapter 7
Monday Morning

If she had been alone, Miriam would have laughed. It was clear to her that none of the men in the room could think in the presence of that amazing beauty. No one made jokes about the other Dr. Jones of movie fame. No one wondered how such a beautiful woman had become involved in such an offbeat area of study. Apparently, they were all reduced to blithering idiocy.

Miriam admitted that Dr. Calla Lily Jones was the dictionary definition of "beautiful." Her face, framed by long, lush auburn hair, featured enormous gray eyes over alpine cheekbones, an elegant nose, and the kind of mouth writers describe as generous. Her clothing, what Rose called the middle-aged lady uniform, dark trousers, untucked, light-colored shirt, and dark jacket, didn't hide her hourglass figure.

The only problem, as Miriam saw it, was the woman's height or rather lack of it. She barely hit five feet. She wore flats, too, as if her height didn't matter to her. At five foot seven, Miriam felt like a giant, a gawky, middle-aged, ethnic giant of curly salt-and-pepper hair, muddy brown eyes, large nose, over-wide mouth—

Jones's shortness and beauty seemed to bring out the men's instinct to protect. Even the Lieutenant, a happily married man, stared at the woman almost rudely. Offers of a better chair, tea, Starbucks, temperature adjustments, all were declined graciously in a throaty Kathleen Turner voice with a hint of a Southern drawl.

If the woman had come to consult on any case but the impossible bodies, Miriam might have enjoyed watching the men around her reduced to foolishness.

But Dr. Jones *was* there for the bodies. She had arrived on Monday morning specifically because of the inside out bodies. They were sitting, Lieutenant Winewski, Detectives Garber and Prentice, Dr. Jones, and Miriam, waiting for Downie to come to the conference room with a print file of photographs of the body found in the apartment building on Asylum Street.

Miriam felt no inclination to say anything. After Jones arrived, Prentice asked how the doctor had come to consult with the Sergeant and Detective Fine. Miriam left it to the woman to explain the case of the levitating minister, how Miriam and Downie had found her, how she had demonstrated various methods of levitation.

The most likely explanation for the minister who seemed to float at the pulpit was toe-walking under the long robe, so Downie had gone to church with a tiny camera and obtained the evidence. Which success, Miriam didn't say out loud, had confirmed for the brass that they were correct in assigning the so-called *X Files* to her and Downie.

And here they were again. *O wondrous day.*

Downie finally walked into the room, carrying the file and a heavy china mug that he set down in front of Miriam.

"Decaf," he said to her, then set the file down in front of Jones.

"Sorry it took me so long. A couple had to be reprinted. But the file is complete now." So saying, he took the one free chair and sat. "They're...graphic."

Jones nodded and began rooting in her oversized purse for something.

"Is there something you need, Dr. Jones?" Downie asked.

Smiling brightly—shaming the fluorescent lights in the room—Jones pulled a leather case out of her bag and unzipped it. "My magnifying glass," she husked and pulled the file folder closer to her. "Let me see."

The first photo, which Miriam had seen, was a wide-angle shot that took in the body and the pentagram and circle. From a distance, things looked artificial, like a scene from a TV show.

The next shots covered the pentagram, first a wide view of the entire figure, then each segment and each candle. Jones paid attention to each picture, but didn't use the glass.

A prop?

Jones flipped over the last candle picture and came to the first close-up of the body. "Oh, my," she said.

"Oh, my?" Seriously? Southern girl training must be rigorous. Because "Oh, my" had not been the reaction of anyone else who had seen the body or pictures of it. Far from it.

Now Jones picked up her magnifying glass and leaned over the picture. "Truly inside out," she murmured.

Miriam kept her thoughts to herself, but really, had the woman thought the cops couldn't tell the difference between inside-out and flayed? *Really?*

Each subsequent photo received the magnifying glass treatment. And when Jones reached the last picture, she turned the whole pile over and began again, this time studying each one, including those of the pentagram, with deep attention.

Miriam finished the tea Downie had brought her and watched as Jones frowned over each photograph. She was as slow as Button, who could spend an hour examining the heel of one shoe through a magnifying lens, tweezers at the ready. Miriam had watched him do it.

"Oh, yes," Jones said. "This was a sacrifice. A murder for the blood." She tapped an elegant finger, short nail, no nail polish, on the photo.

Obviously, Miriam didn't say. The painted circle and pentangle, the candles, the body, all of it showed intent. "What do you mean?" was what she decided to say.

"The circle is whole. There are no breaks in it or the pentagram. So the body was part of a ritual curse requiring a blood sacrifice, a great deal of human blood. More than just the few drops of blood most curses require."

"What does that mean?" It was Downie who asked, not Winewski, Garber or Prentice. Were they so spellbound by that beauty they couldn't speak? Or just as disbelieving as Miriam now felt?

Jones set her magnifying glass down carefully, licked her lips—stalling? Composing an answer? "Any curse requires a lot of energy, and the best source is blood. Human blood."

Garber snickered. "What are you saying? A magician did that?"

"A practitioner did that, Detective," Jones said, her voice and face calm and composed. "A practitioner cast a spell that turned that body—"

"Practitioner?" Downie sounded just as calm as Jones did.

Jones smiled. "Some people might use the term 'magician,' others prefer the term 'spell-caster,' but—"

"What kind of goddamned bullshit is this!" Garber's chair exploded back, and he banged the table with a fist as he stood up. "I *told* you this was bullshit. A total fucking waste of fucking time," he snarled over his shoulder at Prentice as he marched out of the room and slammed the door behind him.

For a second or two, no one else moved. Then everyone spoke at once. "Magician?" Downie repeated as Prentice said, "You have to admit—" and Miriam said, "No magic. It's not possible," and Jones said, "Not an uncommon reaction."

Winewski quietly stood up. "You stay, Prentice. I'll take care of Garber," he said and walked out of the room.

Everyone stopped talking at that point.

Jones cleared her throat. "That is not an uncommon reaction," she repeated. "The idea that magic is real is difficult to accept, particularly when we are taught relentlessly and all through our lives that magic is certainly not real, that the physics described by Newton, Einstein, and so on describes the absolute limits of possibility. But the fact is, you are looking for a practitioner of some skill, one I am not familiar with."

"You know practitioners?" Downie asked.

He sounded as if he believed Jones; he didn't sound sarcastic or ironic or sardonic, and Miriam, who hoped for, who *needed* rationality somewhere in her life, decided that the woman sounded like Rose in lecture mode. She would concentrate on the fact that professors lecture whether they know what they're talking about or not. Rose happened to agree with her on that point.

"I do, Sergeant Downs. I am…a point of reference for people in the special abilities community. Because I have studied their gifts, and I do not judge, and I try to help when I can. I help them to 'police' themselves, if I may use that term."

"Oh, *that* you have to explain," Downie said. "It sounds like vigilante justice, which is not acceptable. Ever."

Miriam carefully didn't smile. Downie was open to the world and experience, but he had standards. He would enjoy seeing a real levitator or a real practitioner, but he would never accept someone policing their own community by their own rules. "We have the laws we have for a reason," he would say. "They're not just arbitrary crap."

Jones had an argument to make. "I would like to agree with you, Sergeant," she said as she began to replace the photographs in the folder. "But what would you do with a telepath who steals by twisting people's thoughts so they think they're making a gift to him of their valuables, their money, perhaps all that they have?"

"A thief is a thief," Miriam said. She desperately wanted that to be true. Because if this shit was real, then it was possible that Izzy and her father were right, that there was a bearded Old Man out there somewhere, and He required—

"This particular thief would have twisted your thoughts so you'd let him go."

"What did you do with him, then?" Miriam asked.

"I located another telepath who could resist his twisting. After that, I do not know what was done."

Miriam caught Downie's eye. "A little hand-washing?"

"Perhaps so, Detective," Jones said. "But no one involved in the...incident would allow me to stay."

Prentice finally spoke. "You're serious," he said.

Miriam knew Jones was serious. Miriam wanted Jones to be wrong, but she knew Jones believed every word she said. That didn't mean what she said was true, but—

"I am perfectly serious, Detective."

Silence fell until Downie nodded. "The body isn't possible unless we accept the possibility of magic." He looked directly at Miriam as he spoke. "The possibility, that's all I'm saying."

Even the possibility weighed on her chest, turning every breath into a struggle.

"I would like to see photos from the previous case," Jones said. "Is that possible?"

Prentice nodded and stood up. "It's being pulled. I should have it by the end of the day."

"I have classes to teach later, but I am free tomorrow morning."

"I can be here," Downie offered.

Again, Prentice nodded. "I'll be here, too."

"Your partner?" Dr. Jones sounded concerned for Garber.

Prentice shrugged. "Thank you for your help so far, Dr. Jones. See you in the morning."

After he left the room, Jones turned to face Miriam. "I do see how unhappy you are with the facts here, Detective. The way physics is taught—"

She stopped because Miriam held up a hand. "I'm not arguing with you, Professor Jones. If you help us solve these cases, I'll accept that we're all Venusians and you're the Queen of the Universe." Miriam stood up. "I'm babysitting for my grandchildren tomorrow morning, but Sergeant Downs will catch me up. Thanks."

Miriam took herself out of the room and to the parking garage before Downie caught up with her.

"Mir," he called.

She stopped and waited until he stood next to her. "As long as the case is solved."

"I've never seen you rude before."

"You need me to be charming?"

"No, Miriam. I need you to tell me what's wrong."

She rejected several sarcastic responses while he waited with that expression on his face. No anger, no impatience, just kind interest. The way she dealt with perps, with the look that said we're all just humans here, fallible humans. She could tell him the truth safely.

Instead, she shook her head.

"I know you're not scared."

"You don't know anything."

"Mir," he said and spread his arms wide. "It's me. We used to—"

She sighed. "No."

Downie didn't argue, just dropped his arms. "Mir." He sounded...tired, sad maybe.

It didn't matter to Miriam. Feeling the heat start to rise on her face, she turned and headed to her car.

He didn't follow her.

As she let herself into the car and the hot flash rose to her ears, she shook her head. *That was some magic, Kiddo. A few words and the man is no longer interested. Good show.*

Chapter 8
Monday

Sunday had turned into a wasted day. Once the police report had been made—well, Rose had hoped it would be an interesting experience, but the detective who took the report barely bothered. She was just another middle-aged woman, utterly uninteresting, totally ignorable. Invisible. Too bad, really, because she'd been looking for some insight into a real police investigation so she could compare it to the investigations in the murder mysteries she analyzed and wrote about. Detective Capelli had bordered on rude, so she didn't even consider talking to him about her ideas.

And once she got home, she hadn't been able to settle down to anything. TV, reading, paper-correcting, crocheting, nothing held her attention for more than a minute and a half. The girls hadn't picked up their phones or returned her calls. She just couldn't do anything. All because she wanted her Nana.

She, Rose Sherman, Ph.D., 52-year-old college professor, wanted her *dead* Nana. She wanted to call her dead Nana Pearl and smell the lavender that had always meant safety.

Ridiculous.

She'd distracted herself with concocting an elaborate eggplant salad, which required careful peeling, slicing, and cooking of the eggplant, tossing it into various greens and pasta, which also had to be cooked and drained, followed by eating that salad and storing the leftovers, a lot of leftovers, cleaning up, and then reading a few student essays, a couple of which showed a hint of original thinking. She'd taken herself to bed early, but now, Monday morning had arrived and she decided she would not be calling Nana Pearl anytime soon.

She was afraid, wasn't she? What if she called and Nana didn't come?

Worse: What if she called and Nana *did* come?

The precognition, telekinesis, ESP, Psi, whatever label anyone used, that was explainable in terms of electrochemical phenomena, right? But ghosts?

Ghosts were supernatural shit. Like vampires, werewolves, elves, fairies, trolls—what she'd heard her students call *woo-woo*.

So she didn't want to call Nana. Nothing supernatural for Rose Sherman, Ph.D., extraordinary intellectualizer that she was.

But she had to do *something*. Chocolate, tempting though it was at 8 on a Monday morning, had to be reserved for serious emergencies; it triggered hot flashes, not terrible, really, her private tropical vacations, but still. Chocolate could be used only when nothing else worked.

No. It was time to try something new. Rose walked into her small kitchen and considered the various small items in that room. She needed something light enough to move easily.

The cookbooks were too heavy, most of them; the phone was an enemy already—and if it broke, she'd have to buy another one because it was the landline for the alarm; the enamel tea kettle would chip if it were dropped, and besides, she liked it. There were the ugly salt and pepper shakers on the table that sat short edge against the wall. They'd been a Mother's Day gift from the girls many years ago.

Two black and white cows, fat, sitting like puppies, grinning, and with four holes between their perky little ears. Those cows were nothing Rose would ever have bought for herself, not even at her meekest.

At the time she opened the box and saw what Harry had helped them buy, she assumed the girls picked out the set, and he, being the loving, supportive daddy, had simply gone along with the atrocity.

Later, Rose had good reasons to doubt that assumption.

If one of those ugly little suckers broke, she would claim an accident, a tragic accident. *Poor thing.*

But okay. Even filled with salt and pepper, the cows were light enough to work with. She grabbed the yardstick from her office, laid it across the table, set the salt shaker alongside it, and sat herself down to stare at the ugly little cow.

She had no idea how to make it move without using her hand. She couldn't remember how telekinesis worked in the science fiction novels she'd read. Hannah wasn't answering her phone calls, so no help would be forthcoming there.

Instead, she stared at the little thing and thought at it: *Move, you ugly little stinker, move.*

Nothing happened.

Maybe she *couldn't* move it.

On *Charmed*, each sister had one particular gift. Maybe the writers on that show knew how the gifts, so called, worked.

Maybe she was supposed to imagine waves pushing from her head.

Nothing happened. That hideous thing just sat there grinning stupidly as if it knew something she didn't.

Rose squinted at the thing, getting angry. Hannah, who didn't want to be able to do it, could do it, so why couldn't Rose, who wanted to?

Stupid cow. Stupid, hideous, revolting cow. "Move," she snarled. "Move!"

The cow jumped along the yardstick. Rose jumped, too. "Shit!"

When her heart slowed down and she caught her breath, Rose checked the yardstick and saw that the cow had moved two inches away from her. That stupid, ugly cow had actually moved. Her hand had never touched it.

Rose slapped the table. "Ha!"

Ignoring the tingling in her hand, she pulled the cow back—using her hand—to its original position along the yardstick and thought about what she'd done to move it. She'd gotten angry. The cow moved with her emotion.

"Huh." Rose leaned back in the chair and stared at the salt shaker. She hated the phone, found it intrusive and annoying at best, and she knew when it was going to ring and who was calling. She hated the cow, too. She'd gotten angry because it wouldn't move—and, *let's be honest, Rosie*—because Harry, good old cheating Harry had encouraged the girls to choose the things for their mother. Evidently, some kind of emotional reaction was necessary to the phenomenon, at least to start with.

Poor cows. After Harry left, she kept them to remind herself that he hadn't wanted her for a long time before he asked for the divorce.

Stinking, cheating Harry. Poor ugly little cow. Come here now.

Damned if the cow didn't slide along the yardstick toward her, toward the edge of the table. Rose shoved herself away from the edge so the thing fell onto the floor and shattered with a satisfying noise.

"Oh. Oops." Rose smiled. She'd have to clean up the mess of china and salt the old-fashioned way, with broom and dustpan, or she'd be late for her appointment with Aunt Fanny's lawyer, but who cared? She had moved that stinker just by thinking.

And there was nothing supernatural about it. All she'd done was engage in electromagnetic phenomena, right? She was going to practice and master the skill.

Who knew what else she might be able to do?

Rose Sherman, superhero? Definitely a possibility.

Take that, *Harry Sherman. And you, too, Hannah Levine. Who needs you? Not your safe little Rosie anymore. Ha.*

She would be as easy with it as Hannah and...

Hmmm. There was the question: What was she supposed to do with these talents or gifts or whatever they were? Maybe it was time to speak with Cal Jones, who was said to know about these things.

And in the meanwhile, she needed to drive down to Colchester to see Teddy Breslow about Aunt Fanny's estate and then office hours and classes beckoned. Life had to be lived.

Still, Rose smiled. Maybe all this stuff would turn out to be okay. Maybe Rose Sherman was going to be okay. Time would tell.

60

Chapter 9
Monday

Granted it was Monday, not Hannah's favorite day of the week at the best of times, but particularly not during the school year. She didn't mind getting up early; she always got up early. The problem was that the kids took their time settling in after their weekends, and her colleagues likewise took their time settling in. God knew *she* took her time.

But the day had turned seriously weird before she'd even left the bed. Her cell buzzed with a text alert: School cancelled, call the usual number for information.

School was cancelled? Not for snow. It was far too warm for snow. Weird March weather, so warm she didn't need a jacket.

Now, she left David sleeping, went into the hall, and dialed the alert number, expecting a recording from the principal, and she got it. "Vandalism has been perpetrated in the pool house. This vandalism is egregious and is being investigated by the Wethersfield Police with assistance from the state's forensics laboratory. After their investigation is complete, the pool house must be cleaned and tested before we can reopen. You will be notified of the school's status each morning by alert. Thank you."

Hannah stared at the phone. Vandalism in the pool house so bad that they had to cancel school? She couldn't imagine what it might be, didn't want to. But still, it had to be serious.

"Egregious," she muttered.

"Egregious" was one of the principal's favorite words. Kids running in the hall was "an egregious deviation from the rules," not to mention chewing gum and wearing flip-flops rather than shoes.

But school *had* been cancelled and the state forensics lab *was* assisting the local police. Maybe the vandalism *was* egregious.

It was entirely possible. The swim team kids could be serious brats. Champion athletes, often given a pass for a lot of behavior like bullying and cheating that other kids would be suspended for, they could easily have provoked other kids into significant retaliation.

But retaliation bad enough that the state crime lab had to get involved?

Very strange.

On the other hand, she'd had the day off anyway because she had an appointment first thing with Aunt Fanny's lawyer about a bequest. Aunt Fanny had been gone for several years now, but the call from the lawyer's office had been clear. She had a bequest coming from Aunt Fanny's estate.

So she got dressed, ate a buttered English muffin, sipped her one cup of coffee for the day, suffered her hot flash triggered by the caffeine, kissed David, got in her car, and drove down to Colchester and the offices of Martindale, Martindale, and Breslow. Very nice offices, pearl grey and lavender, discreet, quiet, calm. Silver tea service, bone china cups and saucers, brewed tea, no tea bags, and carefully laid out lemon slices and sugar cubes with silver tongs.

Young Teddy Breslow was very polite. "Mrs. Levine, this," "Mrs. Levine, that," "Mrs. Levine, Mrs. Hertzkowtitz instructed me particularly. I must read her bequest to you. But first, I must ask you whether you continue to use Winkler as your middle name."

A bit of family weirdness: Every child in the family carried Winkler as his or her middle name. When she had asked her mother why, the answer was "because."

"Yes," Hannah said. "It's traditional. We're all Winklers."

"It's a condition of the bequest, which is as follows: 'To Hannah Winkler Levine, my Bösendorfer piano, to be delivered and tuned at no expense to her, after she has been married to David Levine for one year—'"

"Excuse me?" Hannah frowned at the lawyer. "I'm sorry, but when was this will written?"

Breslow didn't hesitate. "It was signed by Mrs. Hertzkowtitz in 1998."

"Oh, but that's..."*Impossible,* she'd been about to say, but it wasn't impossible, was it? She could move things by pointing at them. Cousin Rose knew things were going to happen before they happened. Not *years* ahead, but the principle was the same, wasn't it.

Hannah smiled. "It's a wonderful bequest. I love that piano."

Breslow smiled, too. "Even *Chopsticks* sounded brilliant on that piano."

It took Hannah a second or two to remember that Teddy Breslow's grandmother used to play canasta with Aunt Fanny and some other old ladies, even Nana Pearl, until Mrs. Breslow died. His grandmother had given up driving for some reason or other, so he drove his grandmother to and from Fanny's house. He knew Fanny and had heard her play. "It did," she said, suddenly uncomfortable.

Not suddenly, really. It was all the same problem: David. He could never know about the specifics of the bequest. *Never.*

"I am going to be home for at least a couple of days this week—school is closed...for repairs—"which he hadn't needed to know about—"so if you could arrange something by Wednesday..."

"I'm sure we can. I'll call you later today with the details."

"Perfect," she said, already making a mental to-do list: Decide what had to be moved to make room for the piano, call the handyman to arrange the moving, and decide whether to give the displaced furniture away or store it. "I'll wait to hear from you."

She picked up her purse, smiled at Breslow one more time, and left his office.

It was all just so strange. Aunt Fanny had known, long before Hannah even considered coming back to the States, that she would come back and marry David Levine. Long before Hannah knew that David Levine even existed, Aunt Fanny had named *him* specifically. Aunt Fanny had been possessed of *serious* precognition. And she'd married into a family in which one member was also a precognitive and another was a telekinetic, and it was all just too damned strange.

If she'd been able to go to school, she could have buried herself in *Animal Farm* and *Romeo and Juliet* and all the drama teenagers generated.

That avenue of distraction was closed, and the day stretched out in front of her. No Rose, no Miriam—she couldn't talk to anyone about any of this.

Well, she had to call Andy and get some furniture moved. That would take some time. There were books to read, gardens to plan....She would be fine. She had to be.

Chapter 10
Monday

S tanding in the front hall, Miriam checked the caller ID on her cell, slid the phone back in her jeans pocket, and kissed the baby sleeping on her other arm. His mother was stowing groceries, and Gramma Miriam wasn't interested in phone calls from the job. She was Gramma first and a Cold Case consultant second or maybe a hundred thirty-second.

Besides, it was Monday morning, and the baby's big sister was waiting in the living room to read to Gramma before the bus came to take her to kindergarten.

The phone chimed again in her pocket.

"Ma," Maddy called from the kitchen. "Shouldn't you answer your phone?"

"I'm not on duty," was the simple answer. Miriam wasn't going to explain that Lieutenant Winewski wouldn't accept facts, that he wanted his detectives when he wanted them, or that she wasn't even actually one of his detectives anymore. The Lieutenant was a good cop and a good boss most of the time, but he could demand too much from his detectives—and she wasn't one of his detectives anymore. Maddy didn't need to hear all of that. She'd never needed to know about the job.

The phone stopped ringing as Madeline appeared in the kitchen doorway, tomato in hand. "From the job?"

Maddy looked tense, even strained, her lips pulled thin, her shoulders up.

"They don't own me, for—"

The phone rang again. *Damn it.*

She was a volunteer, a retired volunteer. Winewski could kiss— But she wasn't supposed to use that kind of language anymore.

The phone stopped.

"Ma," Maddy said as the phone rang again.

"Go finish with the groceries, "Miriam said, pulling the phone out of her pocket. "I'm not working now."

Little Mark frowned and squeaked as if he were waking up. She needed to answer the phone to stop Winewski.

"Miriam Fine." She did *not* snarl into the phone. She came close, but she didn't snarl.

"It's me."

"I know, Lieutenant."" The man apparently didn't believe that caller ID worked.

"Has Jones gotten back to you with anything?"

"No. She's not answering her phone."

"Damn it. Richter wants action soonest."

Captain Richter always wanted action soonest. It was a standing joke in Robbery-Homicide. "I don't know what to tell you, Mike. I think she's checking her sources."

"Damn it. Isn't there someone else?"

"If there is, I don't know, and neither does Downie."

Dead air was the response. She shook her head as she tucked the phone back in her jeans and looked up to see Maddy staring at her.

"An important case?" Maddy's eyes were open wide, her eyebrows up. Scared?

Miriam adjusted the baby in her arm. "Not as important as this guy."

Nodding, Maddy turned back into the kitchen. "Dangerous?"

Given that the baby's father had died just seven months ago in a car accident, Maddy's worry was understandable. "The baby?"

"Ma."

"Yes, I know. Sorry. There's a current case that ties into something I handled a while before I retired. I'm just consulting with someone Downie and I know who might have information that could help. That's all. Just consulting."

It wasn't just Big Mark's death that upset Madeline. Three years ago, her father and her brother had walked out, leaving her, no surprise, with *lots* of abandonment issues. "Maddy." Miriam followed her daughter into the kitchen where Maddy was flattening her shopping bags. "I'm just consulting."

Maddy looked up from the bags, her eyes glittering.

Tears? Her daughter was on the verge of crying. "Maddy, really. I'm in no danger. There are more cops around me than there were when I was on the job. I don't—"

"There's a gun in your purse, Ma."

"There's always been a weapon in my purse, Honey. It's a require—"

"You'll get shot again, and—"

Again? "What?" Almost never in all her years on the job had she ever actually pulled a trigger. Weapons had been drawn, yes. Of course. But fired? Miriam Fine talked people out of their weapons, a point of pride. She'd never been shot. Never. Didn't Maddy remember?

Of course she didn't. How could she? Miriam had never talked to her children about the job. She'd protected them from the ugliness. She'd just refused to share information about her overstepping boss. Habit. "Maddy, Honey, it's not like on TV."

Maddy was staring down at the shopping bags so Miriam couldn't read her face. "Madeline. I've never been shot."

Now Maddy looked up, tears definitely shining in her eyes. "That time we had to pick you up from the hospital? When you were on crutches?"

"Because I sprained my ankle."

The baby whimpered. Of course he did. Miriam's voice had gotten too loud too close to his delicate little ears. She had to speak softly. "Madeline. It was a sprained ankle."

"Daddy said you'd been hurt on the job. He cursed about guns."

Daring her to call Izzy a liar? Not a problem. "If your father said or even let you think I was shot, he lied. I actually tripped on garbage in a chase. Really embarrassing, but I'll give you permission to see my medical records if you don't believe me."

The truth *was* embarrassing. She'd chased a guy down an alley strewn with smelly stuff; he threw a garbage can, she ducked and slid in garbage and fell. It turned out okay; the guy actually stopped running to look at her when she fell, letting Downie, who'd circled the building the other way, grab him from behind. "By the way, I'm the one who's supposed to dispense the guilt here."

Maddy's smile was feeble, but it was a smile. "I'm glad you feel guilty."

"But I don't, Maddy, not about the job. I was good at it. And I loved it. That's why I volunteer for Cold Case." She took a deep breath.

"Maybe I should have told you and David about what I was doing. Why the gun had to be in the purse when I was off duty. Why it's there now—unloaded in this house, by the way. The ammunition is in the glove compartment in my car when I'm in this house."

Maddy didn't look convinced. "I guess." She started for the refrigerator. "It's scary, Ma."

Miriam ventured a chuckle. "Like letting a certain 16-year-old go to the prom with Drew Dickerman?" Maddy's first unchaperoned date.

"Oh, my God," Maddy laughed.

"Yeah." Miriam blew her breath out. "Local drug dispensary he turned out to be, didn't he?" Actually, the kid was arrested three days after the prom with at least a kilo of coke in his trunk. Miriam could only thank Whoever for the fact that Maddy wasn't in the car when Wethersfield PD stopped Drew and found the drugs in the trunk hidden under his spare tire.

Hand on the refrigerator handle, Maddy turned to face her mother. "Okay, Ma. I give up. It's okay."

"Obviously not, Mad. But we can talk about it. I can tell you what I'm doing, not all of it, but as much as I can."

Maddy waved a hand. "I'm over-reacting, I know. Sadie is waiting to read to you. We got more books from the library. And Ma? You can put the baby down. He really does sleep all by himself." She smiled.

As if Gramma would voluntarily put her grandson down. She didn't get to hold him enough. "You can't spoil a two-month-old."

And she didn't get to sit with her beautiful granddaughter often enough, either. Sadie pouted a little at the sight of Gramma holding the baby, but she perked up at the compliment on her curly dark ponytail in the purple scrunchie.

Still, it was hard to concentrate on *Hop on Pop* as read by the wondrous little girl, her beautiful Sadie.

Because Miriam hadn't known that Izzy used to keep himself busy encouraging fear in his children about their mother and her job. That's what he'd done. And she hadn't known. She hadn't been aware of what was going on in her own house.

How could Miriam Fine, the great detective, have not known what was going on with her children?

Well. There was the guilt Maddy wanted.

How the hell could she ever have through she was a good detective? How had she thought she could solve *anything? Good God.*

Some detective she was.

***

The drive down to Colchester made a good break from the guilt, even early on a Monday in March, even if it took Miriam away from the grandchildren, even if it was to see Aunt Fanny's lawyer. Sweet Aunt Fanny, who had married one of Nana's brothers, who had helped her *and* Rose *and* Hannah because she knew all about their lunatic mothers. She'd never said anything, but Aunt Fanny used to show up when bad shit happened, especially after Nana Pearl died.

But Aunt Fanny died in 1999. So how did a bequest suddenly happen now, more than ten years later? What sorts of requirements had Aunt Fanny attached to her bequests?

Okay. Miriam Fine was a detective. She solved mysteries for a living. Of course, most of the mysteries she solved weren't so mysterious. The obvious suspect was generally the perp; the rare exceptions were, in fact, rare. And even the exceptions were usually other people's mysteries. She did *not* want or need mysteries in her own life.

Well, okay, Teddy Breslow would explain, and everything would be made clear. As mysteries went, this one was minor anyway, like the story of how a Breslow, Teddy's great-great grandfather, an Orthodox Jew, came to be law partners with two old Yankees like the Martindales.

Miriam had overheard bits and pieces of the story here and there, but never enough to put it all together. And she'd never been curious enough about it to ask because it really didn't concern her, and when she was younger, she hadn't cared about the history. Rose knew some bits and pieces, too, but when they tried to put it together, they'd discovered they knew the same bits and pieces. Now, the only way to find out was to ask Teddy. Maybe she would.

That was a minor mystery that didn't matter in the long run, anyway. What mattered was, she sat in the tiny parking lot behind the Martindale, Martindale, Breslow building when she should be going into the beautifully restored Victorian. Why she was so reluctant to move, she had no idea.

Come on, Detective Fine, let's go.

She went and saw that the understated elegance of the entry was matched by the understated receptionist, a brunette in her thirties dressed in a black suit and modest white blouse. A smiled greeting, a murmur into a phone, and another understated young woman appeared at the reception desk to walk her down an understated hall to young Teddy Breslow's office.

"Mrs. Fine," the young woman announced, and Teddy Breslow stood up to shake her hand and gesture her to a small armchair upholstered to match the rest of the grey and lavender décor.

Teddy had grown up nicely, tall, broad-shouldered and curly haired. She smiled, remembering the gawky kid who used to drive his grandmother to Fanny's house for canasta, mandelbrot, and gossip. God, the gossip those ladies had shared. But Aunt Fanny always gave Teddy some of her amazing almond biscotti—mandelbrot with a more socially acceptable name—and he would sit in the kitchen waiting for his grandmother, and if Miriam was there, they'd sit together and listen to the old women tell the most astounding stories about people they all knew. Some of those stories, she knew now, were morally loaded, like how a particular man had survived Auschwitz, how another had made a small fortune in a way Miriam knew she'd have investigated. At the time, she and Teddy had been most concerned about how long the card game would last.

Now she sat, waiting for him to speak. Like most experienced interrogators, she was good with silence.

He smiled again. "You're still using Winkler as your middle name, correct?"

Miriam nodded. "You don't happen to know why we all have to be Winklers, do you?" She didn't actually expect an answer.

"Mrs. Hertzkowtitz never said, and there's no record of anyone else ever explaining, at least to my knowledge."

Miriam sat up straighter. "There are records of other things being explained?"

"We have records of legal transactions and documents, yes, going back to Moishe Hertzkowtitz and Rachel Winkler who married in...1882, I believe. And I am not revealing any secrets to say that Mrs. Moishe Hertzkowtitz's children all used Winkler as their middle name."

Nana Pearl was the youngest of the six children of Rachel Winkler Hertzkowtitz who lived to adulthood, Miriam knew. So it wasn't some whim of Pearl's three daughters or of Pearl herself. It was more than just "because." And if there was a reason, it could be found like—

"Your use of the name is a condition of the bequest. It has been since this firm started serving the Hertzkowtitz slash Winkler family."

"But we're not—well, I suppose if we were matrilineal, as Cousin Rose would say...if we count descent through women, then...but Aunt Fanny married in..." Miriam looked up at the lawyer, whose face was carefully, politely neutral. *They must teach that look in law school.* "Sorry. Thinking out loud."

"I understand. There's a great deal of, let's call it puzzlement around this bequest." He smiled. "Shall I proceed?"

If the lawyer admitted to being puzzled, it would be a doozy. "Yes, please, go ahead."

He nodded. "I have to read the relevant portion of the will. 'To my niece Miriam Winkler Fine, after her divorce from Isaac Fine has been final for at least one year, the—'"

"What was that?" She *had* been paying attention; she had *not* been drifting or daydreaming or otherwise inattentive. But she needed to hear the words again. "Repeat that, please."

Breslow nodded. "'To my—'"

"The part about the divorce."

"'After her divorce from Isaac Fine has been final for—'"

"Fanny Hertzkowtitz died in November of 1999."

"Correct."

"And the will was written when?"

"In July of 1998."

When Fanny had received the awful diagnosis. "But I wasn't even—Isaac hadn't—How did Fanny know?" Had there been signs? Miriam had missed the unhappiness of her children, their fear, and Izzy's encouragement of that fear. Maybe Fanny had seen signs of trouble in the marriage.

But to be so sure that she would make it a condition of a bequest? *That* was not possible. *Not possible.*

Like the inside-out bodies. Not possible, but there it was, in black and white, on the page Teddy Breslow was reading. "Sorry. Go ahead."

Breslow cleared his throat and went on. "'To my niece Miriam Winkler Fine, after her divorce from Isaac Fine has been final for at least one year, the pin called *Tannah*. She may decline this bequest on condition that she name an alternative heir.'"

"Why would I turn it down? It's a beautiful piece of jewelry."

"We had it appraised for Mrs. Hertzkowtitz when the will was made," Breslow said, picking up another piece of paper from his large, mostly clear desk. "We used Halmey and Kronen in Hartford, and, as you can see..." He passed the paper to her. "In 1998, it was worth approximately $10,000. The pin is at least 400 years old, conservatively. I can tell you that Mrs. Hertzkowtitz believed from family stories that the pin was older. The appraisers thought so, too, but no one could find any documentation older than 400 years."

He opened a drawer, from which he lifted a small black cloth bag that looked like fine wool, which he set gently on the desk between them. He tugged open the draw-string closure and withdrew a box of dark wood covered in cracqleur. Carefully, as if he were afraid it might fall apart in his hand, he lifted the lid and slid the bottom toward Miriam.

There lay *Tannah* on a bed of black silk. A marcasite dragon, maybe an inch and a half long, four-legged, wingless, with a ruby chip for an eye.

She had to smile. *Tannah* used to be Nana Pearl's, back when Miriam, Rose, and Hannah were young girls. She wore it everywhere and on every outfit, including bathing suits and nightgowns. And then, quite suddenly, Aunt Fanny was wearing it.

"We all wondered where *Tannah* went after Fanny died."

"Let me read you the rest of the bequest. I quote: '*Tannah* carries a great responsibility, and if Miriam Winkler Fine believes the responsibility to be too great, she may decline this bequest, provided she names an alternative heir, who must also be a Winkler in the female line who is willing to assume this responsibility.'"

He looked up at her. "I don't know what the responsibility entails. It isn't specified here or in any of the Winkler wills or documents in which the pin was transferred or bequeathed. I did look, because I thought you would ask, but I could find nothing specific."

Miriam frowned. "Aunt Fanny didn't know?"

"No. I am betraying no confidence when I say she herself was puzzled. And she specifically gave me permission to tell you that she thought you might be able to investigate and find out what *Tannah* represents. She thought your being a police investigator would help. She also said it was appropriate that the pin belong to a police officer."

Miriam shook her head as if that action could stop the circling thoughts. Puzzle after puzzle. "Well, I do want the pin. Whether I ever know what the responsibility is or not, it was Nana's and then Aunt Fanny's, and I love it."

Nodding, Breslow produced another piece of paper and slid it across to her. "There is one more stipulation. As you can read here, you must promise to wear it all the time, and you must name an heir for the pin now. The assignment you make now will override any other bequest of the pin—"

"Is this the usual—or should I say, is this the way *Tannah* has been passed along since Rachel Hertzkowtitz. I'm assuming she originated the bequest, correct?"

"Yes. At least as far as Martindale Martindale Breslow has been involved with the family's legal interests."

"So. Every woman who's had the pin—oh, but Nana Pearl didn't leave it in her will. She must have given it to Aunt Fanny. How—"

"You mean Pearl Winkler Hertkowitz Kasner?"

Miriam smiled. "Also known as Nana Pearl."

Teddy smiled back. "I can tell you that Mrs. Kasner came in with Mrs. Hertkowitz and they signed the required papers to transfer the pin from Mrs. Kasner to Mrs. Hertkowitz."

"Huh," Miriam huffed and leaned back in the chair. "Okay. It's weird. But no weirder than anything else that's been going on lately. So I'll take a cup of tea and think about who might be an appropriate heir."

Breslow picked up his phone and asked for tea, then set the phone down and smiled at her. "Remember: it has to be a Winkler in the female line. I can't explain why, but those are the requirements."

She nodded. There were three possibilities: her own daughter, Maddy, and Rose's two daughters, Pena and Tava.

Maddy had recently suffered the sudden loss of her husband and was raising two children with help from Miriam and, when she wasn't traveling, Big Mark's mother Rosalind. That was enough for Maddy to handle.

Pena always took the practical approach to life. Rose said her older daughter rarely read fiction, her choice of rebellion against her English-teacher mother, but also, Rose said in a rare bit of gossip, Pena had a practical imagination and a quiet sense of humor—that much Miriam knew from personal experience. Pena was a serious young woman who worked hard as an emergency room nurse and might not want the mystery of *Tannah* in her already busy life.

That left Tava. But Tava was perfect. The opposite of her older sister, funny and imaginative and about to graduate from medical school, she would take *Tannah* seriously and probably goad Miriam into solving the mystery surrounding the pin if Miriam took too long to do that.

So while Teddy Breslow's secretary poured tea, Miriam and the lawyer began the paperwork that would make *Tannah* hers and Tava's after her.

It took a while to get everything signed, but finally *Tannah* was pinned to the lapel of her blazer and she was ready to drive back to Hartford.

"I know I'm presuming, Mrs. Fine, but if you ever do find out what *Tannah* represents, I would love to know. We could put it in the family file, so the information can be available to other family members."

"If I ever find out. There's no one of Fanny's generation left to ask, as far as I know. And of my parents' generation, the only person I know who is still alive abandoned his wife and daughter and has refused any contact with us, so it may be difficult to get any kind of information at all. But I *will* look into it, and anything I learn, I'll get to you so you can put it in the family file. Definitely. And thank you."

Breslow stood up and walked her out to reception. "Your grandmother and your aunt were my grandmother's very good friends. And both of them were always kind to me. Besides, Fanny's mandelbrot—I've never had anything so good since."

"Oh. Yes, well. Rose, you know my cousin Rose Sherman? She has the recipe and hers comes pretty close. Maybe we can get some down to you."

He laughed. "That would be wonderful."

"I'll see what we can do." Miriam smiled and turned to go, then turned back. "Here's a mystery you can solve, nothing to do with this business, and if I'm being nosy, tell me, please. But Rose and I have always been curious about how Martindale and Martindale became Martindale Martindale and Breslow. Two Connecticut Yankees and an Orthodox Jew?"

Teddy laughed. "It is a funny thing, isn't it? But it was really just a matter of practicalities. When the firm was founded, there weren't many Jews in the area. But then, you know the story of how Baron Rothchild bought land in Colchester for Jewish refugees from the pogroms in Eastern Europe?"

Miriam nodded, beginning to see how the story would end.

"So now, there were a lot of Orthodox Jews in the area, and not just in Colchester. People brought over their relatives, who bought land in East Haddam, Chester, and Deep River, and those people needed a lawyer who could speak Yiddish and English. At first, Great-Great Grandpa Chaim had a solo practice, but James and John Martindale knew a business opportunity when they saw one, and Chaim had more business than he could handle alone. So, they got together." He laughed again. "Not much of a mystery, I'm afraid, not even a very good story."

Miriam chuckled, too. "Not much of a mystery is a relief, to be honest. I'm sure Rose will think so, too. Thanks. I'll see about getting you some of Rose's mandelbrot."

She made sure *Tannah* was secure on her lapel before she left the office.

Back in the car, Miriam pulled out her notebook and pen and wrote down everything about the bequest so she could put it all aside to think about later. She would have to think about it because it was just...more than strange. It was weird. And irrational.

God, but for a woman who hated irrationality, she was becoming mired in it. And the harder she fought it, the worse it got.

Chapter 11
Monday

• ——————— •◆• ——————— •

Hyperventilation did *not* help the situation, but Rose panted anyway and felt the warm flush hit her ears. At least she'd waited until she sat in her car to panic.

Definitely panicked. *At last.* After months of developing precognition, deliberately cultivating telekinesis, talking to a ghost, a *ghost, for God's sake,* the old familiar panic had struck.

And what broke through the calm produced by two years of meditation? Aunt Fanny's will. Which she could quote, the words now engraved permanently on her brain: "With respect to the following bequest, it is my wish that it not be implemented until the divorce of my niece Rose Winkler Sherman from Harold Sherman has been final at least one year..."

Aunt Fanny had been a precognitive just like she was. It wasn't just Rose and Hannah, but there was no one to talk to about it. No one. What was she supposed to do? Be glad for Aunt Fanny's record collection, the old seventy-eights she'd learned to foxtrot to—good thing she'd kept her turntable even after Pena thought she should give the old thing away, because who needs a turntable anymore—and the jewelry, beautiful jewelry, of course, some of it old-fashioned but all things she loved because they'd belonged to Fanny. She was glad, grateful, surprised—but Aunt Fanny's precognition? It was too much, too damned much. The woman had known years, *years* before.

Okay, Rosie. Pull it together. You have an office hour, you have students to take care of, you have a meeting to go to, you have two classes to teach, and you will, by God, do it all.

Because no one else was going to pay the bills, Rose sat in her little red Toyota, two years older than Miriam's little red Toyota, breathing deeply until she felt steady. Then she pushed in the clutch, eased back on the brake, eased up on the clutch, missed the gas pedal, and stalled the car.

Maybe not so steady, Rosie. Try again.

She had to go to work. She had to meet with Cal Jones at three. After all, Cal Jones was going to help her. Assuming, of course, that the lady's room stories were true.

Come on, Rosie. You've dealt with worse. Take, for example, your mother.

She smiled at the windshield. Her mother probably would have scared Charles Manson into behaving well. Or running away. And she, Rose Winkler Sherman, had escaped her mother, hadn't she? Yes, she had.

This time, the clutch, brake, and gas pedal went in the proper order. First gear came under her hand the way it did, with no thought on her part, just muscle memory, and off she went.

The line of students outside her tiny office in Hillyer Hall reassured her. She wouldn't have a lot of time to think about the visit to the lawyer or much of anything else.

In fact, she barely had time to set her tote bag down and boot up the computer when Susan Wheaton bopped into the room, pulling ear buds out of her ears. Her jeans looked sprayed on, but that wasn't unusual. Pretty much every female student on campus wore jeans that molded to the body. Pena, Tava, and Maddy did, too. Rose didn't. But okay.

"Hey, Professor Sherman." The standard greeting.

"Ms. Wheaton. What can I do for you today?"

"I won't be in class after today."

"Okay." The Intro to Narratology paper was due Friday. "Are you ill?"

"No. I've got a flight home tomorrow afternoon."

Rose carefully did not roll her eyes, but Chicago isn't exactly off the beaten path, *forgive the cliché*. There are multiple flights out of Bradley to O'Hare every day, including Friday. Not to mention that Susan Wheaton, like every student on and off campus, had multiple means of accessing the academic calendar and knew exactly when spring break started: Friday evening at 8 pm.

"So either your paper will be in my mailbox before you leave tomorrow afternoon, or you are going to email me a copy by Friday at 2, when class ends."

"Well, um, I thought I'd turn it in after break." Ms. Wheaton bestowed a perky smile, accompanied by a perky hair flip, on Rose.

"Then your paper will be late."

"Late? But—"

Rose counted acceptable reasons for late papers on her fingers. "One: your illness. Two: illness or death in the family. Three: class cancellation—and spring break is *not* a cancellation. Four: a significant emergency on campus. The reasons are all listed on the syllabus."

Her smile no longer perky, Ms. Wheaton nodded. "I'll email it to you before the end of class Friday."

"I look forward to reading it."

"Yeah," Sara said and walked out, making way for Julio Gonzalez from the Tuesday first-year comp class, who wanted to turn in *his* research paper after break. He'd known about the assignment since the first day of class, but Julio was a perfectionist, therefore a major procrastinator. Rose could sympathize, having overcome the same problem herself because a professor hadn't given in to her pleas for more time. So no mercy. "Progress, not perfection, Mr. Gonzalez. Keep repeating that." He left, not looking particularly convinced of anything except that a due date really is a due date. Or maybe he was convinced of his doom. One way or the other, however, he understood that he had to turn in that paper.

So the hour went. Rose smiled and gently denied all but one request, that being from a student whose father was actually seriously ill, per the Dean's office. *Thank God for all the normal weaselly behavior. So nicely distracting.* And then she taught her classes, after which it was time for her appointment with Cal Jones, whose office was two flights up, whose overt specialty was folklore but whose lady's room reputation labeled her an expert in—call it the paranormal. *That* Cal Jones.

Also, the Cal Jones whose stunning, even shocking beauty made Angelina Jolie look like a wannabe. Just what every 52-year-old recently divorced woman needs to face on a Monday afternoon after major weirdness.

Of course, Cal wasn't responsible for what her genes had created, so Rose marched herself up the two flights of stairs and down the hall to the Religion and Folklore office, passing the department secretary with a "Hi, Kathy," and a wave.

Kathy, a plump, dark woman around Rose's age, stopped her. "Just a moment, Dr. Sherman."

"I have an appointment."

"I know, but Dr. Jones had a family emergency and had to leave. Actually, she went flying out of here as if the devil were after her, but she did leave this for you."

"This" was a large manila envelope taped closed, marked "DR. ROSE SHERMAN PERSONAL AND CONFIDENTIAL." It felt light in Rose's hand; therefore, it was papers of some kind.

"Thanks, Kathy. See you at the next Women's Wednesday?"

"Absolutely."

They chatted for a few minutes about the upcoming meeting, a presentation by a woman on the University staff who traveled to all sorts of places by herself, some of them places Rose wouldn't go with an armed escort. But then, Rose was notoriously careful about traveling, alone or otherwise. Always sure she would become hopelessly lost, even with a GPS system, she planned and over-planned and planned some more, then suffered bouts of anxiety all through her trips.

Rose finally excused herself to go back to her office, where she unfortunately had plenty of time to read the contents of the envelope. Except she sat for several minutes staring at the thing. *Honestly, Rose, such a cliché, frightened of papers in an envelope. Besides, you've had your allotted ten minutes of panic today.*

She used the blade of her scissors to open the envelope and pulled the papers out, four typed sheets stapled together to which a handwritten note had been paper-clipped.

"Dr. Sherman," the note read. "Forgive me for not being able to keep our appointment. I am eager to discuss your paper on Martha Grimes in *Modern Fiction Studies* with you. Your approach is interesting and different from the usual 'double narrative' papers I've read."

Rose snorted in surprise and felt herself flush and warm. She hadn't expected anyone to actually read the paper or to find it interesting. Hoped maybe. But, okay, back to the note.

"Forgive, too, my presumption in offering you the attached pages. Your reticence on the telephone leads me to believe they are relevant. If I am mistaken, you must feel free to laugh at my expense.

"If I am not mistaken, I also suggest a call to Dr. Mikhail Petrovsky, who lives in Mansfield Center, at 860-492-0077. He is far more expert than I in the development of these matters and can advise you on learning to manage them."

The pages themselves looked like photocopies of photocopies, fuzzy and speckled, but all legible. The first page was a glossary of terms: clairaudience, clairvoyance, telekinesis, nothing she hadn't already Googled for herself.

The second page was labeled "An Extended Physics." It began: "What is conventionally referred to as the paranormal is completely within the realm of the 'normal.' Even 'magic' can be explained by physical rules now known and understood—"

Magic? Abracadabra presto change-o magic? The woo-woo stuff? Not woo-woo?

Well, Dr. Sherman. Here is a fine how-dee-do. All that nifty, logical education you worked so hard for—

Just shut up and read, Rosie.

There was a lot of physics, actually. Rose caught a bit: "On the quantum level, particles are not defined in time and space but rather by probability. Particles can be in two places at the same time and communicate instantaneously regardless of distance.

"On the macro level, the human level of observable phenomena, definition in time and space occurs, and the speed of light is the limiter of all phenomena. Such is the physics of Newton.

"So-called magic, along with all other paranormal phenomena such as telekinesis, is merely the application of quantum physics on the macro level. Practitioners of magic..."

"Huh," Rose said and skipped down to the subsection labeled "Genetics." "Four genetic mutations, inherited—"

"Inherited?" she said out loud. That was the word on the page. Right there. "Inherited." Hannah had a gift, she had gifts, but Aunt Fanny, whose precognition outdid Rose's by *years, for God's sake, years,* had married in. She was a Winkler by marriage, had adopted the middle name for some reason never explained. *Off the point, Rosie. Read.*

Because there was more to read. "Families in whom the traits occur generally hold the information closely, but they have been identified—"

Holy shit! "*Identified?*" She said it out loud, repeated it in a whisper, went back to the paper, which didn't go on much longer and didn't say *who* had identified the families.

Rose straightened the four pages out, replaced the paper clip, slid them into the envelope, and taped over the slit she'd made, lips compressed all the while, her heart tap-tap-tapping like a woodpecker going after a meal.

If only Cal were there to answer her questions. Except only the family could answer some of the questions. If the trait—that's what the paper called it, a trait—ran in families, why hadn't she known? Another secret in a long line of secrets? Did Hannah know? Did Miriam? No one had ever said anything. *Ever.*

But they were all pros at keeping secrets, the Winklers were.

And the kids? What about the kids? Did they—would they—

Hyperventilation did nothing. She had to teach one more class, just one hour. After class, she'd go home and think about this stuff, figure out what to do. She was good at thinking; that's what the Ph.D. was about, after all. And no one could intellectualize better than Rose Winkler Sherman. No one.

Her chocolate stash was empty. She'd just have to breathe and get home as soon as she could.

This was so not okay. *God. Not okay.*

Chapter 12
Monday

Having notified Phillipe that he wished to discuss his will and certain related matters, Peter found he could focus on reports from the Trust's agents. He summarized each report as he read, planning to compile the summaries into the quarterly financial report to the *phyle* that he and Gerard issued. He was very good at overseeing the Drakon Trust and the Ladon Fund, good at reading spreadsheets and identifying trends and problems before they became trends and problems, even good at explaining the complex behavior of markets and so on to people who didn't understand much about money other than how to spend it.

He had started life as a fisherman. Now he helped to move billions of dollars around the world, a task he supposed he would perform until he died. If he died.

He worked through the morning until his phone rang. He glanced at the caller ID and felt surprise.

His caller was Arlo Braxton, one of the three unaffiliated vampires remaining in the Hartford area. None of them had ever been part of the *phyle,* finding the association with casters, in particular, unseemly, but they cooperated in the effort to stay hidden. No one wanted exposure and the resulting unpredictable, yet almost certainly unpleasant, consequences. However, Peter had cut off William Lowell's head, and the other three simply cut him and the rest of the *phyle* off. They did nothing to draw human attention to themselves, but they behaved as if the *phyle* and Peter in particular did not exist.

Yet Arlo was calling Peter.

The news would not be good.

"Good morning, Arlo," Peter said as warmly as he could. "How are you?"

"Smith." Arlo sneered at Peter's pseudonym. "You've got a rogue wolf."

Shocked, hoping the rogue wasn't a LeBeau wolf, Peter had to arrange his thoughts before he could ask, "Can you give me more information, please?"

"Not one of your pack. He smelled different. And he didn't look...well-fed. Not starved but not...sleek. Your wolves always look sleek and clean. You know what I mean."

Relieved to know it wasn't one of Martin's wolves and determined not to argue with Arlo over whose wolves the pack was, Peter simply agreed with the other vampire. "I do know what you mean, yes."

The *Phyle* took good care of all its members. The wolves didn't look scruffy and flea-ridden, not even after a hunt. That was not important, however. "But, Arlo, where did you come across this rogue?"

There was a moment's pause before Arlo answered the question. "In an alley off Homestead Avenue, near Woodland Street. He was chewing on a homeless human, or so it looked to me."

Peter understood Arlo's hesitation before answering the question. That neighborhood is centered on St. Francis Hospital and various medical facilities. The hospital, in particular, had a blood bank. Peter did not want to know whether Arlo was stealing blood from the hospital again. He could hardly blame the other vampire if he was. Human blood was the vampires' natural drink, after all, and nearly irresistible.

The hospital was an easy source if one were careful, kept the theft small and of a common blood type easily replaced. The humans seemed to consider a missing pint or two the result of sloppy record-keeping, particularly if there had been a busy night in the Emergency Department. At least, that's how it looked to Peter.

However, as much as one could, one had to resist the urge. Making a habit of drinking human blood, that nearly irresistible combination of iron, salt, and—

Even thinking about it made Peter's fangs ache for it. He had to think clearly now. "I take it the wolf is not there now. Is the human body still there?"

"No," Arlo said. "Something startled him, not me; he couldn't see or hear me, I promise you. But something startled him, and he took the remains and ran off."

"So he was in half form."

"He could hardly manage to carry the body in full, could he?" Arlo's sneer was back.

"Of course. I suppose I am surprised by the presence of a rogue. The LeBeau pack marks territory regularly."

"He looked hungry," was all Arlo had to say on that account.

Hunger could make wolves risk themselves foolishly. Peter had seen it. "May I ask a favor, Arlo?"

"You want me to call if I see the bastard again."

Peter breathed before he answered to make sure his voice stayed calm. A rogue wolf could cause trouble for every magical in the county. "If you would."

"I will. And I'll ask the others to do the same. None of us wants to be exposed because some damn wolf is hungry."

On that point, they could all agree. "Thank you. I will inform you when we have settled the matter."

"Thank you for taking care of this business, Peter. It's...unsettling."

An understatement. "Of course, Arlo."

The call ended, and Peter sat back in his chair. Arlo had it right: A rogue wolf who preyed on humans, even the throwaways, if the dead human was a throwaway, endangered them all.

But Arlo could have taken care of one wolf, even in half form, by himself. Strong as wolves are, vampires are stronger. Nevertheless, Arlo had called him to take care of the matter.

Arlo obviously had stolen blood again, but Arlo wanted Peter to make sure the magicals stayed safe. Although he was afraid of Peter after the William Lowell business, Arlo acknowledged the need for order.

Grateful that Arlo had called him, Peter now called Martin.

That wolf answered after the first ring. He was alone since he did not bother with the formalities. "Peter?"

The vampire responded in kind. "Martin. I have received a phone call from Arlo Braxton."

The wolf huffed. "A problem, then."

"A rogue wolf, not one of the pack by his smell and appearance, preying on a human."

Martin swore fluently in French before he responded. "You'd better come here so we can discuss this matter."

"I will walk over now."

"Good." The call ended.

Peter made sure his morning's work was saved, then stood. Before he left his office, he stared out the windows at the trees. He had been doing that regularly lately, not that the view was particularly beautiful or even interesting at this time of the year. It simply offered a rest for his eyes and the opportunity to make sure he was calm before he went to the basement and walked up the tunnel connecting his house to the others in the compound.

He knew this business with the rogue would hold his interest for a time. He had to make sure his *phyle*, his magicals, and the few other magicals in Hartford were safe before he asked Martin for the sword.

He also had to pay attention to the cookies presented with tea in Martin's office. The big room was lined with books, but a glass and metal desk and leather and metal chairs occupied a large Aubusson rug. However, the chocolate chip cookies from Rosie's on Park and gunpowder tea, well brewed, made a pleasant break. Though he hadn't used any of his magic this morning, the calories were good to have. Besides, Rosie and her partner were wonderful bakers. Their goods were delicious.

Martin joined him with a cup of tea and a fudge brownie and resumed his staring.

"You smell different today," the wolf said after a good minute's gaze.

"I did shower this morning." Peter took a small bite of cookie and waited for the response.

"Don't be a pain in the ass. You know very well what I mean."

Peter swallowed and nodded. "I am concerned for the *phyle*. This rogue was in a busy neighborhood, Martin, in half form. Arlo assumed the prey was a homeless human, but that is an assumption. Most of the streets around the hospital and along Homestead do not receive...call it strict attention from the police. People go missing, the police assume they are just criminals on the run and do not bother to look, or they make *pro forma* attempts just to be able to say they investigated. But the people in the neighborhoods know something is wrong. And if they were to see a wolf..."

Martin finished his brownie. "Rosie packages sugar very nicely," he said and licked a finger. "Yes, I do know what you mean. But one rogue is no threat. I've already sent the twins to sniff out the situation, with Robert to watch."

"You are assuming it is one rogue. Everyone is making assumptions this morning."

Martin stared at him.

Peter chuckled. "You do remember I am a vampire. Staring does not work on me."

"I remember you can be a pain in my ass. That's what I remember."

It was Peter's turn to stare at his friend. "You usually take threats of exposure more seriously. Assumptions and bad jokes will not take care of this threat."

Martin reached for another brownie. "Right now, I'm more concerned about you, Peter. I'm glad you're smelling alert and interested, but you are still not entirely engaged. Not close. The despair is still obviously there. You smell like a copper penny with notes of despair."

Peter would not argue with the truth. He shrugged and took a sip of the tea, followed by another small bite of cookie.

"Peter." Martin set his second brownie down and breathed loudly. "We need you. The *phyle* needs you. Your abilities as a vampire help to keep us all safe. But besides that, you are my friend. You are the one male who does not instinctively bare his throat to me. You do not apologize to me before you argue with me. I do not wish to lose you."

Peter snorted. "You are the Alpha. You are supposed to receive bare throats. And then you bare your throat to me. So how—"

"I do not know another way to show another predator that I trust him." Martin spread his hands wide. "What else can a wolf do to demonstrate friendship and trust?"

Surprised, Peter straightened and stared at Martin. "I did not think about it. All this time I thought...I thought it is just what wolves do. But that is not so. You are the Alpha. You bare your throat to Robert and to me, but not to any of the others except in formal situations..." Peter shook his head as if that would straighten his thinking. "I never bothered to think about it."

The wolf cocked his head, a faint smile barely curling his lips, and tapped his neck in the vicinity of his right carotid and jugular. "I trust you with my life, Peter."

Peter nodded now. "I simply never thought about it this way. I have always known that when a wolf bares his throat, it is not an empty gesture, but...I must apologize, Martin. I never asked myself why you bare your throat to me. I took it as a politeness, that is all." He had never stopped to think about Martin's behavior toward him at all.

Martin nodded. "I never thought we had to discuss it. But, Peter, your despair is something we must discuss."

"What is there to discuss? I am alone, I am tired, nothing holds my interest for more than five minutes." Peter imitated Martin's cocked head. "Until this business of the rogue."

"We have dealt with rogues before. Quickly and easily."

"But it is something different, Martin. It is not the same as yesterday's routine. It is not the same as tomorrow's routine is likely to be, you understand? In the seventy years since we settled here and built this compound, I have largely lived the same day over and over. I am truly tired of living the same day again and again. Unlike what happens in that movie, there does not appear to be a formula for changing the day."

Martin grimaced. "And the *phyle?* What..." Martin's phone rang. Martin answered and put the phone on speaker. "My Beta," he said.

"My Alpha," Robert answered. "We found the alley where the rogue took his prey and followed the scent to the culvert in front of the Little League field at the corner of Trout Brook Drive and Asylum Avenue."

"I know it," Peter said. Robert could hear him, he knew, almost as well as he could hear Robert. "The pipe that opens there is small. I would not be able to enter it." He was only six feet and two inches tall, with a build best described as wiry. All the wolves were bigger than he, even in their human form. So the rogue was small, even undersized. Chronic hunger could stunt growth in a wolf.

"We could not follow," Robert confirmed. "But we checked the area, sir, to be sure the rogue actually used the culvert to escape. We found the scent of three other wolves we do not recognize."

Martin leaned over his phone. "Three more?"

"Yes, my Alpha. And we believe someone else is watching the culvert or something in the vicinity. In the UConn branch parking lot close to the ball field, there is a black Lincoln Navigator with heavily tinted windows. Four human males, young, we think, with military haircuts, white shirts, black ties, and black suit jackets."

"And there is no indication of what they are doing there?"

"They simply sit there. They appear to be doing nothing more than watching."

The vampire and the wolf both breathed loudly. That big SUV might mean nothing, but it might also mean more danger to the *phyle*. They would have to be careful in their attempt to determine which meaning applied.

"Where are *you* parked, Robert?"

"At St. Joseph College. We walked down through the trees until we got to the ball field."

Not a long walk, a quarter mile at most if they left their vehicle in the west parking lot. "The trees offer you plenty of cover to get the license plate," Peter suggested.

Robert waited until Martin said, "An excellent idea, Robert. We must know with whom we are dealing."

Then Robert said, "I will do that."

"Excellent, my Beta. Come back to the house when you have that information, please."

"Yes, sir." Robert ended the call.

Martin grimaced at Peter. "You are right, my friend. I was making assumptions, perhaps out of wishful thinking."

"I am nevertheless sorry to be correct, Martin."

Martin huffed and shook his head. "One good thing, however. I do not believe tomorrow will be the same day as today, vampire."

Peter had to agree. "You are not mistaken, wolf. Tomorrow will be an interesting day."

Chapter 13
Monday

Elbows on the counter, Hannah stared at the eggplant as if it were going to tell her how to prepare it. It didn't respond. It just sat there looking...purple.

"Purple is not a meal," she sighed. "Parmesan it is. Again."

On the other hand, considering how weirdly the day had started, plain old eggplant Parm wasn't a bad idea. Something normal and reassuring.

Rose probably had 60 ways to make eggplant, from simple to elegant enough to serve the Queen of England. That woman could probably cook an old shoe to taste like ambrosia or soma. Good old Rose—who was strictly off limits, not to be called, spoken of, thought of—What could Hannah think about instead? Not the piano, though it was going to look wonderful in the living room.

Andy had arrived a little after one o'clock as promised to rearrange the couches and chairs to create space for the piano. It turned out the living room was big enough for the piano and the furniture without looking crowded or fussy at all. And the lawyer was arranging for delivery and tuning tomorrow, late afternoon, so if school did resume, Hannah wouldn't have to play hooky when it was installed, and the hell with how Fanny had known about the marriage to David.

But Fanny *had* known. What if Fanny had started out like Rose, just knowing small things a minute or two in advance? What if—what if Rose started knowing things backward, things people had done long ago and was kept secret.

"No, no, no." Hannah Levine would *not* allow herself to go down *that* path. Absolutely not.

Instead, she would pay close attention to laying the slices of eggplant in the glass casserole dish. Luckily, she hadn't included a finger with the eggplant, given how little attention she'd paid to the cutting operation. After she finished a layer of eggplant, she poured sauce, not homemade, unlike Rose, who always made her sauces from scratch, then another layer of eggplant and more sauce.

After she filled the dish with eggplant and sauce, she grated cheese from a small hunk she'd bought on her way home from the lawyer on top of everything. An acknowledgement that real Parm, real mozzarella, did taste and cook differently than the cheap stuff. She had to give Rose a point for that information. Grudging, but a point.

The casserole went into the oven and Hannah turned her attention to making a salad. Unfortunately, salad didn't require close attention. Washing spinach leaves and cherry tomatoes she could do on autopilot. So her thought returned to Aunt Fanny and Rose. Again.

Why couldn't she just think about something else, like when school would re-open, or how she would teach *Animal Farm* to kids whose minds were definitely *not* going to focus any better than hers did?

Her cell phone buzzed on the counter behind her. She looked over at the caller ID.

Rose.

The granite countertop amplified the buzz nicely, or not so nicely since Hannah wanted to ignore it. She picked up the phone, opened the utensil drawer, dropped the phone in, and slammed the drawer shut.

Slamming the drawer felt good, but since she could still hear the phone, the good feeling didn't last even a nanosecond. If she left the room, maybe went to the den, she wouldn't hear it anymore.

But she'd know. She'd know the freaking phone was buzzing for her, *damn it.*

And now, to top it all off, another flash was working its way up her neck to her face. Rose could call it her private tropical vacation and laugh it off, but to Hannah, it was an infuriating sign of aging.

There was only one thing to do.

Hannah jerked the drawer open, snatched up the phone, and stabbed the Answer button. "Rose. Don't call me any—"

"Hannah, it's inherited. The whatever you call it, trait, talent, gift, curse, my knowing and your whatever," Rose blurted. "It runs in families. Do you understand? It's genetic. You can't undo it. What are we going to do?"

"What do you mean, what are *we* going to do? *We* aren't going to do anything except keep our mouths shut. And you are not going to call me anymore. Do you understand me? Leave. Me. Alone."

She punched the phone off. Slamming the receiver onto the cradle of the old rotary phones used to be so satisfying. Nothing to slam now, but she had let Rose know. No more phone calls. *Hallelu...*

No. Wait. It ran in families? That's what Rose had said, it was genetic. A trait. Like her blue eyes and dimples and curly hair.

She couldn't call Rose back, could she? Not without groveling, which was absolutely out of the question, but she needed information, because the Big Secret involved family, *yes indeedy*. Despite what she'd said to Rose, there was a we. And she had no easy way to get more information now. She'd just isolated herself from her source of information. Pretty conclusively.

Way to go, Hannah.

Chapter 14
Monday

Hannah had just told Rose to never call again.

Because Rose had babbled, the way she did when she was upset or frightened. And she was frightened at the thought that someone or someones unknown knew about the gift and the family. And she was angry. Oh, yes, she was angry. If the gift or whatever it was ran in the family, then her mother and her aunts must have known about it. And Nana—had Nana Pearl known?

Would Nana Pearl have kept such a secret from her? Maybe she thought Mother had told her about whatever this was? And then she had died.

But she could ask Nana…

Right. And she was going to tell Pena and Tava that she knew what was going to happen before it happened and that she could move things just by thinking they should move. Because the girls would accept the information cheerfully, so cheerfully they'd have her locked up at the Institute for Living, assuming her insurance would pay for such a nice room with no sharp edges.

So she sat there in her cozy little kitchen, deciding to keep secrets. Just like the rest of the family. *Yep. Way to go, Rosie.*

Really, all she wanted to do was talk to someone who knew she wasn't crazy. But Hannah had put herself off limits, and Miriam certainly was out of the question.

Which left the man Cal Jones suggested in her note.

Seriously? You're going to call a stranger to talk about this...whatever it is? A stranger, yes, but one who apparently knows about it. And since Cal Jones isn't available...

Babbling and *dithering. Wonderful.*

There it was. She could make the call or talk in circles to herself.

Concentrating on her breathing, she picked the cell phone up off the table. Slow and steady kept her calm while she tapped the numbers and listened to the phone ringing.

A pleasant male rumble answered after the second ring. "Petrovsky here."

"Dr. Mikhail Petrovsky?"

"*Da.* Yes. Who is speaking, please?" He spoke with a thick Russian accent, so that "please" became "plis."

"I'm Dr. Rose Sherman? Cal Jones gave me your number?" *Why are you asking him?*

"Yes? So you call from the Hartford area?"

"Wethersfield, to be specif—"

"Good. I meet you tomorrow at Teahouse of August Moon in Hartford. You know this place?"

"Yes, but—"

"There is a time that is best for you?"

"Yes. After my 1:30 class, so about 3:30? But—"

"I will see you tomorrow at 3:30 at Teahouse of August Moon."

"But—"

"We do not speak of certain matters on the phone, yes?"

"Yes, but—"

She was speaking to dead air. *Oh, brother.*

And now the phone was going to ring. Miriam was calling about...Aunt Fanny. *Just wonderful. Now I definitely know why people are calling.*

Rose took a deep breath and let the phone ring a couple of times before she answered it.

Miriam cleared her throat before she spoke. "Rose. Did Aunt Fanny leave you something in her will?"

Typical Miriam. Straight to the point, the point unfortunately being uncomfortably close to the secret. Unless...if the whatever it is ran in families, then maybe Miriam...What an interesting possibility *that* was. Miriam insisted that logic and reason would always lead to an answer. "Yes. Her jewelry. Minus *Tannah*. And her records, those amazing 78s. Why?"

"I got *Tannah*."

"Oh, Mir. That's so nice. Are you going to wear it all the time the way she did?"

"Actually, I *have* to wear it all the time. It's a stipulation of the inheritance."

That was odd. "Seriously?"

"Seriously. But, Rose, when did you get the inheritance? Back when Fanny died?"

And here came the secret. "No. Why?"

"So, recently?"

"Today, actually. Before I went to work, I drove down to Colchester to see the lawyer."

"I saw Teddy today, too. And it was very strange."

Miriam had *no* idea. "Oh?"

Miriam must have been fighting a cold because she cleared her throat again. "Fanny...um. Yeah. Fanny stipulated that the lawyer couldn't give me *Tannah* until my divorce from Izzy had been final for a year."

And there it was. One enormous secret looming over everything. "Um." *Where is the babbling when I really need it?*

"Rose?"

"Yeah. Yes. I couldn't have the things from Aunt Fanny until my divorce had been final for a year, too."

"You know she wrote the will in 1998, right?"

Time to say it. *Just say it.* "It's called precognition."

"What?"

Rose cleared her throat. Apparently, the condition was catching. "Knowing things before they happen is called precognition."

The silence stretched out until Rose thought Miriam had ended the call.

"Mir?" she asked.

"You sound so calm, Rose. Not puzzled." That sounded like an accusation, not a comment on Rose's state of mind.

Rose sighed. "Yeah, no. Come on over and I'll tell you all about it."

"It? What it?"

"Family stuff, Mir. I'll make supper.

"Half an hour."

Half an hour felt like the run-up to her execution. But Miriam was smiling when she walked into Rose's kitchen with a box from the Crown's kosher bakery, and she was wearing *Tannah* on her blazer lapel.

"The pin looks nice, Mir."

"It's nice to have."

"Come sit and I'll tell you all I know."

Rose handed Miriam a mug of tea and the envelope from Cal Jones. "Read this while I finish the salad."

She kept her back to Miriam deliberately, nervous about what Miriam would say. When Miriam did speak, all she said was, "Okay. Aunt Fanny's family is, what did you call it? Precognitive? I have to believe it, right? The will—but that's Aunt Fanny's family."

Time for the big reveal. Rose turned around so she could see Miriam's face. "Ours, too." She took a deep breath and slid Miriam's mug of tea down the table from where she stood. No hands. "That's called telekinesis. Hannah can do it, too. I also have precognition, but nothing like Aunt Fanny's. Maybe five minutes ahead. I knew you were calling me and I….."

She stopped because Miriam had stood up. She held up a hand to stop Rose and swore under her breath in English and then in Yiddish, the latter much more fluently than Rose could ever manage. Then Miriam sat back down and closed her eyes.

"Mir? Are you—"

"Give me a minute, please."

It was more like four or five minutes before Miriam opened her eyes, shaking her head. "I hate this, you know that."

"It's frightening and strange, I'll give you that, but—"

"No. It's...not rational or reasonable or solvable. It's Izzy's version of the world."

"Frightening," Rose repeated.

"And there's—I have to tell you a story, Rose. But you have to swear you will not tell anyone. Not Pena or Tava or Hannah—"

"Hannah has cut me off. And anyway, you know I don't gossip."

"No, you don't." Miriam nodded. "Hannah gossips. You don't."

"Is it a long story, Mir? Should I put supper on the table or—"

"I—we should eat. Can I help?"

"If you set the table, I'll put the food out. And you can talk while we work." Difficult subjects were easier to talk about without eye contact. The girls used to bring up all sorts of interesting things in the car when her eyes were busy with the road, things like boys and illicit drug trials and questions about sex.

And it worked with Miriam, too, who cleared her throat yet again. "You remember my apartment on Prospect?"

"The tiny place? With the round windows?" Rose had loved that place, even if it was far too small except for a person who didn't own much furniture.

"You remember that Victorian next door?"

"That place was beautiful. But it burned down years ago, didn't it?" Rose remembered that after the wreckage of the house was removed, the lot stood empty until someone bought it and turned it into a neighborhood garden.

"Before it burned, a murder was committed there. Do we need knives?"

"Yes. I made southern fried baked chicken fingers and fries. What does a murder next door to your old apartment have to do with anything?"

Miriam stopped laying out silverware, straightened up and stared at something not anywhere near Rose. "The body had been turned inside-out and laid out in a pentagram inside a circle painted on the floor and with black candles at the places where the points of the star met the circle." Her voice sounded oddly flat.

"You mean flayed, don't you? Because inside out is impossi—Oh. Not any more impossible than telekinesis or precognition is. Right? Right. Sorry for the interruption."

Now, Miriam looked over her shoulder at Rose and smiled. "Right. So that was six years ago. Fast forward to the day before yesterday. Another inside-out body, this one in an apartment in the building David Levine lived in before he and Hannah got married."

Rose pulled the baking sheet with the chicken and fries from the oven and set it on top of the stove, began to transfer the food to a small glass platter. "The fancy-schmancy place with the kitchen bigger than my entire house?" *Fancy-schmancy? You're talking about inside-out bodies here, Rosie. Dead human beings. Try to be respectful.*

Miriam nodded. "Here's what Downie and I think. The first body was found near where I used to live and the second was found near where Hannah's then fiancé used to live." Miriam sat down at her place at the table. "We think this has something to do with us. Hannah and me, anyway."

"But why? It could be coincidence, right? And there's—"

"There's no such thing as coincidence."

Frowning, Rose set the platter on a trivet next to the salad bowl, then sat herself down. "So should I be worried? Should I warn Pena and Tava someone is after them? Should I—"

"I don't know." Miriam sounded bleak. "Two days ago, I would have told you that you were crazy. But I saw the bodies. I *saw* them, Rosie. It isn't gossip from my sergeant's nephew's brother-in-law's cousin twice removed like some urban legend, okay? And then I saw you slide that mug across the table from about ten feet away. And I hate it. I hate it. Because if Izzy is right, and my father was right, then I'm wrong, and…"

"Either or? Not a little bit of gray in there somewhere?"

"Rose. If Izzy and my father are right, there is no gray. It's God says this is the way, so this is the way."

"No. No, Mir. Just because I can slide the mug across the table doesn't mean you should stone a disobedient son, okay? What I can do is a result of genes, that's all. You read the papers." Rose pushed the salad bowl toward Miriam using her hand. "But those inside-out bodies sound awful. Really."

Miriam nodded. "We have an expert. Your Cal Jones, actually. Doesn't she teach in your building at UHart?"

Shaking her head, Rose frowned. "Didn't you see the note? Oh, no. I took it out. She's the one who gave me the pages. And makes me feel like a dowdy old lady."

Miriam chuckled. "Gawky giant, that's me. But she didn't warn me. She didn't say we should be worried. She did say the person creating the inside-out bodies is a very powerful practitioner. That's Jones's word: 'practitioner.'"

"But we shouldn't worry?" Rose grimaced. "Okay. I know in my head I can go from this house to living under the Putnam Bridge in a cardboard box in under two seconds flat. So maybe I tend to catastrophize. But really, Mir. If this person can turn a human being inside-out, why shouldn't we worry?"

"Because Jones didn't seem worried. And I don't worry about my cases, you know that."

Rose had to take a deep breath before she could speak. Because Miriam and her partner carried guns, they didn't have to worry. Rose carried embroidery scissors and pens. Sharp but not the same level of defense. "Do you and Sergeant Downs think we're okay?"

Shrugging, Miriam picked up the salad bowl. "I'm worried because of the Izzy angle. But not about the perp. Not now anyway. I think we'll learn more and get it taken care of one way or another. Jones will help us and we'll be okay."

Rose nodded but couldn't respond. How could she be okay? She was alone and—

"Downie and I will make sure you're okay, Rosie. Really."

"That obvious, am I?"

"I'm a cop. I was paid to notice—although..." Miriam sank back into her chair. "Listen to this."

As Miriam told her about Izzy's behavior back in the old days, Rose felt her stomach unclench. Maybe it would be okay. Maybe *she* would be okay.

Rose leaned forward and served Miriam chicken and fries. At least she knew the food was okay.

Chapter 15
Monday

As Miriam walked out of Rose's house toward her car, she decided she had to talk to Downie. Tonight, and face to face. She had to know whether her sense that Rose, Hannah, and she were safe, at least for now, was right.

Yes, Cal Jones had been calm and confident, but no one had asked the obvious question until Rose did. Miriam had been so busy resisting the idea of all the irrational *shit*, she'd missed it. She'd missed what Izzy had been doing while she had been enjoying her job, and she'd missed this question, too.

Downie would confirm or deny. He never said things because he thought she wanted to hear them. He told the truth as he saw it. She could trust him to do that for her.

So she sat in the car and punched Downie's number on her cell. He answered after the first ring.

"Miriam? Everything all right?"

"I'm not sure." She cleared her throat. "I need to talk to you. I have questions. Can I come over?" His place was the first-floor apartment of a three-family he owned on South Quaker Lane. She'd never been farther than his dining room. And why was she thinking about *that* now?

Because it was his place she was going to visit. *Yes, Downie's place. And isn't he a good, decent man? Just a good, decent man you happen to find attractive, damn him.*

"Of course. Now?"

Nothing has to happen that you don't want to happen, so just go.

"Mir, you there?"

"Yes. I mean, yes, I'll come over now. Thank you."

"I'll be here."

"I'm on my way."

She ended the call, had to take a deep breath before she could insert the key into the ignition.

Crazy to be nervous about going to see Downie. The man was her partner, after all. She'd worked with him every day for over twenty years, and she was working with him again. So she shook her head, started the car and pulled out of the driveway. She was simply going to consult with her partner about a case. Yes, the case involved her and her at least one of her cousins, but it was a case and nothing but a case.

Fine. She could do that and enjoy driving, too. Thanks to daylight savings time, she had enough light to see the scenery. There were buds on bushes and daffodils opening, or maybe they were jonquils.

Rose knew that kind of thing. Miriam knew things like how to tell whether a person is lying and whether a person is nervous because she's talking to a cop or because she's done something she shouldn't have done. Flowers had never been especially interesting to her, not even as a gift from a man. Too impermanent maybe. Too fussy. But nice to look at as she drove.

As she made the slight turn from Ridge Road onto Maple Avenue next to the golf course and then the left onto Fairfield at the monument company, she also could see that the black car behind her had been following her since she'd left Rose's. But how did she know? A black Camry is a black Camry, after all.

Not with that weird license plate, it wasn't just any black Camry. She couldn't read the plate, couldn't even tell whether there were letters or numbers or what combination of letters and numbers was on the plate, not even when they stopped for the light at Fairfield and White. Because the plate was blurred. Not obscured by dirt or mud, truly blurred, as if someone had run fingers through the digits while making the plate. Miriam could see the plate itself but only smudges of blue where the numbers and letters ought to have been.

Now that she thought about it, she had seen that same plate in the morning, too. After she pulled onto Albany Avenue from the condo's driveway, a black Camry with that plate had been behind her until she got to Asylum Avenue. There was too much traffic in downtown Hartford during rush hour for an untrained tail.

But the son of a gun had found her again.

Miriam Fine, Detective Retired, was being followed, and she was followed all the way past the Quaker Meeting House to Downie's place.

Miriam pulled down the long driveway and parked in front of Downie's bay of the three-car garage. Getting out of her car, she casually looked back to the row of three-family houses across the street. Sure enough, the black car had parked there, but as she watched, the car took off heading north, toward Farmington Avenue and all sorts of possible destinations.

Downie had come out onto the little wooden deck behind his kitchen and leaned against the railing while she watched the car.

"Mir?" he called softly.

She walked across the driveway to the brick walk leading to the bottom of the wooden stairs at the foot of the deck. "I was followed here. And the same car followed me downtown this morning. And as long as I'm thinking about it, maybe yesterday when I went to Maddy's."

"Call it in?"

She smiled but shook her head. He hadn't asked how she knew she'd been followed or why she thought so or any doubtful question. He trusted her judgment. "No license plate number."

He huffed his surprise.

"The plate is there, but the number is blurred out. All I can say, it's a recent Camry, black. I didn't see any special stickers or tags, anything like that."

"Come on in, let's talk."

In the bright kitchen, blue tile splash backs that matched the blue tile floor, white cabinets with glass fronts, blue checked café curtains, he pointed her to a stool at the wooden island counter painted white to match the cabinets. He'd done all the work himself. *A talented man, George Downs.*

"Tell me." He plugged in a blue electric kettle, pulled two white ceramic mugs out of the nearest cabinet.

"It's more than the car," she said, suddenly unhappy about talking to him.

"Nice pin, by the way."

Trust him to make things difficult by being so...nice. "Yeah. That's part of the story." She had to tell him the whole story. She had to. So she did, all of it: *Tannah,* Aunt Fanny, Aunt Fanny's will, Rose, Hannah, precognition, telekinesis, all of it. *All of it.*

It took her two cups of tea and a small plate of chocolate chip cookies, not homemade, but he made the effort, at least. Downie let her talk without interrupting, and then, when she finally stopped, he raised his eyes, nodded and said, "Yeah. Makes sense."

She stared at him. "Makes sense? Seriously?"

"There's always been, I don't know, stuff. In the background. *Not* the sacrifice in the cemetery, and not our favorite levitating minister. Not the fakery. Like the inside-out bodies but more subtle. Like, you remember the woman who knew Marcia Botello had been raped and strangled and left in a dumpster in Yonkers? You remember that case?"

Of course, she did. A fourteen-year-old girl had been missing for three days when a woman, Anna Restolli, an ordinary woman who just occasionally "saw" things, came to the department to tell them where the girl could be found. Restolli, her relatives, her friends, her acquaintances, all had been investigated thoroughly because the Yonkers cops found the body exactly where Restolli said it would be, but seriously? How could she have known? Within a few weeks of Restolli's appearance at HPD, Forensics determined that the DNA on Botello's body matched the DNA in eight other cases, mostly in suburban New York, the work of a serial killer who turned out to have no connection to the victim or to Restolli or to anyone else anywhere near the case.

Miriam breathed before she answered him. "Restolli said she saw the murder when she was praying to St. Anthony to help her find her missing car keys." St. Anthony, the woman said, sometimes directed her to other missing things, too.

Downie nodded. "Stuff like that goes on all the time. We pretend it doesn't, right? We ignore the inconvenient, the contradictory evidence, but it's there. Restolli *knew* where Marcia Botello's body would be found. She did. I don't know whether St. Anthony told her or her belief in his power opened her to the knowledge, but she knew."

"It's not rational." She didn't care for the broken-record quality of her whine, but there it was.

"It has nothing to do with rational or irrational, Mir. It just is."

Miriam shook her head. "That does *not* help."

"It's a lot to adjust to—"

"You're not having any problem with it," she accused.

He shrugged. "It isn't happening to me, not directly anyway. And I always just figured there's more to this—" He waved a hand around the kitchen—" than Newtonian physics. I figure the Buddhists are closer to the truth than western science." He cocked his head and stared at her.

"What?" Even she heard the defensiveness in her voice.

He shook his head. "You don't need me playing shrink."

"You're right. I just came to ask you whether we should be worried, Hannah, Rose, and I, about this person and the curse."

Again, he shook his head. "This person is trying to work magic, and not very well, so we're being told by Jones, right? So I think you're good for now. And the person following you? Let's watch."

That was what she'd come for, straight-ahead, what-you-see-is-what-you-get George Downs. The business about Marcia Botello and all that could be set aside for now. "I have to get some sleep." She lifted her purse from the counter and stood. "I'll see you in the morning."

"'Kay." He spoke softly, walked behind her to the door. "Do me a favor? Call me when you get home, let me know if you're followed again, okay?"

"I will," she said and walked out, grateful he had her back even if he knew all the secrets now. She had a partner, a damned good one.

Chapter 16
Tuesday

Sara strolled up the sidewalk toward the porch of C. Jones's house as if she belonged there. *Not* as if. She *did* belong there. No question about it. The books said to be kept in that house—only she had the knowledge and power to use them.

The collector, the dilettante who occupied this pathetic little cottage, five rooms, maybe six if the rooms were small, surrounded by a porch on three sides, front steps painted blue, gardens all around, shouldn't own—

Sara hit a wall about two feet from the steps leading up to the front porch, an invisible wall powerful enough to knock her onto her back on the cement walk and drain the power away from the charms on her necklace and bracelet. As she sat up, she felt the power wash away like water running off her body in the shower.

Wards. She'd walked into protective wards stronger than anything she could manage, and she could lay protective wards that moved with her. The wards around this little house stopped her while letting bees through. She'd watched them work the plants hanging from hooks from the porch roof, and she'd seen a sparrow chase some bug around one of the porch columns. Damned good blood wards.

And now that she was paying attention, those plants on the porch and in the gardens weren't fuchsia or snapdragons or gladiolas. No, they were licorice and wolfsbane and—witch's herbs.

But the rumors, the whispers she overheard when she hung around the *botanica* down on Park Street or sat in the Cuban restaurant a couple of doors down, all agreed that Jones didn't cast because he couldn't. So someone, a powerful, resourceful someone, had laid those wards, grown those plants, protected him and those books.

And Sara was sitting on her ass on the sidewalk, clearly visible in the early morning light to anyone who happened to look. Still, she wasn't ready to move. She wanted those books, so she had to get through those wards. There was a way through, of course. There always was. She could find the objects that anchored the wards. Of course, they could be buried anywhere along the borders of the house, in pots, in the gardens, under rocks, anywhere. She could spend *days* digging everything up. She didn't want to spend days digging everything up while maintaining an invisibility spell, especially not now when she had to spend time and energy to recharge her charms.

She could prepare a counter-spell, something maybe to make her feel like an insect to the wards, so they would let her through. It would take time and thought, but not days. And it would be well worth the effort, given what those books were said to contain. The necromancy alone—

Yes. To hell with following the cop. She had the blood spell ritual almost ready to go on Farmington Avenue, and once the Winkler bitches were taken care of, she could work out a spell and own the books this C. Jones collected.

Sara smiled. She would have the power she deserved, finally, and she could show her bitch of a so-called mother who she really was.

Chapter 17
Tuesday

━━━━━ ◆ ━━━━━

Hannah ran a hand along the piano bench and smiled. The piano was such a beautiful piece of furniture, and the sound the Bösendorfer created was resonant, remarkable. She sat and played an arpeggio, awkwardly to her ears, but she also heard possibility. Maybe she could take lessons again. It would be good to pick up the music she'd left behind when she went to France.

France. God, there was something to think about. It had been such a...relief, being where no one knew her, no one had expectations, no one thought she was spoiled, foolish, or rash. She'd found a solid job as a publisher's rep, and she'd made a good life there. There had been one problem, a large problem, admittedly, but the American Embassy in Paris had been wonderfully helpful, and off she'd gone to her good life.

No family, it was true, but she'd never had to look for company, always had a man, friends, acquaintances, not a huge number of people, but she'd done well for herself, and she'd had a lot of fun. Of course, she was younger then. Effortlessly thin, effortlessly pretty, effortlessly charming.

Now? Now she had to work at staying thin and wore makeup to leave the bedroom, and most days, charm gave way to tiredness, thanks to the damned night sweats. Rose said exercise—

But Rose said a lot of things, including that business about the...trait, the ability being genetic. If that was true—and why, really, would Rose lie about that? Then so many questions had to be asked, questions of obligation.

What did one owe a person one had never known but who might be considered family? Genetically, of course, the tie couldn't be denied, but otherwise? There was nothing.

It had been the right thing to do, walking away, never looking back. She had been wildly irresponsible in those days, so she had never doubted, never had second thoughts until now. But, really, why would she have worried? Not quite thirty years ago, she hadn't even mentioned the mental...difficulties that also ran in the family. This new wrinkle—what a nice clean way of labeling these so-called abilities—was no different. The child would develop some "gift" or other when she went through menopause. So why should Hannah worry now?

The woman would probably have awful hot flashes just like her mother. No one was going to tell her about that, either.

It didn't matter. No need to panic.

Still, maybe she ought to call...what was his name? At the embassy, not that he was likely still there. But she'd think about it. He'd been cute, tall, and kind, though the kindness was probably just part of his job.

She'd actually considered asking him out, at least to have a drink, but she'd met—what was his name? Roland, that was it, who'd introduced her to Claude, the publisher. She'd moved on quickly after that.

And she didn't look back. She never looked back. She would stop looking back now. She would go down to Scott's Music on the Silas Deane Highway and ask about piano lessons.

To hell with Rose's news.

Chapter 18
Tuesday

Rose usually enjoyed the ride from the university to the Teahouse of the August Moon. She always took Prospect Avenue to Farmington Avenue so she could watch the seasons progress in the landscaped grounds of the mansions that stood along the street until it crossed Asylum Ave at Elizabeth Park. She recognized magnolias and tulip trees, Japanese andromeda, and forsythias by their blossoms.

There were other brilliantly flowering trees and shrubs she didn't know the names of, and then at the Governor's Mansion on the corner with Asylum Avenue, there was a whole hillside blanketed by jonquils visible through the tall wrought-iron fence. She didn't especially care for Wordsworth, but his poetry always came to mind when she saw that hill in the spring.

Today, she could have been driving past concrete bunkers. Her breathing was tight, her hands cramped on the steering wheel.

Thank God there was parking in the lot at the Teahouse. If she'd had to parallel park on Farmington Avenue, she would have given up and driven home.

In fact, nothing prevented her from changing change her mind now. She had an idea for a possible paper on the Nero Wolfe mysteries, and she wanted to sit and think about it, make a few notes about the competing voices of Archie Goodwin and Nero Wolfe and how they worked against each other, but always along the main narrative lines and still contributed to the narrative of the solution to the mystery. To make the work juicier, Archie was no Watson, worshipfully reporting Sherlock's achievements. He was a skeptic and a smart aleck—

But there she was, resisting the urge to intellectualize, getting out of the car, walking into the Teahouse of the August Moon. She ignored the scenery here, too, the occupants of the little round tables and the murals on the walls of idealized Japanese life, and wound her way to the counter to order a large cup of Darjeeling and the hell with the caffeine. Hot flashes and potential sleeplessness were the least of her worries today.

The barista was a skinny girl sporting so many studs in her lips and over her eyebrows, Rose wondered whether she could go outside in a thunderstorm. *Voluntary lightning rod doesn't seem like a vocation with a future.*

Nice distraction, Rosie. Find the man you're here to meet.

Over by the big windows that looked out on Farmington Ave sat a handsome older man with a full head of curly white hair, wearing a red plaid flannel shirt under a leather bomber jacket and jeans. His face was lined but strong, and he was tall, Rose could tell even though he was sitting, quite relaxed, not looking at anything in particular. He was the only person sitting alone in the big room.

Okey-dokey, Rosie. Yet again, she wound her way past tables and stopped by the empty chair opposite him. "Dr. Petrovsky?"

He stood—at least six three or four—and smiled. "Dr. Sherman." He extended a hand and she shook it. Well-calloused that hand, so he wasn't just an academic.

She should have touched up her makeup.

She glanced quickly down at his left hand as she sat—*Oh, God, I did not do that, did I? Oh, yes, I did do that; I checked for the wedding ring. He didn't wear one, but—*

Business, Rosie, business.

She sat and took a deep breath. "I called you because Cal Jones suggested that you could help with—what is happening to me."

Smiling, he cocked his head a little to the left. "It would depend on what is happening to you, Dr. Sherman."

"Of course." She pulled the list she'd prepared for Cal out of her jacket pocket and slid it across the small table to him.

He picked it up and began to read, sipping occasionally from his oversized mug.

Her tea arrived, delivered by the multi-pierced barista. Rose thanked her and leaned over the mug to inhale the lemony fragrance.

"So," Petrovsky said as he refolded the paper and held it out to her. "You develop many talents. What is it you wish to know?"

Her chuckle took her by surprise. What *did* she want to know? "What to do with it, I suppose. Is it just, I don't know, inconvenient? Something to whip out at Halloween to impress the children?"

"You and your unnamed friend saved a life. That is very good. But life does not always offer such opportunities."

"That's the question." She shook her head. "Well, no. It's not the only question. But I'm still so surprised by it all that it's hard to think about it with any kind of clarity."

"No one in your family told you to expect this development?" He sounded surprised at the idea.

"No. My mother, well, let's just say she didn't share much." A gross understatement. "And she died years ago along with her sisters, who were all professional-grade secret keepers, and my father and one of my uncles are also dead, and the other is estranged. So no. No one shared information about any of this with me." *Why am I sharing personal information with this stranger? Control yourself, Rosie.*

"Ah. Well then, I will explain. You have read Dr. Jones's little handout, so you are aware now that the talents are genetic, though sometimes they arise spontaneously in people with no family history of such things, yes?"

She recognized lecture mode and responded in kind. "Yes, but I have reason to believe this is in the family."

"Very good. So. These talents normally are latent until puberty or, in many women, the change of life. Occasionally, a child may exhibit them before puberty, but that is rare. And that is not the case here, so we speak only of the later development.

"*Da.* Okay.

"What we know is that, even if you ignore them, do not practice, do not attempt to use them, they persist. They do not disappear. So it is better to acknowledge them, learn to use them—"

"But is that safe? Practicing, I mean. What if people find out? Honestly, that's my biggest fear, that people will find out and I'll lose—"

"No, no. Please, Doctor Sherman, calm yourself. Truly, most people nowadays do not believe in the possibility, *da?* You did not. Before these talents appeared in you, you thought them myths, fantasies, material for Joss Whedon, yes? And those who do believe, the religious, whom I think it is you fear so very much, are so extreme, insist that witches kiss the ass of the devil—"

"But if these talents exist, then who knows what's out there?"

"These talents do not prove the existence of God or the devil or anything else but themselves. We see only these human abilities here. And the people we care about, the people who decide our success, do not listen to the extremists, you see."

"I don't see." She took a sip of her tea, the faint lemony heat helping her to stay calm. "But it seems I don't have any choice about what happens—"

"You choose what to do with the talent. I will quote Professor Dumbledore about choice, if you wish."

She had to laugh. "Oh, very good. Very good. I know exactly what you're referring to." *"It's our choices that show us what we truly are..." We're all just geeks here. And he's such a nice-looking geek. And age-appropriate. My, my.*

He smiled and cocked his head again. "So. You might learn to meditate or perhaps perform yoga."

"Actually, I practice *Vipassana* meditation. Every day. Does it...affect the talents?"

"It is not known why," he said with a shrug, "but meditators and yoginis do better with the talents. So you must continue your practice, relax with the knowledge. Continue to practice the telekinesis and attempt to perform small, delicate tasks. Talk to your grandmother."

Thank God for the tea, because otherwise? This conversation would be very hard to take. "And?"

"I do not understand your question."

"So what? So I know about things before they happen. So I can move things." She wouldn't say talking to Nana Pearl out loud, but that *was* a gift, definitely a gift.

"It may be that there are opportunities, *da?*" He smiled. "Occasionally, I am called about a problem to be investigated and solved only by our abilities. If you become very good at what you do, you may also——"

She stopped him with a raised hand. Because as he spoke, her gut had been taken over by an elephant marching up and down. The message it stomped out wasn't clear, only that something terrible, involving—*oh, God*—terror-filled dying— and someone else was about to die, and she couldn't call the police this time because she didn't know where or who—"Oh, God," she whispered. "Bad."

"You are not ill," he said, leaning across the table toward her.

She had to control her breathing, slowly fill her lungs and slowly empty them, to keep any hint of fear from her face and voice. "Something awful. Very close by."

"You have some emotional connection to someplace near here? Or to a person who lives near here?"

Emotional connection? What kind of question was that? She had no idea, but the answer to his other question came almost immediately. "Yes. The first apartment that was just mine, no roommate. It's up the hill at the corner with Prospect." Three blocks up, a quarter of a mile away.

As soon as she said the words, Rose knew. "That's where it happened. Just now." The stomping faded to tap-dancing because the worst was over. The terror had ended. Her breathing eased on its own.

Petrovsky watched her, concern in his eyes. "A strong emotional connection is key, you see, crucial to the talents. They do not work randomly, *da?*"

His quiet logic helped her calm down. "Keep talking, please."

He nodded as if he understood why she wanted him to talk. "It is why studies on these talents do not succeed in laboratories, *da?* That is something not understood by many scientists. Oddly, emotion is studied in computer and robotics laboratories where it is recognized as necessary in decision-making processes. But elsewhere, it is discounted. Foolishly. Emotion is the survival mechanism that suffuses all mental processes—But you are easier now, yes?"

Only fluttering butterflies remained. "Yes, but I need to call my cousin—she's a retired detective, and she'll know how to find out. She'll know—"

An ambulance screamed up the avenue toward Prospect. Toward her old apartment building.

Rose shut her eyes and swore. When she opened them, Petrovsky was watching her, looking more concerned than before.

She couldn't reassure him. She couldn't reassure herself. Especially not when two Hartford patrol cars and another ambulance, sirens howling, zoomed up toward Prospect.

"Damn. I'm sorry," she said, standing up. "I have to talk to Miriam. I have to find out what's going on up there."

"Yes." He stood. "But you will not want to do it here, not here in front of so many." He gestured for her to go ahead of him.

Somehow Rose avoided tables and people and ended up in the parking lot, next to her car, cell phone in hand. More cars, marked and unmarked, sirens so loud she winced at the noise, streamed up Farmington Avenue.

The sirens died quickly. When she looked up the street, she could see where they had parked.

Right there, three blocks up. It didn't have to be that particular building, her old building. There were two other red brick apartment houses and a big, brown single-family house that now served as psychologists' offices on the side facing Farmington Avenue, and more apartment buildings and a couple of small office buildings on the Prospect side. Any of those places could be where the deaths had happened.

Just one teensy-weensy, eensy-beensy little problem, Rosie. You know *it's your old building. You* know.

"*Borzhi moi,*" Petrovsky said as yet more police cars joined the group already up the street. "That man again," he muttered.

Rose stopped tapping Miriam's number into her cell and stared at Petrovsky, who stared at a nondescript man in a leather jacket and creased jeans.

The man in question was speaking into a cell phone and getting into a nondescript car, just another bland guy, Mr. Nobody, if not for those jeans.

"This is third time I see him today," Petrovsky said to her raised eyebrows. "In Storrs and here. Is no coincidence, I am thinking."

Calm enough now to notice that upset thickened his accent and worsened his grammar, Rose had to wonder whether Petrovsky was paranoid or Ironed Blue Jeans was, in fact, following him. And then, Ironed Blue Jeans pulled out of his parking space and drove slowly past the two of them, looking right at them as he went.

"Who irons blue jeans?" Rose whispered as Petrovsky said, "He *is* following me."

Rose looked at Petrovsky, who didn't seem so paranoid anymore. "What the hell is going on here?"

"I do not know, but I will determine this and be in contact with you. You are all right?"

All right? Something terrible had happened that she knew about but couldn't do anything about. She felt responsible, somehow, for not being able to stop it. She had opened up to this stranger, who obviously had troubles of his own, and those troubles could easily splash onto her. *Yes or no?* "I don't know. But I'll call my cousin and go from there."

Petrovsky bowed his head a bit. "You are all right to drive?"

That she could answer with a nod. "Are *you* okay?"

He smiled—*such a nice smile.* "That is to be determined." He bowed a bit again. "I am at your service, Dr. Sherman."

Rose couldn't help it; She smiled. Such an elegant man. *Not now, Rose.*

She watched him walk to his car—*the view from behind is as nice as the view from the front*—then watched as some student-looking people walked out of the Teahouse. The place was not private enough for the kind of call she had to make. She needed to go home.

But she would not go up Farmington Avenue past all those cop cars parked along both sides of the street. She could go down to Sisson and the highway entrance. It was faster to take the highway, anyway. *Right. Especially at rush hour, Rosie. You bet.*

Nevertheless, she didn't want to go past the old apartment building. She just wanted to go home and talk to Miriam. Miriam would know something. Something simple and straightforward.

A person could always hope.

Chapter 19
Tuesday

Sitting in the Cold Case Office, reviewing the list of residents at 68 Asylum Street for Prentice did not distract Miriam from everything that had gone on last night: Rose's revelations about the family history, Downie's calm acceptance of that history, the mysterious follower. Trying to make sense of it had kept her awake most of the night, and now she stared at the list, barely thinking about it or the murmuring of the other Cold Case people.

Her part of the list was oddly simple. The names were all well known locally, a mover and shaker here, a slightly bigger mover and shaker there, a minor player on the national political scene, and then a person of interest to several narco-trafficking investigatory task forces, city, state, national, *and* international. That woman couldn't pee without various alphabetical agencies knowing about it, so she probably wasn't using magic to turn bodies inside out—

And there it all was again, the irrational crap. Downie could call it arational all he wanted, Rose could say it had nothing to do with God, but Miriam remained unconvinced. Frightened, too, if she were being honest about it. Everything came back to the whole argument with her father and then with Izzy over God, didn't it?

Izzy believed that God had handed down the rules for living back at Mount Sinai and that those rules, all of them from keeping kosher to observing Shabbat, still applied. He had left his community of *Haredi* for a while, but the beliefs had proven stronger than his ties to the broader world, and he had gone back, taking their son with him.

Miriam herself had been raised with those rules by a father who believed likewise. The problem was, Miriam had come to believe that the Bearded Old Man probably wasn't there, and that most of those rules were just a way to keep fear of the dark and death away.

And control women. But that was another issue.

Now? Now Miriam didn't know what to believe. How could she know? What was she supposed to do? Who could she ask? What did this stinking list matter if—

The phone rang. *Thank God—and there's an ironic statement.* The caller ID showed her Rose's name. But Rose never called her when she knew Miriam was working. *Never.*

"Rose? What's wro—"

"Miriam, what's happened at 660 Farmington Avenue? Something bad?"

"Uh. Wait. Isn't that where you lived? When you first started teaching?"

"Yes. But, Mir, something bad has happened there. I *know,* you understand? I *know.*"

"What we talked about last—"

"Not on the phone, Mir. Please."

Wow. Paranoid. "Okay. I'll find out and call you back."

"Soon, please."

"As soon as I can find out anything."

"Thanks."

"Sure," Miriam said and realized Rose had ended the call.

Tempting as it was to stare at the phone and wonder why Rosie had gone paranoid when she'd been so open last night, Miriam figured it was better to just go across the hall and ask Rose's question. She did look around the room to see if anyone else was aware of something "bad," but the rest, Costello, Capobianco, Krantz, Franco, and Soures, all sat working the phones, calling names on the same list she was supposed to be working. She had to go across the hall.

Cell phone in hand, she stepped into Robbery-Homicide just in time to see Garber snatch his holstered weapon from a desk drawer and fasten the holster to his belt. Winewski came striding out of his office, making sure his jacket covered *his* weapon.

When he saw Miriam, he nodded. "Good. You're here. We've got another one like 68 Asylum, up at 660 Farmington. And the woman who found the body, the old lady who lived across the hall, apparently saw it and had a heart attack on the spot after a good scream. Alerted a neighbor who called us."

Ignoring the chill shivering up her spine to tighten her scalp, Miriam nodded. "I'll get Downie."

First, though, she stepped back into Cold Case and called Rosie.

"Yes," she said simply.

"Oh, God," Rose responded.

"I'll tell you more later. I've been ordered to the scene."

"Thank you."

Rosie obviously wasn't okay, but Miriam needed to find Downie and go. So she ended the call and started to punch in Downie's number, when who walked into the office but Downie.

"We've got another body like the others," she said.

He grimaced and started for the desk where his keys and weapon lived when he was in the building. "Where?"

"Six Sixty Farmington Avenue," she said, making sure that her weapon was in her purse, ignoring Capobianco, who whistled the theme from *The X Files*.

Downie turned around, keys in hand, frowning. "Isn't that where your cousin Rose used to live?"

Eyebrows raised in surprise—*why should he remember where Rose used to live?* —she nodded.

"We need to talk about this," he said. "In the car."

But in the car, neither of them had much to say at first. Then up around the memorial to Gallaudet and the original asylum for the deaf at Asylum Avenue, Downie opened. "Once is an occurrence, twice might be chance, but three is a pattern."

"And Rosie knew beforehand," she said without looking at him.

"Jee-sus."

Silence fell again until he drove up past the address. Patrol units and a morgue wagon, a forensics truck, and several large black SUVs, Lincoln Navigators, lined both sides of Farmington all the way to Prospect.

"Look at them." As he turned onto Prospect, Downie pointed at four men in black suits, skinny black ties, white shirts, dark sunglasses, with buzz-cut hair. "Men in Black."

Miriam looked where he pointed. "And a schmuck wearing creased blue jeans. Who does that?"

"A pathetic attempt at camouflage?" Downie pulled up to the curb about halfway down the block on Prospect.

"They're probably here to take the case," Miriam hoped out loud. Except standing there in a group on the tiny lawn, they weren't exactly taking over. They weren't even taking part in the investigation. They were barely observing.

In fact, the scene was being run by Hartford PD. At least the uniform on the door with the log was HPD. Aware of the feds' heads tracking her as she came up the walk, she showed her badge and spelled her name for the uniform and then stepped into the tiny foyer, 15 mailboxes on one wall, a small dark wooden bench, well polished, on the other, and yet another uniform on the door into the building.

That guy, Downie knew. "What's going on, Tully?"

Tully, an older man with the beginnings of a pot belly, shook his head. "Bad." Then he used a key to let them into the building itself.

A far cry from 68 Asylum, this was a working-class building, neat, clean, well lit, nothing fancy, although people wanted the beautiful old wooden floors in the apartments. Three apartments on the left side of the hall, two apartments, and the staircase up on the right.

Each apartment opened into a narrow hallway running parallel to the building hallway. Living room at one end of the hallway, bedroom at the other, kitchen, bathroom, and linen closet on the wall opposite the door between those two rooms.

The apartment on the wall behind the stairs up to the next floor had a coat closet and a bigger kitchen. Like Rose's place on the third floor.

Let it not be Rosie's old place, please.

A third uniform stood at the bottom of the stairs, holding out masks and a jar of Noxzema. "Rear apartment on the right, second floor. These won't do much."

"That bad?" she asked, knowing the answer, glad it wasn't Rose's place.

"Worse."

Nodding, Miriam started up the stairs, but she stopped because someone up on the second floor yelled in surprise, someone else screamed, and then something—someone? pushed past Miriam, so she had to snatch the banister for balance. Downie was shoved against the wall, the uniform was knocked flat on his ass, the door to the foyer sprang open—

But Miriam saw no one. *No one.*

Downie pushed off from the wall and grabbed Miriam by the arms. "You okay? Did you see anyone?"

"No. My God. Did you?"

They would have run up the stairs, but people, detectives and uniforms, came running down, weapons drawn. Miriam and Downie flattened themselves against the wall out of the way of the chasers who exited the building.

"Shit!" was all Mir could get out before Winewski called to her from the top of the stairs.

"Come on up," he ordered.

Still shaking their heads, she and Downie went up. Miriam could see all the activity at 2C from where they stood at the top of the stairs. She wanted to go back down the stairs, but just stood there instead.

"Why are the feds here, Mike?" Downie asked.

Winewski stopped just short of rolling his eyes. "Those schmucks? Decorating the fucking yard as far as I can tell. Haven't even checked in with me." He turned and started marching down the hall toward the scene. "Common fucking courtesy. And now I've got the invisible man, too."

"But, Mike," Miriam said, "they aren't—"

"Just take a look at this scene, please, and find Jones."

Find Jones? Hadn't she come in to look at the old case? "Didn't she finally show up yesterday morning?"

"That's what I didn't tell you when I got back to Cold Case," Downie said. "She never showed up."

"But she said she was going to come back with information, didn't she? I didn't imagine that," Miriam said. She stopped to pull the little surgical mask over her mouth and nose to deal with the odors she could already smell.

"No, you didn't imagine it. She did say she was going to come in," Downie said. "But she didn't show, and she's not answering home, office, or cell. There's a message on all the phones about a family emergency."

"Yeah," Winewski snarled. "She disappears. Like fucking magic. Another invisible friend."

At least they knew Jones had gone home, wherever that was. It wasn't another irrational mystery. That's all Miriam could think of as they closed in on Apartment 2C. Jones was one little bit of business they didn't have to worry about. There was enough to worry about, what with inside-out bodies and invisible men.

"My cousin teaches in the same building as Jones, so if we have to track her down, Rose will know how." Too bad Rosie couldn't answer all the other questions about magic and inside-out bodies, and invisible men.

God, but Miriam hated magic.

Chapter 20
Tuesday

Sara stood, unseen, next to a huge beech tree on the lawn of the apartment building across the street from 660 Farmington Avenue. An army of jackasses searched up and down the avenue and Prospect Avenue and never came close. She had to stifle the urge to laugh because the noise would have given her away, but really, they looked like fools.

It was all too easy. And at any moment, that Winkler cop would get sick, and Sara would have everything she wanted. Because if the cop died, the other two Winklers died. Satisfaction guaranteed.

The only hard part of all of this business had been getting access to the apartment in the first place. She'd had to evoke eerie noises and misty visions on and off for days until the superstitious cow who lived there vacated. When the apartment broker called to tell her the place was available, she had trouble controlling her excitement.

The apartment was the closest she'd been able to get to any of the old Winkler residences. It would have been best had she been able to work in the actual apartment Rose Winkler had lived in, but the woman living there, another stupid cow, was excited by the visions, loved the idea of living in a haunted apartment, and even tried to talk to the apparitions Sara produced. So two-C was a close second, really just a few vertical feet of difference.

The apartment broker had tried to talk her out of the place. "Honestly, it's very small, about 800 square feet with no amenities, no parking included. There *is* a super in the building, but that's the only benefit. Honestly, I can't imagine living there if your aunt can afford better."

"It's on a major bus line and near the park, which my aunt loves. So I want to see it," Sara insisted.

The broker wasn't especially gracious about visiting the place, which was a smaller space than Sara believed anyone could live in. Even the house C. Jones lived in had more space.

"Oh," Sara said almost as soon as the super opened the door for them. The place was immaculate, the walls freshly painted, the windows sparkling in the early spring sunshine.

She allowed herself to be led into the living room, with its sealed oak floor. The place was perfect, absolutely perfect. "Oh, dear," she said. "I didn't realize how tiny it actually is. It won't do. Not at all."

The broker barely kept the gloating smile off her face. "There are *lovely* apartments just down Prospect. Close enough to walk to the bus stops on Farmington, and certainly more spacious than this. Also with amenities. Covered parking, doorman on the premises..."

The woman chattered on about amenities, and Sara let her, knowing she had the perfect space for her sacrifice.

The rest of it had been far simpler.

The blood sacrifice himself required a sandwich and a bottle of beer, both loaded with sedatives, of course, offered to him, a beggar, on Church Street near the Franciscans' soup kitchen, and she'd bagged herself a reasonably healthy-looking man. Once he was endered insensible and then invisible, she'd easily transported him back to the apartment building and stashed him in the bitty little bathroom while she painted her circle and pentagram.

The one snag, not really a snag, an inconvenience, occurred when she ran short of candles. The candles had to be physically present, had to be black, had to be tallow.

That had meant a trip back to the one reliable *botanica* in Hartford, where the proprietor knew her business and actually had power that she used as a *Curandera*. The woman had decided she didn't like Sara—a matter for another time. The trip there was just a minor distraction, really, but after the frustration at Jones's house—Sara worried that the failure at Jones's house had been an omen.

But everything went so smoothly once she had the candles. She laid them out and took her place in the circle with her sacrifice. Quickly centering herself, she focused on the flame, and the candles lit in unison with no wavering. The sacrifice awoke exactly at the right moment, his fear adding power to the spell. Then she inverted him, and the blood pooled around him, exactly as prescribed.

It was a bonus when the old busybody from across the hall tiptoed into the apartment through the door Sara had forgotten to close just as Sara dropped the invisibility spell. The old lady's panic and screams strengthened the potency of the sacrifice.

At that point, Sara had re-invoked the invisibility so she could wait for the police, hopefully to hear about the death of one of them. But she'd inadvertently brushed up against one of the uniformed officers and had to run. And when she hit the stairs, working hard not to laugh at the fear she was engendering in all those stupid cops, who stood there? That Winkler bitch, that's who. The cop who was supposed to get deathly ill and die.

Sara knew that any minute now, the woman would start having trouble breathing, would become so ill she couldn't stand. So Sara kept running, out of the building and across the street, where she could wait and watch.

Those other cops ran around like idiots, scratching their heads, trying very hard not to believe in magic and invisible people—and the Winkler woman came strolling out of that ridiculous building, obviously *not* so sick she had to be carried.

Sara wanted to scream her frustration. No dead Winkler bitches, no books. She deserved those books; only she had the ability to use them, while that Jones person could only collect them and admire them. And the Winklers deserved to die. They deserved horrible deaths. Her birth mother had given her up to the unloving people who adopted her. And the other two had turned their backs, had refused to help her mother when she discovered her pregnancy. They all needed to be punished.

She would get those books, and those women would die.

They *would*. And Sara would have everything she wanted. Everything.

Chapter 21
Tuesday

Hannah sat in a booth at Vito's facing the big window that fronted on the busy Silas Deane Highway, waiting for her chicken *Française,* feeling reasonably satisfied with herself. Scott at Scott's Music had given her the names of three piano teachers who took adult students, and now she was treating herself to a restaurant lunch on a Wednesday, a real treat. Of course, she had to thank whoever had vandalized the pool house at school for her unexpected free day. But she knew how to make the best of a bad thing. She always had.

Sipping cold water with a slice of lemon, she felt herself relax into the seat. Then she heard familiar voices up front. At least two of her sophomores, Croce and Minsky, had decided to treat themselves, too. Now they sat in the booth two or three up from hers, not toning down their voices despite the public setting. They never did.

"But it was *blood,*" Minsky said.

"Dog's blood, my father says." Croce would know, her father being the head swim coach.

"Eew!" Minsky almost screamed. "Dog blood? I'll never swim in that pool again."

"They're draining the pool and disinfecting it." Croce sounded calm and reasonable. "It'll be fine. What I'd like to know is what they meant by 'We know what you did'. Whoever it was spray-painted that on the pool deck."

"Who did what?" Minsky asked.

"Nobody knows, but you know how jealous people can be. You'd think we were bad people or something."

So. The vandalism *had* been in retaliation for something a swim team member had done. Of course it had. Exactly as Hannah had thought. At least half those kids shoved people around, bullied people, and generally behaved like entitled brats.

The half that didn't behave like that still got away with a lot. Grades bumped up from C+ to B- to maintain eligibility was just the start. Croce didn't see it, but other people did. And some of those people didn't like what they saw.

But it had nothing to do with her. Someone would discover the answer to Dawn Minsky's question, some kid or kids would be punished, and nothing would change at school. Those graced with certain abilities would continue to be graced.

"Hello. May I join you?"

Startled out of her reverie, Hannah smiled up at her husband, dressed in scrubs and a light jacket. "David! How did you find me?"

"You told me what you were planning, remember?" David sat opposite her and reached for a piece of garlic bread in the basket she'd pushed to the side of the table. "Did you find a music teacher?"

"Scott gave me three names so I can try them out."

"Local?" He pulled his cell phone from a jacket pocket and laid it on the table near the bread.

"One is, but the other two are in Avon and Newington. I'll try the woman in Wethersfield first."

Minsky squealed again.

David chuckled. "One of yours?"

"Sophomores." Hannah sighed, about to expand on Minsky and Croce, when the waitress appeared with her meal and a menu for David.

"Give me a minute, please?" David asked the waitress and turned to study his choices.

Hannah smiled, enjoying his silent company. After a moment, she decided not to let her food cool too much. "Do you mind if I start, David?"

He smiled over the menu at her. "Of course not. Go ahead. I think I'll—"

The phone vibrated and slid slightly on the table.

"Damn it," he said and picked it up. "Levine."

Hannah had read the name on the screen before he picked up the phone. Mike Winewski. That was a new one to her. He hadn't mentioned any Mikes when he talked about Emergency Department staff.

"Right," David said after listening for a moment. "I'm on my way." He ended the call. "Damn it. I should have known." He shook his head.

"Of course I have to go." David pulled his wallet out of his pocket and handed her money.

"At least I can pay for lunch." He leaned down and kissed her quickly, more of a peck on the lips, really. "I should be home for supper. No double shift today."

He was gone as fast as he'd appeared. But that was life married to an emergency physician.

So Hannah returned to her chicken and the girls behind her. Their conversation had moved on to various young men, and they giggled over rumors of alleged conquests and what Mary O'Riley said about Susan Ahern and what Susan said about Mary in return, and so forth. *Animal Farm* absolutely paled in comparison.

Had she ever been so focused on boys and clothes and anything but school?

Had she seriously just asked that question? Of course, she'd been focused on boys and clothes and sex, and there it was, the subject she'd avoided for at least an hour. Sex with a married professor whom she would not dignify by naming had led to a problem.

Not a problem, Hannah. A child. You gave birth to a child. You didn't name the child, you didn't see the child, but you gave that child life. That you can't deny. Especially not now, not after what Rosie said about inherited traits.

Did carrying a child for nine months seriously obligate her? She'd made sure the child had every advantage, money, religion, both in a good family, solid people, thoroughly investigated by what's-his-name at the embassy. So she considered herself finished. She'd done well by the accidental child, better than her own parents had done for her, especially considering that Daddy had left her and her mother. No. She had taken special care to make sure the child was placed well, and that was that.

Hannah finished her lunch, left David's money on the table, and walked past Croce and Minsky with a smile. The girls giggled after Hannah passed them, and Hannah's smile broadened.

She felt good as she threw her purse onto the passenger seat of her car. She was going home to try out the music book Scott had sold her. Everyone needed a hobby, right? And everything would be fine.

Chapter 22
Tuesday

◆

Emile slowed the Subaru as he approached the intersection of Trout Brook and Asylum. Invisible in the passenger seat, Peter said, "Leaving now," and rose up through the roof of the vehicle.

His vampiric abilities to fly, to go invisible, and to pass through solids made him valuable to the *phyle*. Doing those things also felt good to him in a way he could not explain. The feeling had nothing to do with the exhilaration he had experienced when he first discovered what he could do. Deciding to be invisible, to fly, to pass through walls felt...right, as if his body wanted to do those things, wanted to perform his magic.

However, working his magic required energy—any magic did—so he rationed his magical activities. But as he alit near the culvert, he enjoyed the sensations in his body. He was still invisible, after all, standing there between the small waterfall exiting the pipe and the fence around the ball field. There he stood, though no one could see him, and listened.

Despite the heavy traffic, particularly on Trout Brook Drive, he could hear a baby crying in the house on the corner opposite him. He heard a woman crooning comfort to the child. He heard a voice in the house diagonally across from where he stood, a newsreader on television, he thought. He also heard voices behind him, male, complaining about this "fucking assignment."

"Nothing is going to happen."

"The Wethersfield detail is seeing some action."

"This is what we were detailed to do, so just shut the fuck up and watch."

Those voices came from the Lincoln Navigator parked in the lot on the other side of the ball field. What the fools could see through the trees that separated the field from the lot, he had no idea, but there they sat. He hoped they were too bored to pay attention properly if a wolf appeared, even as he admitted to himself that a wolf in half form was hard to miss, stunted and skinny though he might be. The wolf's head on a fur-covered human body with knees that bent the "wrong" way definitely called attention to itself.

He knew from Robert's report yesterday that their license plate was federal government issue. Those men were federal agents of some sort. Chili and Abel, the pack's computer experts, would not hack federal systems, nor would Martin ask them to, so the license plate was of limited value. However, Phillipe and Jean, the pack's lawyers, had instituted discreet inquiries, but even they and their human agents had to be careful not to work too hard for information. Pushing for answers, demanding information drew precisely the kind of attention they wished to avoid.

The hope was that the appearance of federal agents at the same time rogue wolves invaded LeBeau territory was a coincidence, though Peter thought the mention of a Wethersfield detail made coincidence unlikely.

The fools might be looking at a drug connection at one of the several schools in the area. They might be interested in someone living in one of the houses in the neighborhood. Solidly professional and upper middle class, well kept, the area looked innocent. But houses, even pretty houses, could hide secrets. His certainly did.

Peter huffed at his own joke, set aside the question of the Wethersfield detail and the Lincoln Navigator in the parking lot here, and turned away from the streets to inhale deeply. His sense of smell was not as sharp as the wolves', not as sensitive as his hearing, but his senses exceeded any human's, even a perfumer's Nose, in his ability to discern scents.

He rose a few feet to follow the strongest wolf scent along Trout Brook Drive toward Albany Avenue, ignoring everything but the message from his nose. He was not sure that he could follow the scent if the trail followed that street, which carried far more traffic than Trout Brook did. Albany was the major East-West artery for commuters from Hartford to the wealthy suburbs of Avon, Canton, and beyond. So much traffic, so many gasses, would confuse his nose.

But the scent of the wolf he followed crossed Albany Avenue and went into the trees that ran along King Phillip Drive. The noise and stink of traffic faded as he moved along just a few inches off the ground so as not to make noise. The scent avoided the yards and houses along the street until he came to the parking lot of King Phillip Middle School. Instead of staying in the trees that lined the lot, the rogue wolf had chosen to walk across the open pavement.

Obviously not a wise choice. Unlike campires, wolves cannot go invisible or fly or go through solids. He would have been perfectly visible, obvious, to anyone looking in his direction. Perhaps the rogue had been tired. Perhaps he needed to orient himself. Rogue that he was, perhaps he was still hungry and wanted a respite. Or a janitor to gnaw on.

Peter smiled at his foolishness and floated along, inhaling deeply to separate the scent of the rogue from all the other scents in the lot, the humans, adult and child, male and female. Promising scents. His proper prey. Tempting, all those humans in the buildings around him. So easy to take a taste. Invisible as he was, who would know—

Peter stopped there at the edge of the parking lot and blew out his breath. His discipline was usually much better than this. He could sit in his favorite Chinese restaurant and eat a nice dinner without being bothered by the humans all around him. For some reason, his hold on his appetite was not firm just then. But he could not add to the *phyle's* troubles. He would not. He would not drop the discipline that he had developed over hundreds of years.

He had a responsibility to his *phyle*. Therefore, he rose above the pavement and picked up the scent of the wolf again. Through trees, in some places thin, in some places more like woods, he followed the rogue until he came to Simsbury Road. There were large houses along that street, widely spaced out and separated by woods.

Peter followed the scent for a time toward Simsbury. But he was tiring, and that could be a problem. The earlier temptation had surprised him. Now he anticipated the temptation. The discipline held because he kept the vampire, the magic, not a demon, magic, well fed and rested. If he used his magic too much without feeding it, temptation was almost impossible to ignore.

He did the smart thing, alit, settled himself against a tree trunk and called Emile on his cell phone to report his location.

"You're well west of the intersection with North Main Street, sir." That was the closest Emile would come to a rebuke, Peter knew.

"I will need a little something to hold me, Emile," Peter acknowledged.

"I'll be with you in perhaps ten minutes."

Of course he would. He regularly drove Peter on these little forays. No need to leave a car in a parking lot or along the road somewhere when Emile could drive him—and take care that he did not endanger the *phyle* as well.

Peter pushed himself off the tree. "Pet vampire is what you are, Peter, son of Mikal, just the pet kept for your fancy tricks. That's what you are."

He maintained his invisibility until Emile cruised slowly past the spot where Peter exited the woods. He slid into the car, announced, "I am here," and let himself be seen.

"There are two thermoses under your seat."

Emile drove quietly until Peter drained the first thermos. "Shall we go up into Simsbury?"

"They could be anywhere in these woods, Emile. The farther we get from West Hartford, the thicker the woods there become. And there are ponds and lakes everywhere. We need to put wolves on the scent with me."

Emile nodded. "We could go to Plan B up in Simsbury.

"As good as their burgers are, Emile, I think we must speak to your Alpha as soon as we can." He felt uneasy, suddenly, about that big SUV sitting in the parking lot near the Little League field.

Undercover operations generally involve people trying to blend in, not stand out. That Lincoln in a lot where UConn branch students and Little League parents parked was like a neon sign flashing for attention.

Peter finished the second thermos of blood before they reached the compound. Emile went to do what he did, and Peter carried both empty thermoses with him to Martin's kitchen, a cold place, all stainless steel and black granite. Cesar, the pack's cook, took them from him as he bared his throat.

Peter bowed to that throat, now wholly aware of what was offered.

"Lunch?" Cesar suggested when Peter straightened.

"Yes, thank you, Cesar. I *am* hungry."

"Of course. My Alpha is waiting in the dining room. Lunch will be ready in five minutes."

Michael was indeed waiting opposite a place setting with a glass of blood. "Too kind." Peter picked up the glass and drank it down before he reported. "Three wolves went up that small pipe. One must have been too big to fit, so he walked to Simsbury Road and headed west. I followed for a time, until I started to get thirsty and thought it best to call Emile." He sat and finished the glass.

"So Emile reported." Martin nodded. "Thank you for calling Emile when you did, Peter."

"I told you I would not go rogue, Martin. It is insulting to me to think I would after I said I would not."

Martin nodded once. "It is. But I do worry about you."

Peter made his sigh loud and dramatic. "It is very kind of you to worry, but it is unnecessary. I promise you, Martin, I do not plan to go rogue. I *will* exercise my discipline."

"Yet you say you wish to die."

Cesar stopped the argument by pushing his serving cart into the dining room. He transferred a large platter of filets and another of steak fries to the table, followed by one of Peter's favorites, a small bowl of roasted garlic.

Peter grinned at the cook. "Cesar, you know me very well."

"I do know your preferences in food. Thank you."

As Cesar left the room, Martin shook his head. "He's been cooking for you for almost two hundred years, Peter," he said as he slid a piece of meat onto Peter's plate, then offered him the tongs so he could take his own fries.

Laughing, Peter took the tongs. "The look on his face the first time I walked into his kitchen in the morning and asked for eggs was just amazing."

"We'd never known a vampire before. We believed the lore."

"But I had been eating while I healed, Martin. And you knew I had a pulse. I still have a pulse. I am not dead. I will not die in the sun. I will not die of garlic, I will not die of a stake in the heart." To punctuate his words, he took several cloves of the roasted garlic and smeared them across the top of his filet.

Martin shrugged. "We all learn as we go along. Now tell me why you're so worried."

Peter sighed loudly. "One could never make a surprise party for you." He cut a piece of meat. "That Lincoln Navigator was in the parking lot by the ball field again. Or still is. Who knows?" He cut a piece of the garlic-covered meat and popped it in his mouth, chewed and swallowed. Martin still hadn't responded to his news. But Martin was a thorough thinker. The Alpha definitely liked to think before he spoke.

"So our assumption that they are part of an undercover operation must be incorrect," Martin said finally.

"I have to say so. They make absolutely no effort to blend in. They look military to me, and all they do is sit and watch. Who are they watching? They are too far from the houses, which are obscured by trees between the ball field and everything else. They might be watching screens and listening to things reported by cameras and other devices. There is some nicely sensitive eavesdropping equipment available, particularly for government agencies. But they are so openly sitting there, not making any effort to look like a plumber's van or something like that. I am willing to say that if they are undercover, I will kiss an elf." He would never talk to an elf, much less kiss one, unless the sun rose in the west. The wolf knew that about the vampire.

Martin snorted before he responded. "We think they followed the first rogue to the pipe." He began to eat his filet.

"Something like that. Because they do not belong in that parking lot." Peter took a steak fry and held it on the fork. "We know they are federal, possibly military, watching near where rogue wolves used a culvert to travel through LeBeau territory.

And they mentioned a Wethersfield detail. Nothing about it, just that they have people working in Wethersfield."

Martin chewed a steak fry and swallowed before he answered. "I would argue for coincidence, but it seems unlikely that such people would just turn up in the same place twice. Or more perhaps. We patrol borders, not the entire territory, unless we have a reason. So we have a problem."

"We do have a problem." Peter took another bite of meat. "What are we doing about the rogues?"

"We will go out tonight to look. And the question of what is going on in Wethersfield will wait."

"What would you like me to do?"

"You and Emile will resume following that Simsbury Road scent after you check out that SUV. Please."

Peter almost laughed. The pack was, in fact, a dictatorship, and Martin was the unquestioned dictator. He always said "please" and "thank you," though those words were unnecessary in the pack.

Nevertheless, Martin used them, even with his wolves. Peter liked those words, Martin made an effort to use them appropriately, and the vmpire appreciated the effort. "When?"

"Full dark. Emile will fetch you at seven."

"I will be ready."

"Thank you, Peter."

"Of course, Martin." He *would* know the *phyle* was safe before he did anything about his situation. He truly was worried. Martin had sniffed him out. Peter worried about the *phyle*.

No. Peter worried about his *friends*.

Chapter 23
Tuesday

◆

Rose couldn't settle on anything, not television, not her Nero Wolfe outline, not crochet, definitely not practicing telekinesis or anything else. Even cooking, which usually calmed her down, felt too complicated, too fussy. She needed the promised phone call from Miriam.

Miriam didn't call. An hour and a half after the initial call, a description of the terrible something didn't come. Two and a half hours and still no call from Miriam.

After wandering through the house, at 988 square feet, not that far to wander, at least fifty times, Rose stopped in the kitchen, leaned against a counter, and considered what she'd been avoiding: the woo-woo stuff.

Specifically, talking to Nana Pearl. Even though Nana Pearl would know what was going on, talking to her could not be explained except as *supernatural*. It was true that Dr. Petrovsky had recommended that she talk to Nana to strengthen her skills. But, really? It wasn't natural. It could *not* be explained as some sort of electromagnetic phenomenon, or even quantum events on the macro scale. Nana Pearl was a *ghost. Definitely a ghost.*

But it had felt good, hadn't it, to see Nana. Nana loved her. So. A deep breath for calm, which didn't actually work, and she called out. "Nana Pearl?"

Her voice sounded tentative, weak. *Come on, Rosie. It's Nana, for God's sake. Make an effort.*

"Nana, please. I'd like to talk. I have ques—"

The clean scent of lavender suffused the kitchen, and there Nana sat at the table in the spot where Miriam had sat last night. Today, Nana wore a white blouse and a black cardigan. Rose sat down opposite her and noticed the tiny gold filigree star of David in the open collar of the blouse and at Nana's ears the pearl earrings, both of which items also sat in Rose's jewelry box down the short hall—

"Hello, Sweetheart."

Rose needed a couple of deep breaths before she could say, "Hi, Nana." Tears threatened. *Tears? Really?* "I'm glad to see you."

Nana looked sad. "It's nice to see you, too. But I came for a reason, you know."

Rose nodded. In the ghost stories she taught, "The Turn of the Screw" and *A Christmas Carol,* the ghosts always had a purpose for their visitations. Those Victorians definitely knew their way around ghosts. "Can you answer questions?"

Nana's lips thinned. "There are rules."

Rose nodded. "Can you talk about the family history? Whatever you want to call them, the gifts?"

Nana's chest moved as if she were sighing. "You should have been told. Your mother was supposed to tell you before you got your first period, but—"

"Hannah and Miriam didn't know either." Rose heard the accusation in her voice: *Why didn't you say something?*

Nana didn't say anything for a moment or two. When she did speak, Rose was surprised by her approach.

"When I married your grandfather," Nana said, "I was seventeen. I didn't know a lot of important things. Oh—" She waved a hand toward the stove—"I knew how to kosher and cook meat, and I could make kreplach and my own noodles. I even knew how to make babies. But the question I should have asked? Why did two of Jacob's sisters, Pena and Tava, beauties both of them, never marry? Especially when they had rich dowries. Who knew to ask such a thing? I was a poor girl, surprised and grateful for the match." Nana's chest rose again as if to sigh.

"Nowadays, everyone understands mental illness, personality disorders, and chemical imbalances. By the time I knew I had to ask, I had three children, your mother, and her sisters. You understand what I'm saying to you?"

Rose knew, had known for a long time, that her mother and her two aunts had been ill, her mother paranoid, definitely the worst of the three sisters, and Miriam's mother probably the least, but still off in her view of the world, always seeing the worst in everyone and everything that happened. None of them, not Aunt Ruth or Aunt Chava or her mother, had a cheerful take on life. "Laugh in the morning, cry by nightfall" was the sisters' motto.

"What's your point?" Again, Rose heard the edge in her voice.

"In those days, no one went to a psychiatrist, even assuming they had the money to pay for such things, not unless they couldn't function. And I didn't understand how bad your mother was. Honestly, at first, I thought marriage would help them, especially your mother, reassure them that they were loved, that no one wanted to hurt them. So I waited." Nana shrugged. "I even waited for your mother to tell you about the other thing, the special gifts. I would have explained about the illness myself, but I truly thought she would tell you about the inheritance." Nana shrugged again and made her who-knew? face, that half-smile, half-grimace.

"I hadn't planned on dying at 62, you know."

Despite the urge to have answers *now*, Rose smiled. "I've missed you."

"You were my sweetheart. You still are." Nana's smile disappeared. "Which is why I am back."

Afraid to say anything in case she said the wrong thing and stopped Nana's willingness to speak, Rose raised her eyebrows instead.

Apparently, that was the correct response. Nana kept talking. "I knew, you see. When she broke your arm. I knew you hadn't fallen off your bicycle."

Suddenly light-headed, Rose stopped breathing. Thoughts, ridiculous thoughts flooded her: *How did Nana know? Why hadn't she done something? Who was going to remind her to breathe? What was she supposed to do with this information? If her mother's ghost came back now, she'd have to throw something at her, find an exorcist, do rabbis do exorcisms?*—"Why didn't you say anything? Why didn't you take me away? How could you just leave me with her? I know she was your daughter, but—"

"In those days?" Nana reached across the table, but her hands stopped short of Rose's. "In those days, Sweetheart, no one took children away from their mothers unless there was absolute proof of abuse. But it was only my word against hers, and she knew it. She told me that if I told anyone, even your father, she would make sure everyone thought that *I* was the crazy one and that I would never see you again. I told her that if she ever touched you like that again, I would tell the police, regardless of the consequences—"

"She never touched me again. Not a hug, not a kiss, nothing."

"Now, I know that. Then? I only knew that I was a widow, an older woman with no power to do anything. I had the ability to see what was happening, but nothing more—"

"Oh," Rose said, suddenly understanding. "That's why you couldn't prove it. You *knew,* but you had no rational way to explain it."

Nana smiled crookedly. "Some gift, eh?" She shook her head. "That's why I gave *Tannah* to Fanny. I couldn't even protect my own granddaughter properly. How could I keep that legacy?"

Legacy. *Tannah.* Miriam. A better topic. Safer, at least. No threat of tears there. "What is *Tannah,* Nana? Why is it so important? And why couldn't you keep it?"

Spreading her hands wide, Nana shrugged. "Some kind of protective amulet. There must have been a story about her, an explanation, but it was lost, forgotten, long before the pin came to me. The only thing my mother knew was that *Tannah* came into the family during the Chmielnicki pogroms in Poland in the

1600s. Supposedly, *Tannah* protected the family then, but by the time I inherited her, no one knew how to make her work. If it was *Tannah* that protected us, the information is gone."

Nana shrugged again. "I can tell you this. The lawyer who passed her to me from my mother's estate said the pin must be worn by a woman, and the woman must be morally fit." Nana shrugged—they were a family of shruggers—"He didn't know why." She chuckled. "Like everything else, *Tannah* is—" Nana held her hands out, palms up—"a gift—" one hand reached closer to Rose—"or a burden." The other hand reached closer to Rose. "Maybe a curse." She dropped her hands. "I only knew I wasn't fit to wear it, not if I couldn't protect you, Rose."

Rose sighed loudly—she'd been doing that a lot lately—"What do we *do?* Why can't it be simple? Everything is so damned complicated."

"This question I cannot answer."

The question had been rhetorical anyway. But—"Wait, what? You *can't?* Does that mean you know what's going on but aren't allowed to say? Because there are rules about saying things that might...I don't know, interfere with what's supposed to happen? Who makes these rules? Why can't we just know what—?" Rose stopped because she heard herself starting to demand and accuse.

Besides, Nana's face had gone neutral. "Please, Rose," she said. "I can't answer you. But you must be careful, Sweetheart, you and Miriam." Nana smiled sadly. "And next time, Rose darling, offer me a cup of tea."

"Tea? But you're a—" She spoke to an empty chair. "Ghost."

The scent of lavender lingered at the table.

Rolling her eyes, Rose groaned to the ceiling. "Seriously? Do you think I *want* to go crazy? Dear God in heaven, do you really—No." Rose stood herself up, still talking. "Okay, Rosie. You talked this out with a therapist a long time ago, number one. Number two, you have a P-H-fucking-D, for God's sake. You are not that helpless little girl, not for a long time now. And you have information now, at least about *Tannah*. You can use what Nana told you and do some Googling, can't you? Yes, you can. And Miriam will call when she has information. So go do some work."

Rose Winkler Sherman could intellectualize anything, and she would do it to *Tannah*. She had the names of the towns where the family had lived in Eastern Europe, most of them now in Poland, at least one in Ukraine, before they moved to Germany and then to the United States in the 1880s. She had the original family names, she had Google, and she had time. It was something to do, and it would let her feel useful. Pretending to be okay helped, too. "To the computer, Rosie. The game is afoot."

Chapter 24
Tuesday

Staying in the little apartment, getting in the way of Button and his team, and maybe contaminating the scene were not good choices. So, along with at least a dozen uniforms, Miriam and Downie spent a frustrating hour trying to find a trace of the invisible person who had fled the apartment building.

No one said the word "invisible" out loud, not a single searcher, not once. Neither did anyone question people at the gas station diagonally across the intersection, or at Tangier directly across Prospect. What could they possibly have asked? "Did you see anything odd?" Define "odd." That older woman at the gas station wearing a fur coat on a day when most people weren't even wearing a lightweight jacket? Or how about that young guy in a kilt across the street with a safety pin through his eyebrow? Or the two Goth kids, heavy black liner around their eyes and more piercings on their faces than Miriam ever considered possible, who just got off the Connecticut Transit bus at the corner of Farmington and Prospect? *Wow.*

Besides, how can you ask if anyone saw an invisible person? By definition, the person is unseeable. "Pardon me, but did you see a stray shadow or hear a noise, but there wasn't anyone there?" Right. That would get you a good stare, maybe even a phone call to the Lieutenant, but nothing productive.

Finally, standing in front of the CVS at Whitney Street, three blocks down from the scene, Downie shook his head. "This isn't even futile. It's...impossible. We don't know what or who we're supposed to be looking for or even how to look."

Miriam blew out her breath. "What can we do? I can't find Jones at all, and..." she looked away from her partner. "We have to talk, you and I, to Rose. Now. Is that okay? You can tell Mike we're following a lead on Jones."

Downie stared at her for a few seconds before he pulled out his cell phone and pushed a number. "Hey, Mike. Listen. We have a lead to Jones."

"Is she in the city?"

"No, we don't know, but we know someone who does..."

"Sounds pretty tentative."

"Well, yeah, but Jones can definitely help us, so we want to follow up. We'll call when we have something."

"Fine. Fine. That's fine. We'll talk later."

Downie ended the call, slid the phone into his jacket pocket, and grimaced. "Mike is not a happy man. C'mon."

As if Miriam gave a rat's patoot whether Mike was happy. She just chuckled as they turned to walk up the hill toward Prospect Avenue, ignoring the Men in Black, who were still congregated on the tiny lawn of 660. When they got to Downie's car, Miriam announced an errand. "We need to swing by the Crown, please, so I can pick up some lemon squares."

"Bribing, are we?" he asked as he pulled out into traffic.

"Bribing is such a harsh word. Softening, maybe. Comforting. Something sweet to let Rose know she isn't alone." Actually, something to let Rose know she wasn't deliberately being betrayed, wouldn't have to move to a cardboard box under the Putnam Bridge. Rose joked a lot about the box under the bridge, but Miriam heard the fear in the joke. And talking about the family inheritance, not the craziness, the other stuff, in front of Downie might be considered a betrayal. Rose might consider it a betrayal. She wasn't like her mother, but this stuff could damage their carefully constructed, carefully conventional lives.

Downie drove up to Bishop's Corner and waited in the car while Miriam went into the kosher market. He didn't say anything until they were well on their way to Wethersfield.

"What's the plan?"

Miriam had to laugh. "You don't know me by now? Seriously? A plan?" She played interrogation by ear, he knew damned well. Besides, "I'm barely thinking straight as it is, and you want a plan?"

His calm remained unshaken. At least his voice stayed calm. "Rose isn't going to be happy that I know her secrets. And you've been followed. Not to mention there's been a death in an apartment in the same building she once lived in. Rose should know all that, too. Besides which, we don't believe in coincidence, so..." He glanced quickly over at her. "Will Rose accept my knowing? And maybe help us?"

"She's not police, but I think, if we're careful—"

"This case isn't police." He shook his head. "And those bastard Feds are leaving it alone for a reason. It's about you, Rose and Hannah."

Miriam laughed again. "*You* obviously have a plan."

He grinned at the windshield. "Only if Rose can accept my knowing about all of this. I'm not family. I may be your partner, but I am not family."

Sighing, Miriam stared out the passenger window. He didn't have a plan; he simply faced reality. "Okay. I plan to eat a lemon square. How's that?"

Still smiling, Downie nodded. "Go with the certainty. I like it."

She laughed, but the laugh died as they pulled into Rose's driveway. "God, but I hate this," she said, getting out of the car.

Rose was slow answering the door, and when she finally pulled it open, she seemed distracted, more interested in the papers in her hand. "Oh, hi. Um. C'mon in."

Miriam held out the box from the Crown. "Lemon squares."

"Oh. Thanks. I'll make tea. You drink tea, don't you, Sergeant Downs?"

"Downie. Call me Downie."

"Okay." Rose still hadn't moved aside so they could walk into the house.

"Rosie. Wake up."

Rose snapped her eyes open wide and smiled. "Sorry. Research. Interesting possibilities. Come in." Now she stepped aside and let Miriam lead the way to the kitchen.

"Listen, Rosie," Miriam said, facing the stove. She couldn't look at her cousin, having given major secrets away. She really did feel as though she'd betrayed Rose. "Downie knows. About Tannah and the other inheritances."

Nothing. No response from behind her. She had to know what was going on, so she turned.

Rose stood there in the kitchen doorway, lips pressed together, breathing.

Downie stood beside Miriam, apparently just waiting calmly.

"You okay, Rosie?" Miriam asked, barely above a whisper.

For several seconds, Rosie said nothing, did nothing. Then she breathed loudly and shrugged. "You had to tell him, I guess. If these murders have anything to do with us, he'd have to know what he's potentially dealing with, right?" And she walked around Miriam to the counter. "Decaf all around?"

"Rose." Miriam didn't quite trust Rose's easy acceptance of the situation. Just yesterday, her fear had been palpable, right on the surface, ready to take over. And today? This afternoon? "Seriously, Rose. Are you okay?"

Rose just kept working, placing the freshly filled kettle on the stove, pulling mugs from a cabinet, placing tea in the infuser for the teapot, cutting the string on the box of lemon squares—

"Rose," Miriam insisted.

Rose turned around, a small plate in one hand, a half-smile on her face. "I don't know what 'okay' is anymore, okay? I spilled the family secrets to a stranger earlier today, and all I could think about was how handsome he is and that he's most likely single. Is that okay? And then I knew about a murder. A *murder*, Miriam. Me. The one who buries herself in books and stories on TV because reality hurts too much sometimes. And then, because that all isn't enough, I spoke to Nana Pearl, who, in case anyone here has forgotten, has been dead for somewhere in the vicinity of 40 years." The smile actually grew a little bigger. "So you tell me, Mir. Am I okay? Are *you* okay?"

Rose went back to the box of lemon squares. "Oh, before I forget. I have information about *Tannah*. Not definitive, but highly suggestive. And strange."

Miriam glanced over at Downie, then walked to the counter, picked up the mugs. "I'll set the table. And I promise, no more questions about state of mind. I'm not in any state of mind to be asking anyway."

Rose chuckled. "Neither of us does well with change, Mir. We all know that."

"Who does—well, Downie does. How, I can't figure out, but, okay, we'll—"

Downie took plates from Miriam. "I don't try to figure everything out at once. That's all. I figure out what's right in front of me right now. Then I go on to the next thing." He shrugged. "It works most of the time."

Rose huffed. "That's a meditation trick. One breath at a time." She huffed again. "Apply it to everything." Then she added under her breath, "Huh." She raised her voice. "Well. Tell me about the old homestead. I assume that's why you're here."

"It wasn't in your apartment," Miriam said as she laid spoons on the table. "In two C—"

"I don't think I knew the woman who lived there except to nod at her. She was very quiet, I remember that, but that's it. If she was the one who still lived there, although people did tend to stay. I was the first person to move out since 1960-something."

"Well, the tenant moved out about a month ago now," Downie said. "Long enough for this person to find it and make another blood sacrifice."

"And go invisible." Miriam sat down. "Don't forget invisible."

"Invisible?" Rose echoed. "Not invisible, that's not poss— Is that possible?"

"Oh," Downie said, rubbing the back of his head tenderly. "Definitely possible. I've got a bump to prove it."

"But how do you look for an invisible person?" Rose took the whistling kettle off the stove and began to pour water into the teapot. "You can't exactly ask people what they've seen. Even if they've seen something odd, they'll find a way to ignore it or explain it that doesn't involve...what are we calling this all? The new physics in Cal's photocopies? I don't think Dr. Petrovsky totally believes that explanation either. Nana Pearl isn't quite...well, now I'm babbling."

Miriam felt Downie sit up a little straighter beside her. A sign of his interest. Sure enough, he asked. "Who's Dr. Petrovsky?"

Smiling, Rose set the three mugs and the teapot on the table. "Lemons or milk, Sergeant?" She sat.

"It's Downie," he said. " I've been hanging around with your cousin for more than 20 years, so call me Downie. Lemon, please. Who is Dr. Petrovsky?"

"You'll always be the sergeant to me," Rose said as she passed the small glass dish of lemon slices across the table to him. "Anyway, Cal Jones gave me his name. He's a professor of religion at UConn, but he knows a lot about the development of these, I'll just call them gifts, okay? He's a very handsome man. And kind. Patient, I think. Very patient. But he's being followed; he's not imagining it. I saw the man following him, this utterly innocuous-looking man, almost forgettable, except he irons his jeans. A perfect crease right down the—"

"Ironed blue jeans?" Miriam's heart beat a little faster. Not fear, not yet. Just uneasiness that she didn't want to talk about loud. Not yet.

Ever the perfect partner, Downie stepped in. "We saw a guy wearing ironed jeans, perfect crease right down the front of each leg, at our scene. At 660 Farmington. With a group of federal agents. Men in Black I call them, but—"

"No," Rose said.

Just the flat word, that very short word, but Miriam recognized Rose inching up to panic. "Rosie?"

Rose sat very still, almost frozen in place, and did not respond.

"Rose?" Miriam repeated.

"They know who we are," Rose whispered. "That's what Cal's paper said, and now they're at your magical crime scene. They know."

Panic is catching. Miriam's gut seized and she gasped.

"Wait," Downie spoke firmly. "The feds cannot hurt you. You both live very public lives, with jobs and friends and family. Anything they do would be noticed and—"

"But they know," Rose said. "And they can take everything away. If they know, they could call us terrorists or something like that and just—"

"No," Downie said in a voice good cops have and use, the voice that commands attention, that brooks no exceptions. "Look at me, both of you. They may know about you, but I think they just watch for people paying too much of the wrong kind of attention to you. That has to be why there's been no press coverage of any of these murders except the bare mention that they happened. I think that's right. Besides, I won't let anything happen to you. I promise."

Miriam knew he meant it, but Rose kept arguing.

"Sergeant, the invisible person, he could be here right now and we wouldn't—even if the federal people don't—You can't—"

"Rose!" Miriam smacked a hand on the table to stop her own escalating fear as much as to stop Rose, who clearly had gone into panic mode. "Panicking isn't going to keep us safe. Please." She blew out her breath loudly. "Help me stay calm, too."

Rose stared across the table at her.

"Tell me what you learned about *Tannah*, okay? We can't figure out the feds now, but we have *Tannah*, right?" Miriam said.

"That's your new pin, right?" Downie asked.

Rose transferred her stare to Downie, and Miriam braced for the screaming and weeping. Not that Rosie had ever so much as shed a tear in front of other people, at least not in front of Miriam, but in this situation, the screaming and weeping, maybe even some wailing, might actually have been appropriate. It was awfully tempting. You could just scream and cry, and someone else would take care of everything, right?

But Rose continued her new habit of not doing the usual or expected. She clasped her hands to her chest, shut her eyes, and breathed slowly and deeply, as if she were trying to inhale all of the air in the kitchen, once, twice, three times.

Her eyes opened. She didn't look happy, but she nodded and spoke in her normal voice. "Yes," she said, sounding almost calm. She definitely wasn't babbling. "I did some research. I spoke to Nana Pearl first—" she smiled feebly. "I will deny ever saying that if asked by anyone other than you two, by the way. Anyway, Nana didn't know very much, except the pin came into the family around the time of the Chmielnicki uprising in the seventeenth century."

Downie frowned. "Say that name again, please."

"Khmyel-NYET-skee," Rose pronounced. "Cossacks. Ukrainians, actually, who were rebelling against the Polish ruling class. Poland controlled a lot of Ukraine then. The borders moved every few years, Polish today, Russian tomorrow, Polish again, then independent for about four and a half minutes before the Poles came back. The borders kept changing even into the twentieth century, which is why Nana's family spoke so many languages.

"But anyway. Some Jews worked for the Polish rulers, Court Jews they were called. At first, the Cossacks killed just those Court Jews. And their families, of course. But after a little time, it became Jews in general. Pogroms. And not just Jews, though we were the main target. The Cossacks went after Catholic priests, Poles..."

Miriam didn't let herself smile because of the subject matter, but she could have. Rose was in full-on lecture mode. And calmer. Much calmer.

"Suddenly," Rose continued, "the plot thickens. The Cossacks came to a small city called Brody, which is still there in Ukraine, by the way, and which I am probably not pronouncing properly, but anyway, they came to Brody and started in on the usual: rape, pillage, kill.

"And then, suddenly—" Rose threw her hands wide—"for reasons no one in any history I have access to can specify, they stopped. There are suggestions of illness or possibly a shortage of food. It's odd because so much of the uprising is quite well documented, usually in nauseating detail, but this turn of events is mentioned without any detail at all, which I find very interesting. Because the Cossacks simply announced that the Jews of Brody weren't involved in the mistreatment of Ukrainians. They did take a pile of gold in tribute, which is the polite name for bribery, and left the city alone. Almost all of Brody's Jews survived the visit."

Rose smiled, a cat-who-swallowed-the-canary smile. "You want to guess who lived in Brody?"

Miriam shrugged. "Not even a hard one. Winklers."

Rose nodded. "An odd name for Poles or Ukrainians, being German, but definitely our family. Mother, named Miriam, father, Shmuel, seven or eight children, as far as I can find. The youngest was a girl of about 14 named Raizel. Shmuel was a fairly well-to-do merchant who traveled regularly to the German states. Anyway, Raizel is our founder. She kept the name Winkler even after marrying Chaim of Lvov, who was also a reasonably well-off merchant." Rose nodded, more to herself than to anyone else. "I suspect Winkler is a link to the maker of the pin and necessary to maintain a link to the pin itself."

Frowning, Miriam wrapped her hands around her mug. "But you have no proof that any of this story actually relates to *Tannah*."

"I forget you're not an English major—we do love ourselves some good ambiguity." Rose smiled. "But put aside your cop's need for physical proof, Mir, and take that inductive leap of faith. Consider: The pin has to be held by a woman who is morally fit in a family in which all the children, but especially the women, have to carry the Winkler name? That's what the lawyer *and* Nana Pearl say. There are all kinds of legal hooha surrounding the passing of the pin. I mean, when Nana decided to give *Tannah* away, she didn't just give the pin to Fanny. She and Fanny went to the lawyer and transferred ownership formally, right? And Fanny said it was fitting that the pin belonged to a police officer."

Downie grunted. "You think the pin is magic somehow."

Wincing, Rose nodded. "Let's not use that word. Let's call it...I don't know, special, okay? But yes, it's not just a pin. I mean, no historian has been able to offer a solid, provable reason for the Cossacks to have left Brody relatively unscathed. Brody wasn't especially important, and while Raizel's father was a relatively successful merchant, he wasn't an important man. He wasn't a scholar, which was the far more important profession among Jews back then. He wasn't a Rabbi or a Rabbi's student. He wasn't a learned man. He traveled for a living. Raizel's several times great-granddaughter, also Raizel, whose name is anglicized to Rachel, is the Winkler who came to this country, by the way, in 1860 or thereabouts. She came alone, as far as I can tell, and met her husband here. And she is the only way *Tannah* gets to this country still attached to Winklers."

"Damn," Downie said. "You found that all out this afternoon?"

Rose swallowed that canary again. "The Internet is a wonderful thing."

But Miriam sighed. "You really think *Tannah* is ma—special."

"The word *Tannah* in Hebrew is related to monsters of some kind, most likely winged dragons, whereas *Tannah* the pin is wingless. But yes, I do. I think she's special."

"Seriously?" Miriam did not want the possibility of magic on her lapel.

"If a magician—" Rose started.

"Practitioner," Downie corrected.

"Fine," Rose accepted. "If a practitioner can bend light around him to be invisible, then why can't a pin be more than just a pin?"

"Because I don't want it to be more than just a pin, okay? I don't want magic. I don't want Izzy to be right."

"Ah," Downie said as if experiencing an epiphany.

Miriam glared at him. "No 'ah.' You don't know anything about—"

"But I do, Mir. I was studying to be a priest, remember? And I have to tell you, this does not prove anything about God or the devil or werewolves or wizards. Or anything else."

Rose shook her head. "No, Sergeant Downs. You're applying logic. Logic doesn't work. This is fear. We're frightened. I mean, think about it. How do I deal with an invisible person? And by the way, if I can see dead people, then maybe there are angels and demons and other supernatural things, too."

"Wait," Miriam remembered out loud. "He opened the door." She sat up straight and nodded in relief. "When he left the building, he opened the door. Yes. He had to open the door."

Downie nodded slowly. "Yes, he did. Yes, he did. So. Set your alarm, Rose. The sensors will pick up any opening doors, windows—"

"That's okay for the invisible guy," Rose said. She sounded utterly unconvinced. "But—"

"We can only deal with one problem at a time," Downie said. "One thing at a time."

And they *had,* in fact, dealt with one problem. They could, in fact, protect themselves from Mr. Invisible just by setting their alarms. About the rest of it, "Listen, Rose, do you think this Dr. Petrovsky could help? With this stuff, I mean?" Including Miriam's own fears about proof of Izzy's god. "Until we can locate Cal Jones—"

"Oh. Cal's gone home, at least according to the department secretary. She had to go home early because someone in the family is seriously ill, so—"

"She didn't tell us about it," Downie said. "She made an appointment to come in to help with our case, but she never showed up."

"It was sudden, apparently. I'm told she practically ran out of the office," Rose said. "She probably wasn't thinking very clearly about appointments. But I will be talking to Dr. Petrovsky again. He seems...a little nervous about the police, to be honest. And he won't talk about it on the phone—"

"I'm pretty sure the feds listen to the phones," Downie said. "Especially cell phones. All that digital data..."

"That does *not* help the paranoia here." Miriam glared. She knew he was probably right, but hearing the words did not further the cause of calm and rational thinking.

Her lips pressed thin, Rose sighed loudly, then shook her head. "I could clean out my bank accounts, shred my credit and debit cards, smash the cell phone, and run. But the gifts would still be with me. And Pena and Tava need to be told."

Miriam could only nod. She would *not* think about Maddy right now.

"And the feds probably are tracking us anyway, right?" Rose actually smiled. "So I'll reheat the tea and call Dr. Petrovsky."

Miriam sat back in her chair. "I think we also have to talk to Hannah."

At the stove, Rose chuckled. " Good luck with that. Hannah isn't talking to me. Maybe we could send the Sergeant. Except she's terrified that David will leave her if he finds out about her gift. Verging on paranoid. And I don't mean metaphorically."

Miriam turned to Downie. "Let's have a lemon square, and then you drop me off at Maddy's and go to Hannah's. Just to see if she's okay. Maybe if I'm not around—And you can't talk about the gifts, not directly, not if David is home, but you know what to do."

Downie smiled. "I do know how to be circumspect. I've done this sort of thing before."

Not quite this. Not magic, for God's sake, and gifts, and maybe-magical pins—Miriam stopped that line of thought before she wound herself up again. "Right," she said. "Sorry. Nerves." Oh, so much more than nerves. So much more. But she had years of practice setting nerves to the side while she took care of business. "You'll be okay, Rosie," she said and squeezed Rose's hand. Not just for Rose's sake.

"Alarm will be set and lights will be on, but, yes, I'll be okay. And I'll call Dr. Petrovsky and talk to him about everything."

"It works," Miriam said. And not just for Rosie.

Chapter 25
Tuesday

<hr>

Really, it was just so *frustrating*. Sara kept coming back to it: the fact that she absolutely *knew* she'd carried out the ritual perfectly according to the instructions she had, not once but three times. However, since those Winkler bitches weren't catching so much as a cold, something wasn't right. She had an incomplete set of instructions, obviously, and no easy means of finding a better one.

The old caster was dead, her book of shadows and collection of spells not found. As for Jones's collection, a means of bypassing those incredible wards eluded her. The books she herself owned did not offer anything that could void the spells warding Jones's little house. It is almost impossible to void blood wards short of removing the blood that was used to lay the wards in the first place. And since she didn't know where the charms containing the blood had been hidden, that meant she couldn't remove them.

On the other hand, she could simply take a gun and shoot the three Winklers dead. She would see them limp and lifeless at least. But shooting, stabbing, burning, all of that was so obvious. And so easy for the police to notice and investigate.

Murdering the three Winklers wasn't the same as sacrificing homeless men no one could identify, either. Connections would be noticed, studied, understood, and traced. She had spells that destroyed traces of herself, but she couldn't destroy the connections that no one would think twice about if those women simply sickened and died.

So the question was, obviously, what to do, aside from finishing her grilled cheese sandwich and French fries, which she planned to follow up with a chocolate malted. Not wonderful food, not like what she could have had in her parents' dining room, but she needed the calories. She might even order a double mint chocolate chip sundae with strawberry *and* chocolate sauce for a second dessert. Wasn't Friendly's Restaurant supposed to do delicious sundaes?

On the other hand, she was in Wethersfield. Hannah Winkler and Rose Winkler both lived in Wethersfield. So did Miriam Winkler's daughter and grandchildren—

Oh.

Sara set the half-eaten triangle of grilled cheese on rye carefully down on the plate, sat back, and breathed.

Because, *good Lord,* how could she have forgotten one of the first things she'd learned about casting spells? Children and blood. The blood of an innocent child contains enormous power. *Enormous* power. The kind of power that might void blood wards or invoke blood curses.

And there lived two innocent young children, a five-year-old and an infant, just up the street. Well, a few streets over. But close. Sweetly close.

She didn't have a space prepared, didn't have the necessary supplies, and wasn't mentally set for another ritual. But she could look, just look for now, and then find a space. It wouldn't take long. There were a couple of empty houses, or better still, that vacant factory just down the Silas Deane Highway from where she sat.

The place was big, and it was surrounded by parking lots. Nothing else was close, and if she waited till midnight, when blood magic is most potent, no one would hear screams or cries. No one would accidentally stumble on her there. She could, if she were willing to do a little hustling and bustling, carry out the ritual tonight.

Yes, and with two children, one to kill the Winklers tonight and one to vanquish the wards at Jones's tomorrow night, she would be done, finally, with everything here. Afterward, she would stay only long enough to confirm that the Winkler bitches were done, and then she could take Jones's books and go home to deal with her so-called parents. Yes. She had a good, solid plan.

The ice cream sundae could wait. The bill and the drive to Cedar Street were all quickly done. Cedar Street was another street of tiny homes, what most architects called ranch style, not even two stories, though the house she was looking for stood two stories tall with an attached two-car garage set in a tiny yard like all the yards on the street. Everything looked well-tended, but so *small*.

Sara parked three houses up from the one she wanted and invoked her invisibility charm before getting out of the car. After making sure the license plates still were blurred enough to be unreadable, she walked back toward the house where the two lovely little children lived with their mother, Miriam Winkler's daughter.

And here came the daughter's SUV down the street and into the driveway. Synchronicity, not coincidence. The Universe liked her plan.

She stopped at the end of the driveway, stood watching as the older child released herself from the car, jumped down, and ran to the front door.

"Sadie," her mother called from the open driver's side door of the car. "Please don't do that. It's not—"

"Mommy." The little girl pointed at Sara. "Who's that?"

Impossible. Sara *knew* no one could see her. It was simply impossible.

"Who is who, Sadie?" the woman asked.

"There. At the end of the driveway."

"Sadie." The woman sounded tired. "There's no one there."

"Yes, there is, Mommy. A lady like you."

Sara understood then that the child did, in fact, see her. The woman couldn't, but the child, Sadie, could, and she might create a lot of fuss. Sara needed to leave.

As she turned to go, a car came to a stop just before the driveway, and the damned Winkler cop got out.

"Look, Gramma. There's a lady there," the little girl called out.

The cop, still standing with her car door open, was focused on the car three doors up the street. "Downie," she said. "That's the car that followed me."

"There, Gramma." The little girl left the front door of the house and started up the driveway. "Right there in front of you."

The man who had driven the car with the Winkler cop as passenger stood in the street now. "Sadie, go back to your mother right now," he ordered and threw something.

It hit Sara on the shoulder—Could he see her, too? It wasn't possible—

"Oh, my God," the Winkler bitch gasped.

Sara knew then that her concentration and the spell had faltered. She was *flickering*.

No more. Fully invoking the charm again, Sara ran to her car, jumped in, and had to try twice to get the key into the ignition. When she thrust the gear shift into Drive, she glanced in her mirror.

No one was running up the street after her. It was a relief, but shouldn't someone be following her? In the ridiculous cop shows on television, someone chased—

They didn't have to chase. Those stinking people would be calling their stinking cop friends with a—what did they call it? An APB? about her. And the car. Even with blurred license plates, it was identifiable in the light. She had to abandon it somewhere and figure out what to do from there.

Damn it.

That child had actually seen her.

How could that possibly happen?

No. One thing at a time. Find a place to leave the car, wipe it down—

Better yet, burn it.

Sara pulled over on the side of the road, whatever road she was on—Ah. The start of the Berlin Turnpike. A lot of traffic, but she had to hope no one but that damned little brat could see her. She got out of the car, still invisible, and walked a few feet away.

"*Exuro*," she whispered as she pointed at the car.

Flames exploded from the car with a satisfying *whomp*. Smiling, she started walking away from the heat of the burning car. She could see a restaurant up the street a little bit. She could go in, have something sweet for calories, and call a cab.

Everything would be fine. She would have to plan a little more carefully, but everything would be fine. Everything would be *fine*. She'd get both brats, carry out her rituals, and have everything she wanted, including a mint chocolate chip sundae with both strawberry and chocolate sauces.

Chapter 26
Tuesday

◆

Hannah watched the spacemen lumber in and out of the pool house. Why the cleaners had to wear that cumbersome gear when they knew the blood in the pool wasn't human, Hannah couldn't guess, but there they were.

And there she was, sitting in her car, deciding whether she actually needed to go into the building. She and all the teachers had permission to fetch anything they needed from their classrooms because school would be closed for the rest of the week, the plan being to reopen next Monday. She'd left her notes for next week's lessons in her desk, but did she need them?

She did. She needed to prepare for her classes. Teaching off the cuff had never been her strength. Rose could do that, ad lib—

To hell with Rose. She needed her notes. Levering herself from the car, she made her way around the pool house to the main entrance of the high school. A Wethersfield police officer sat on a chair just inside the glass doors.

As she pushed the door open, he stood up, clipboard in his left hand.

"Ma'am," he said.

Hannah hated being called "ma'am," knew the young man whose nameplate identified him as Calloway thought he was being polite, so said nothing but, "I'm Hannah Levine, Classroom 6 in the East Wing, second floor?"

She heard herself asking, remembered laughing with Rose over the girls who up-spoke, apparently thinking it made them sound cool, but who actually ended up sounding so young and unsure. And there she was, doing it herself--because she felt nervous about being in the empty building.

"Yes, ma'am. Classroom 6, East Wing." Calloway opened the inner door for her and waited for her to step through.

The door closed behind her, and Hannah looked around the foyer. Without kids walking around and adults watching them, the place felt wrong. It needed the noise, the hustle, the drama, the hormones.

She started up the hallway past the guidance office, the trophy case with the swim team's honors and photos, which she ignored. She did glance at the next trophy case, the one with the basketball and volleyball honors, and she stopped for a minute at the art display, featuring self-portraits and life masks of the seniors. Some of them were quite good, even original, she thought.

Hannah was delaying the walk; she knew she was. She felt uncomfortable, maybe nervous. She'd never felt nervous in the building before.

Because now she knew. ESP, telekinesis, precognition, those abilities were real. And if those abilities existed, then who knew what else existed? Magic, real magic, *abra-cadabra*-you're-a-toad magic? Vampires? Werewolves? Elves? Fairies? Dragons? Ghosts?

Her footsteps echoed against the lockers in the long hallway leading to the stairway. And her mind populated the emptiness with all kinds of entities, none of them human, none of them kind.

Up the stairs to the east wing, down that hallway, Hannah's heart pounded in her ears to tell her she was frightened. But there was her classroom, exactly as she'd left it, *Animal Farm* on the corner of her desk, blue coffee mug of pens and pencils, extra paper for the quiz she'd planned on Act I of *Romeo and Juliet*. Clearly, no one, not even the cleaning crew, had been in the room. She set her tote on her chair and began straightening the rows of desks. Neatening the room felt good, distracting.

"Excuse me."

Hannah jumped. "Oh," she yelped and turned to see a young man in a sports coat and chinos standing in the doorway.

"Sorry, ma'am, didn't mean to startle you. But Officer Calloway told me you were here." He stepped into the room holding out a small leather folder. "I'm John Sanio, detective with the state police. Looking into the vandalism."

Hannah walked over to study the ID in the folder and noted that the photo did look like the man. "How can I help you, Detective Sanio?"

"I'm told you teach a number of swim team members in your sophomore and junior English classes."

"I do, but I don't know what I can tell you. They're teenagers." She shrugged. "Drama comes with the hormones."

"We're hoping someone overheard something, kids talking about something they did that would provoke retaliation."

"Like dumping animal blood in the pool?"

"You know it's animal blood."

"The daughter of the head coach of the swim team is in one of my classes. And she was talking with a friend in a restaurant where I happened to be having lunch."

"Ah. Right. Have you heard anything else?"

"Not really. All the kids gossip, but the really important things they generally don't talk about in class. I wish I could help, but..." Hannah shrugged again. "Has anyone been able to help you at all?"

The detective smiled. "I can't share that kind of information, ma'am."

"Of course not. Sorry." Hannah moved over to her desk, opened the drawer where she kept her teaching notes, and pulled the top folder out. "Notes for next week, assuming you let us open."

"Very likely, ma'am. Once the pool has been decontaminated, we'll have no more reason to keep the building closed. Would you like me to walk you out?"

Smiling, Hannah slid the thick folder into the tote. "That would be very kind, thank you."

"The empty building is eerie," the detective said.

Neither of them had anything more to say all the way to the front door, until Hannah thanked him and he went off to wherever he had to go. She walked to her car, set the tote bag on the roof, and watched the spacemen walking in and out of the pool house.

It was all very strange, but really? In the end, it had nothing to do with her. The police would figure out who committed the vandalism, and life would resume its normal course.

And her secrets would stay secrets. She'd been worried for nothing. There were no monsters in the building, there were no monsters anywhere, the baby she'd given away was probably happily off doing whatever wealthy young women did, and her secrets were safe. Hannah Levine was safe.

Chapter 27
Tuesday

How could *anyone* think *anything* would be all right? Not even deep, slow breathing could convince Rose that anything was all right or ever could be. Running looked better and better.

She had enough money in the bank to get her to...Montana, say. Too cold. Maybe North Carolina. Find some clerical job to hide in, live a quiet little life—

A major question loomed: Could she leave Pena and Tava? Really leave them? Not just go away for a few weeks, but disappear. Like being in witness protection. No phone calls, no letters or postcards, no emails, no carrier pigeons, no contact, no hints, nothing forever?

Of course not. Rose knew. First was the fact that Pena and Tava didn't deserve that kind of treatment from their mother. Despite being a classic introvert who could go a long time between phone calls to friends, Rose regularly called, texted, and emailed her daughters. She loved them. And she was proud of them for being loving, kind people who could take care of themselves, too. Just the thought of never seeing them again made her chest ache.

So the fantasies of running had to cease. She would call Dr. Petrovsky. She had told Miriam and the sergeant that she would call him, but he also offered a calm attitude about the gifts. She would feel better if she talked to him.

Besides, he had a lovely accent *and* he was good to look at. Out came her cell, in went the number.

"Hello, Dr. Petrovsky. It's Rose Sherman."

"Yes, Dr. Sherman. You are well?"

So polite. "No. I have some information for you, and I need to talk to you. Tonight. Please."

"Something is wrong."

"Very wrong. Can we—"

"I have finished my work, so I will come to you, yes? One hour."

Her breathing eased as soon as he said he was going to come to her house. "Yes. I live at 60 Timber Trail in Wethersfield. Thank you."

"I am simply glad that I can help you."

"Thank you," she repeated to dead air.

It didn't matter. She would talk to him. He would advise her. He'd lived his life knowing about the gifts, this alternate physics. He managed whatever gift he had that interested Ironed Blue Jeans—the fed. God, the feds—

What did the feds want? Would they take her to some secret facility and—

"Rose Winkler Sherman," she pronounced out loud. "Stop now. It's all fantasy. Just stories you're telling yourself. You don't *know* anything yet."

She also hadn't eaten any of those lemon squares Miriam had been so kind to bring over. They still sat in her refrigerator.

Fine. Clean up and eat.

A lemon square wasn't a nourishing meal, but Rose felt better once the sugar hit her. Now she could think about supper and the fact that she'd have a guest who also needed to eat. She'd make a vegetable frittata. Chopping vegetables would feel good and consume plenty of time.

When her doorbell rang, Rose was just taking the meal out of the oven, the house redolent with garlic and onions and peppers. She peeked out the window to see who was at the door. Dr. Petrovsky stood on her front stoop, wearing jeans and a crisp white shirt under his leather jacket. *Very nice indeedy.*

"Come in." She smiled as she opened the door. "Thank you for coming. I hope you'll eat. I made a vegetable frittata with onions, green peppers, broccoli, and a lot of garlic." He followed as she babbled all the way to the kitchen and pointed at the table. "Please sit. What would you like to drink?"

Smiling, he sat. "It smells wonderful, thank you. Water is perfect."

"I have seltzer, or I can squeeze you some orange juice, or—" Rose stopped herself and chuckled. "I babble when I'm nervous. Sorry."

"Something has happened to upset you."

His accent was minimal tonight. So he, at least, was calm. "A lot has happened. Let me put the food on the table, and then I'll tell you everything."

His first bite of the frittata brought an appreciative sigh from him, so she let him—and herself—eat in peace for a few moments before she began.

First came the inside-out bodies in places connected to her and her cousins.

"A blood curse." He shook his head. "But badly done. No, not badly. Incorrectly. Yes, that is the proper word."

"Incorrectly? What does that mean? I mean, why—"

"The Caster has misinterpreted the requirements of the curse. That is it. A misinterpretation." He smiled—*such a handsome smile, warm and kind, too.* "And very lucky, or you would not be here to share this most excellent meal with me."

That news did not calm her, not at all. "Explain, please. *Please.*"

"Yes. Of course. A blood curse requires a sacrifice of blood close to the intended victim. Yes. But what is required is closeness to *blood*. Now we say genes, yes, family, kinship. The problem for this person who is trying to cast the spell is that this curse is an ancient one, much translated, and can be misunderstood as closeness in place, you see?"

She did. "So the people who died—The practitioner should have killed someone related to us. Not strangers. And you're also saying that *where* the sacrifice is performed doesn't matter. The practitioner misinterpreted the word."

Petrovsky beamed at her. "Exactly. But it is most fortunate for you. And me, too, since I am enjoying your cooking and your company."

He was flirting with her. *Yes, indeedy.* And she hoped his smile wouldn't disappear when she told him about the invisibility factor.

It didn't. All he said was, "A well-practiced spell-caster, that is all, or perhaps, he has a charm that he can use. I am thinking that because he does not understand the wording of the curse, he does not have a teacher. Even so, he is good enough to use charms to make things easier for himself. And if you are still worried, even with a charm, the invisibility is not perfect. There is noise and, in bright light, even a shadow. Doors must still be opened and closed, lights turned on and off, you see? The person is detectable. And still vulnerable."

"And still frightening," Rose added. "Along with the damned feds—"

"Feds?" That lovely smile disappeared entirely. "This is people who work for government, yes?" The accent was thicker now.

"Yes. Downie—my cousin's partner calls them the Men in Black. They know—" She stopped because he had gone pale and still. "Are you all right?"

"They are government," he said again.

"Yes." She felt the urge to babble again, took a deep breath because she needed not to babble. "Yes. And that man in ironed blue jeans is one of them."

"*Borzhi moi*," he breathed. "This is—"

"Are they—are they going to take us? Or—God." She already saw herself in shackles in a cell deep in a secret government facility, being forced to move oil or diamonds from a vault in another country.

Petrovsky cleared his throat and took a sip of water. "They are not Soviets. They do not take us and use families to force us to do things."

There was a story there, but Rose didn't want to interrupt.

"But," he went on, "they know. They know and they follow us."

"But why? And who are they?" she had to ask.

"Extranormal Special Projects, they call themselves. That much I know."

"E.S.P.?" Rose let him see her roll her eyes. "Are you kidding me? Not even a decent initialism, for God's sake."

"This they choose to call themselves. And they watch. They do not take people away. I have researched and found no disappearances. But they watch."

"They have to want something. No one just watches."

"I do not know. I do not know."

She had a bit more information about them. "Miriam told me that they took over the case of the first inside-out body. Six years ago or so, I think."

"Is true?"

She nodded. "But not the two recent ones. She says they just stand around and watch the police work. And her lieutenant is really angry because he thinks they know something."

Petrovsky shrugged one shoulder. "Who can say? Perhaps Calla Lilly Jones—"

"Oh, no. She went home to take care of someone in her family—"

"No," Dr. Petrovsky said, more firmly than he'd been speaking in the last few moments. "That is not possible. Peony

Jones is dead for many years now. I went to her funeral. Personally I went. And there is no other family but her daughter."

"But she told—"

"A lie. Calla Lily Jones is an only child and orphan."

Rose could only sigh. "I don't understand. Why would she lie?"

"There is better question. What goes on here? Blood curse, okay. Someone with grudge tries very hard to rid world of your family. But Jones and E.S.P. are not making sense, *da?*"

She couldn't have summarized the situation better herself. "Yes. But what are we supposed to do?" Her belly began to tingle. "Phone's going to ring."

The tingle escalated to a buzz. "Miriam. Because...She's upset, but I can't tell why . . ." Rose huffed. "It's as if there's a—curtain, a veil in front of—Oh. *Tannah* must be protecting—"

"*Tannah?*"

She hadn't mentioned the pin until now, but she quickly told him, beginning with the pin itself, then Aunt Fanny and Nana Pearl and Miriam and—

"But this is important," he said. "There is possibility here of—" He shook his head. "It protects. We do not know how, but even from our knowing, it protects without being invoked. Very important. Very powerful."

"I found out some information about it, but we don't know who to talk to to get more—and here comes the phone call. Hi, Mir."

"Rose, can you come to Maddy's?" Miriam's voice didn't quite shake, but it was not her usual solid, strong self that was talking. "Please, Rose. Something—something you don't want to talk about on the phone, okay?"

There was only one topic they weren't going to talk about on the phone. "Dr. Petrovsky is here, so—"

"Bring him if he'll come. Okay?"

"I'll ask, Mir. See you—" And she was talking to dead air. That was getting to be a habit, wasn't it? *Good Lord.*

"There is trouble?" Petrovsky asked.

"Very mysterious call, but yes, Miriam wants me at her daughter's house. It's just down the hill from here, walking distance. And she would like it if you would come."

"She is police." His voice was flat and careful.

Already putting food in the refrigerator, Rose stopped. "Yes, retired, actually, and consulting with the Hartford police on cold cases."

He breathed loudly, didn't answer, only stood up and began helping her clear the table.

"Miriam and Downie, that's her partner, won't arrest you. They—"

"But they are police."

"I can only say that they're not like the Soviets. They won't force you to do things. And they've worked with Cal Jones for a while now on odd cases. But, Dr. Petrovsky. If you are too uncomfortable to talk to them, then it's all right." She did want him to help. But she didn't want to force him to do things he was emotionally unable to do. "I think this is about family, not the police case, if that matters."

As he placed plates and glasses in the sink, he spoke to the window, not her. "You *know* that this matter is family. But *Tannah* weakens your certainty. Perhaps combined with your fear, it clouds your gift, you see."

"Oh," was all she could think of to say.

"So I will go. But it is difficult for me. You must remind me that they are not Soviets if I forget this, *da?*"

He was trusting her with something important. "Yes. Of course."

He turned to face her. "You will allow me to reciprocate for this most excellent meal, and I will relate explanation."

A maniacal magician had taken aim at her family and was turning men inside out to create a fatal curse, but Rose smiled anyway. Because that handsome, intelligent, kind, age-appropriate man had just proposed another meal together. Unexpected, but definitely welcome. "Yes," she said.

Everything was going to be fine. Everything *had* to be fine.

Chapter 28
Tuesday

Miriam Fine had never cried in front of her partner or her children. *Never.* But she was close now. Not because the invisible murderer—a she, not a he, *and aren't we all just a bunch of sexists*—had been doing God knew what there at Maddy's, planning something awful, a thought that tightened Miriam's chest so she could barely breathe. The idea of that woman anywhere near her child or grandchildren—the gun had stayed in its holster only because she was too busy herding Maddy, who carried the baby, and Sadie into the house to pull it.

After she had everyone in Maddy's office sitting on the floor away from the windows, the baby screaming, Maddy shaking and gasping, Sadie crying, Miriam grabbed the weapon, locked the door and faced it, ready to fire at anyone who tried to come into the room. She didn't say anything reassuring because she couldn't think of anything reassuring to say. Dazed with fear and anger though she was, she knew she used to be better than this. She used to calm people down, even with active shooters. Now, she could only wait for Downie—*Please, God, let him be okay*—to signal that they were safe.

Her cell phone rang. Downie. "She's gone. I called it in. We're good for now."

"Okay. Coming out."

First, she shoved the gun into the holster on her waistband. Then she knelt down in front of Maddy, who clutched Sadie and the baby to her as if they might blow away on a breath.

"Maddy, it's okay. The woman has run away, and the police are chasing her down."

Tears running down her cheeks, Maddy looked up at her. "Is it one of your cases?"

"It's someone with a grudge against the family, the Winklers. We thought it was just about Hannah, Rose and me, and we don't know why yet, but we'll make sure you're safe." Not entirely clear, but Maddy needed to know she'd be okay.

"I saw her," Sadie gasped out, trying to stop crying. "I did."

"Before the rock hit her?" Miriam asked. She was a cop. Questions were a reflex.

Sadie nodded.

"Nobody else could see her until Sergeant Downs threw the rock at her."

"I saw her before you got here, Gramma. I really did."

Miriam stood up. "We have to talk, Maddy."

"Yeah, Ma. We do."

Expecting recriminations, feeling as though she deserved them, Miriam wanted to apologize. "I didn't—we didn't think she would come after you, Mad. It seemed—"

The door swung open.

No one in the room had touched the knob.

No one stood on the other side of the door.

"Who—" Miriam's breath stopped again.

"I did it," Maddy said. "And Sadie—"

"Mommy says I can't show *anybody*. But, Gramma, why did we have to run away?" Sadie sniffled. "You *scared* me."

That question she could answer, *Thank God*. "I'm sorry, Sadie. That lady has hurt some people, and I didn't want her to hurt you. The police have to catch her now."

"'kay." Sadie sniffed again.

"Mir?" Downie called from somewhere down the hall.

"In here. All the way in the back."

"Is he okay, Ma?"

Miriam turned to Maddy. "What? He's fine, ob—"

"Not that way, Ma," Maddy let Sadie go and stood up before she finished. "Will he freak out when he hears about...you know?" She gestured toward the door.

A bark of laughter escaped Miriam. Whatever rose up in her chest after the laughter, knowing she would sound hysterical if she let it go, she stopped with a hard swallow. "He knows, and he's calm, calmer than I am, I have to tell you. And you have something more to tell me."

"Okay, yeah. Is the living room safe?"

Downie appeared in the doorway, unarmed and calm looking. "She's long gone, Madelyn. You're okay here."

"How can we know?" Maddy looked awful, as if she barely had herself under control. "She can be invisible. She could be standing right behind you and you wouldn't—"

"Mommy, Mommy, I can see her. She's not inbisible to me." Sadie might have been leaning against her mother's leg, but she sounded confident.

"And she's not invulnerable," Downie added. "She reacted when the rock hit her."

Miriam wanted to believe him; she did. She'd never believed her father or Izzy when they went on about the King and Creator of the Universe, about how everything was according to his plan, *some plan, not reassuring,* but she wanted to believe Downie and be reassured by him. "Let's talk, Maddy."

Maddy took a deep breath. "OK, Ma. In the kitchen, so Sadie can have some supper."

It took more than a few minutes to settle Sadie down, but peanut butter on a bagel and a glass of milk surprised her into sitting at the kitchen island on a stool that Downie lifted her up onto. While Maddy prepared the sandwich, Miriam rocked the baby in her arms, crooning softly till he fell asleep again.

"Wait," Miriam said. "Sadie, you need to wash your hands." So she wouldn't hear about the murders that Downie was going to explain to Maddy.

"I'm scared to go alone."

After a glance at Downie and a tip of the head toward Maddy, Miriam smiled at her granddaughter. "Let me put Mark in his bucket, and I'll help you down and go with you."

"Thank you, Gramma."

The bathroom was next to the kitchen, so Miriam closed the door as Sadie pulled her little step stool, the one Izzy had painted purple and pink for her, in front of the sink. Sadie sang the alphabet song to time her hand-washing, but Miriam could still hear Downie and Maddy, not the words, but the soft hum of their voices.

Miriam wasn't eager to see Maddy, but Sadie finished her alphabet and stepped off the bright little stool.

"Gramma?" she said as she dried her hands.

"Hmm? Yes, Sweetie."

"Was that lady really going to hurt us?"

The child was already terrified, but she'd recognize lies. "She's done some very bad things, Sadie. If you see her again, I want you to yell 'Fire!' as loud as you can and as long as you have to until someone comes to help you."

"But, Gramma—"

"I know there won't really be any fire, but people will run to help you when they hear you yell that. So she won't be able to hurt you or anybody else." *Please God that's true.*

Sadie stood there, lips compressed—Rose did that sometimes when she was thinking about unhappy things—and then she nodded. "Can I yell 'fire' whenever I need help? Like if I can't open the door? And I can't do it my special way because someone might be watching?"

"No." Miriam had to smile. Sadie could be very literal. Help *was* help. "Only if there's danger."

"Like stranger danger?"

"Yes." Why hadn't she remembered stranger danger? Nerves. A lot of nerves. "Stranger danger is exactly when you should yell 'fire.'"

"How come Mrs. Metz didn't teach us that?" Sadie pushed her stool back along the side of the vanity.

"I don't know, Sadie." Did kindergarten teachers know the trick? "But now *you* know."

Slipping her hand into Miriam's, Sadie opened the door using her other hand. "Thank you, Gramma."

Teaching a five-year-old—*her granddaughter, for God's sake*—she was teaching her five-year-old granddaughter, the beautiful little girl with the same brown eyes and curly hair her grandma had, how to get help when she faced a serious threat. The threat *was* serious. And there could be worse waiting for them. God knew what irrational shit magic could produce.

Maddy's eyes weren't the only ones glittering with unshed tears in that kitchen.

Downie nodded once toward Miriam as he lifted Sadie back up onto the stool in front of her bagel.

"Mommy, Gramma says to yell 'fire' when there's stranger danger."

"Oh," Maddy used fingers to quickly wipe tears from her cheek. "Oh. I forgot that, but Gramma taught me that when I was a little girl, too."

"It's a good strategy," Downie said.

"What's a strat-uh-gee?"

"A plan," Maddy said. "Like the plan we have not to let anyone know about the special things we can do."

"Is it okay to talk about at home?" Sadie asked.

Maddy tried a smile, badly. "Gramma and Sergeant Downs know about it, so here, with them, it's okay."

Miriam took a deep breath, the first in a while, she thought. "Everyone in the family can do special things, we think."

"So the sergeant was telling me." Maddy stared at Sadie, who was working on a mouthful of bagel and watching Miriam. "You should know, David went with Daddy because he thought what he could do was e-v-i-l. He was going to pray it away. Ma?"

The bottom dropped out of her gut. All Miriam could do was grab the counter. "What?"

"Ma!" Maddy came around the counter to grab her mother by the arm. "Ma."

Unable to speak, Miriam shook her head. Her son had thought he was evil and he hadn't come to her, his mother—

"Here, Miriam." Downie slid a chair behind her, and she let him guide her into it. "Breathe."

"David," she managed to gasp, and then she saw Sadie sitting straight up on the stool, wide-eyed and pale, staring.

She had to pull herself together. She had to be Detective Fine, not Ma or Gramma. Detective Fine took information and followed it to understanding. She certainly didn't frighten her granddaughter, her beautiful little Sadie. Neither did she collapse—

"Okay, okay." She breathed deeply. "Okay. I'm okay."

A glass of water appeared in front of her. She took it, saw that the hand offering it was Downie's, and drank.

"Okay." And she was okay, the awful despair locked away, the detective in charge. "When did you start, Maddy? The telekinesis, I mean."

"Thirteen or so." Maddy sounded very matter-of-fact about it and maybe a little relieved to be sharing the information. "A little after puberty."

"And David?"

"About four years after me."

"So he would have been about twelve." So young. "And Sadie?"

"When I turned five, Gramma. That's when I could move things without touching them." Sophie turned to pick up her bagel again. "But I didn't know about the imbisible people till today."

And no Cal Jones to help—but Rose's new friend might be a good substitute. "Rose. We need to tell Rose. And ask her to get Dr. Petrovsky to help. He may be able to explain."

"We still haven't warned Hannah," Downie added.

"Why don't you ask Cousin Rose to come over so we can talk this out, Ma?"

"Are you sure, Maddy? We've all had a bad fright, and the rest is a lot to take in."

"We all need to talk, Mir." Downie nodded. "And I'm going to call Mike and get some protection here. And someone to do a welfare check on Hannah." He walked out into the hall.

Maddy's eyebrows rose. "What's the matter with Cousin Hannah?"

"She showed Rose her telekinesis—she can move things like you and your Mommy—" she explained to Sadie. "Now she won't talk to us. She thinks that her David will leave if he finds out what she can do. But she doesn't know what's been going on. So…Maddy, does your father know about—” Miriam tapped her temple—” this business?”

“No! God, Ma. Is that what—No. We didn’t tell anybody, especially not Daddy. Pena and Tava can do it do and we talked and—”

“Wait. All four of you can—”

“Especially Tava. She’s really, really good at it, but yeah, all four of us.”

“Rose doesn’t know.” Miriam made her words sound like the accusation she meant them to be.

“We made a pact, the four of us. To keep it a secret. From everyone. Forever. It was just so weird.”

“Oh, God, Maddy,” Miriam sighed. Another family gift, the keeping of secrets, at which the Winklers were better than good. A secret in the heart of a Winkler was safer than information in a black hole. *Pfft*. Gone. Never to be revealed, its very existence unknowable.

“What could you have done, Ma? If I’m understanding the Sergeant correctly, you didn’t know—”

“But we could have tried to figure it out, Mad. We could have tried together. There were people we could have asked.” In fact, had Madelyn come to her when she first started, Miriam’s mother and aunts would have been alive and could have been pressed for answers. They might have known a long time ago. Too late now.

“Sorry, Ma. We were—well, David was panicked, really panicked.”

"I get it, I get it." Miriam sighed. "Some detective I am. All this going on, and I didn't have a clue. Not a clue. Okay. Let me call Rosie. God." Such a great detective, couldn't even see that her kids were going through changes and scared about those changes, never mind Izzy's lies. Out saving everyone else, while her own kids—she'd let them down badly. So badly.

All she wanted to do was cry.

Chapter 29
Tuesday

"So here we are," Rose said. "And I am on the verge of babbling, so would someone *please* tell me what is going on?"

No one in Maddy's living room looked ready to talk. In fact, Miriam looked like she was fighting tears, Sadie and Maddy looked scared, and Mikhail Petrovsky, perched on the edge of an armchair, looked ready to run. Only Sergeant Downs seemed relaxed, but he always looked relaxed. At least the baby slept. Maybe he was having happy dreams.

Miriam looked over her shoulder at Downie and nodded.

Downie cleared his throat. "The invisible woman—the practitioner we've been chasing, the one who's been doing all those things we talked about at your house, turns out to be a woman in her mid-twenties, I think. Maddy's age, maybe a little older. Anyway, she showed up here at Maddy's. No one else saw her, but Sadie could—"

"Wait. What?" Rose grimaced. "Sadie?" She turned to Mikhail Petrovsky, trying hard not to glare at him. "You said puberty. Sadie is five years old."

"It is very rare," he muttered vaguely in her direction. "Unusual."

"Unusual? I'll say—Wait." Rose's breath caught in her throat. If Sadie had a gift, then—"Maddy, can you—are you—"

"Hmm." Maddy nodded. "I have to point, though. Sadie just thinks it's done."

God help me. "Your brother?" *No, no, no, no.*

Maddy nodded again.

"For God's sake, Rose," Miriam practically snarled. "Yes, Pena and Tava, too. At puberty. Madelyn told me tonight."

Rose could only stare at Miriam, her mind refusing to form words. She didn't know what she felt, if she felt anything, or even why she was stunned into this blankness. The papers from Cal Jones said the trait was inherited, after all. She should have known. She should have at least expected it. But all she could do was stare.

"Yes," Petrovsky said. "All of the generations of the family always come into the gifts together. You and—"

"Really?" Miriam said. "I—"

"Why?" Rose suddenly felt the words form. "Why did you keep it a secret, Maddy?" It was fear she felt, fear that, despite her best efforts, she had failed her daughters. She had wound up being the bad mother she had sworn she would never be. "We would have tried to help. We would have—"

"We didn't understand," Maddy said and shrugged. "We had no idea what to do except keep it to ourselves. I mean, we only wanted to be like everybody else, you know?"

Rose did know. She remembered how much she had wanted to be like everyone else, wear the same clothes, like the same music, have a sane mother—"I remember. But—" *That was then; this is now*—"No. Okay." She reached into her purse for a copy of the papers Cal Jones had given her. "Here. You should read this. I have copies for everyone who wants them. And I'll mail them to Pen and Tav."

Miriam stared at her again, muttered something about "Whiplash."

Rose compressed her lips and nodded. "Dr. Petrovsky here...ah...knows about all of this."

"You know Cal Jones?" Sergeant Downs asked.

"Not so well as I was thinking," Petrovsky said.

"She lied," Rose added. "Her mother is dead and has been for a long time, and Cal doesn't have any other family. So we don't know where she is. And—"

"She's running from something," Miriam said.

"Maybe," the sergeant said.

"*Da.* I think so. Perhaps she runs from the woman who threatens you, perhaps those men from E.S.P.—"

"Who?" Maddy asked.

Rose smiled despite the situation. "Wait'll you hear this. Extranormal Special Projects."

"But not a joke," Petrovsky said gently. "I must remind myself they are not the Soviets. The—"

"The Soviets?" Miriam said as the Sergeant asked. "What do the Soviets have to do with this?"

Petrovsky sighed. "They took people like us and tried to force us to do things. They took our families hostage, making threats against us. It was...no good."

Clasping her hands to her chest, Rose closed her eyes. "You don't think these guys will do that, do you?" *Goodbye, cardboard box; hello, concrete bunker.*

"Ma?" Maddy sounded panicky. No surprise. She had two small children to panic over, two little hostages to fortune. Not such a cliché when it comes to people you know and love.

"If they were going to do something like that," the sergeant said, "I think they'd have done it already. Mostly, they stand around and watch."

He sounded quite reasonable. Rose opened her eyes and turned to Petrovsky. "What do you think?"

Petrovsky shook his head. "I am maybe not the right one to ask. I do not think so clearly about these men."

"Right now, they seem content to watch," the sergeant repeated.

"They're watching us? My kids, and me?" Maddy said, and Miriam said, "If they're watching, where were they when that bi—that woman was here?"

"They follow only sometimes, it seems," Petrovsky said. "Or maybe it is that they know only about the three cousins and not about their children, *da?* Because you hid your abilities so well, even from your mother and your cousin, perhaps E.S.P. does not know and so does not watch."

As Rose untangled his sentences, the doorbell rang.

Maddy's hands tightened on Sadie's shoulders, and Rose wished she had someone to hang onto. Beside her, Petrovsky sat up straighter as if he were getting ready to bolt.

"It should be Prentice. After the, um, incident earlier, Mike agrees that we need someone to watch here," the Sergeant said as he walked out into the hall.

Despite her partner's attempt at reassurance, Miriam had her gun half out of her holster. And Rose was glad to see it.

Petrovsky was muttering something under his breath, just above a whisper. Hebrew or Aramaic, she thought.

A spell? Really? He was a witch or whatever those people were calling themselves nowadays. A practitioner, the Sergeant had called it. Rose frowned at him. "So you're a wizard?" she whispered.

He huffed. "A spell-caster."

"Why didn't you say something before?" Even as the words came out of her mouth, she knew the answer. He didn't owe her any information, not really. They were still strangers to each other. She hoped they wouldn't stay that way for long—and she was doing it again, reacting to her loneliness and not the situation. *Pay attention, Rosie. Important shit is going on here.*

And Dr. Petrovsky didn't have to say a thing now because the Sergeant—she could not bring herself to call him Downie in this situation—came back into the room with a young man, maybe Maddy's age, maybe a little older, who looked strong and capable of handling himself if a situation turned violent. He wore jeans and a leather bomber jacket zipped up to the neck and he carried a gym bag. "Madelyn, this is John Prentice, Detective John Prentice. Detective, meet Madelyn Bloom and her daughter, Sadie. And the baby asleep in the bucket is Mark. And that's Detective Fine's cousin Rose Sherman, and next to her is Mikhail Petrovsky. Dr. Petrovsky is an expert on the same sorts of things Dr. Jones is. Have I left anyone out?"

So many handsome men in one room. Rose smiled at her distraction as Sadie looked sideways at Detective Prentice.

"Are you a police officer like my Gramma?" Sadie asked.

"Yes. I am." Detective Prentice had an easy bass voice.

"Do you have a gun, too?"

"Sadie," Maddy warned as Prentice nodded.

"I do, but I don't take it out unless I need to use it." He nodded again. "I've got my sleeping bag in the car."

"Why do you need a sleeping bag?" Sadie demanded.

"I'm going to sleep in the hall in front of the door."

"You are? How come?"

"Sadie, for goodness' sake. Let the detective breathe," Maddy chuckled, a good sound to hear.

Detective Prentice smiled. "I'm used to it. I've got four nephews and a niece, all very curious. So I'm sleeping in the hall so I can stop the invisible lady from coming in."

"Can you see her? 'Cause I can see her. An' if you can't see her—"

"I can make it so she is visible if she comes into the house," Petrovsky said. "Actually, I can fix this house so only good people can come in."

Rose's eyebrows weren't alone in rising.

"I make a spell. Wards," Petrovsky explained. "Special spells to protect a place."

"Are you a witch?" Sadie squinted at him sideways.

"A spell-caster," Petrovsky corrected gently. "There are no witches who wear pointy hats and ride brooms."

"Are you sure?" Sadie sounded disappointed.

"No pointy hats, no warty noses, no cackling." Petrovsky nodded. "I am quite sure. So. I will help to keep you safe. If your mother will permit this."

Maddy frowned at Miriam. "Talk about keeping secrets, Ma. Did you—"

"I had no idea," Miriam protested.

"Neither did I," Rose added.

"I will tell you what you wish to know. But first, I must help here." He stood and spoke to Maddy. "You have a candle? Perhaps a Sabbath candle? A Sabbath candle would be best."

"Um, yes, of course I do. In the kitchen. This way." Maddy started out of the room.

"Mommy," Sadie panicked out loud.

Miriam went to her granddaughter as Maddy led Petrovsky out of the room. "It's okay, Sweet Pea. I'm here. And Detective Prentice is here, and Sergeant Downs, too. And Cousin Rose."

Sadie slipped her hand into her grandmother's. "It's still scary."

Not to Detective Prentice, apparently. He looked excited, even happy. "I'll go get my sleeping bag."

"I'll go with you," the Sergeant said. "You okay for a couple of minutes, Mir?"

"Of course."

Rose sat back with a sigh. "Really, Miriam, I had no idea about him being a spell-caster. Or about the girls. I feel so—I don't know. Nana never said—and what about the case? There are things I don't want to repeat now." She pointed her chin at Sadie, who definitely was too young to hear about blood curses and inverted bodies and all the rest of it.

"No," Miriam agreed. "Things will settle down. And then we'll talk. Later."

"I feel like I've run a marathon. In a maze. Too much information and too little all at once. And—look at that."

That was Dr. Petrovsky, carrying a lit Sabbath candle to the middle of the living room entry. He turned to his left, then to his right, and then shut his eyes for a few seconds. When he opened them again, he didn't seem to be looking at anything at all as he began to chant softly.

Hebrew this time. Rose's Hebrew was weak, but she recognized a few words. *Or*, "light," was repeated several times. But it was Petrovsky's face that held her attention. It was rapt, transfigured. He could have posed as a saint for a Renaissance painter. He chanted with no hesitation, no rasp to his voice. He sounded like a cantor deep in belief—

A chill washed over Rose's skin, greeted by goose bumps and the start of a hot flash.

When he stopped, as abruptly as he'd started, his eyes shut again and the candle flame died. He hadn't blown it out; it simply...stopped burning. And that little wisp of smoke that followed when she blew a candle out didn't happen either. The flame was there and then it wasn't.

"Gramma," Sadie whispered. "It's magic." She wasn't asking.

Sadie was right. Cal Jones could call it alternate physics if she wanted, if it kept her happy and let her feel comfortable, but what Rose had just seen was *magic. Real magic.*

Holy—

Prentice came into the hall behind Petrovsky. "I just had the weirdest—like a cold shower and a hot shower together."

"You felt this?" Petrovsky opened his eyes and turned around to face the younger man.

"That weirdness? I did."

Petrovsky turned to Rose. "You felt this?"

"I felt something, goose bumps and chills. Why?"

"It was the magic, Cousin Rose," Sadie pronounced confidently.

"You are correct, Miss," Petrovsky said, bowing to Sadie, then straightened. "But only people who have propensity for gifts—"

Prentice laughed. "I don't have a gift. Except maybe for trying to date women who don't want to date a cop, but—"

"You have gift." Petrovsky's accent had thickened and his grammar was worse than some of her students'. "This is police having gifts. They can use to control—"

Sergeant Downs joined the party. "Use what to control whom?" he asked.

Detective Prentice jumped in. "Dr. Petrovsky thinks I might have some kind of gift. And since I'm a cop—"

"I worry about those feds," the Sergeant said, holding up a little black box with an antenna sort of thing sticking up. It looked like a miniature version of early cell phones, the ones that looked like bricks. "Someone has been tracking my car."

That did it. Mysterious government agencies and witches—he could call himself a spell-caster all he wanted to, but he was a witch—and telekinesis and precognition and all that, and now Sergeant Downs, *a police officer, for God's sake,* was being tracked by God knew who—Rose jumped to her feet. "I'm done. I can't. I'm sorry, but I can't deal with this."

"Please don't leave, Rose," Miriam protested. "It's not safe."

"I'll find someplace safe. I'm going south. I don't know, but I don't want to—I can't." *A little dramatic, isn't it, Rosie? More than a little dramatic, but enough was more than enough. Truly.*

Sadie began to whimper, and Rose felt sorry about that, but—

"Stop," Sergeant Downs said softly. "Please."

"Easy for you," Rose accused. "You carry—"

"Rose. I know you're scared," the Sergeant said. "I know you don't trust me, and Dr. Petrovsky has good reason to not trust police in general, but we've got problems in common, and I think we can only get through this together. So let's sit and try to work something out."

Shaking her head, Rose turned to Miriam. The voice of reason. "I don't know what to do, Mir. It's like the ground won't stop shaking. I can't get any purchase with my feet at all."

Even when Harry had announced the divorce, she'd known what to do, had known somehow she'd be okay, however long it took. That hadn't been the worst thing that ever happened to her, after all. Her lunatic mother covered that territory.

But this?

Miriam stood there blinking at her. It was Petrovsky who came over to Rose, took her hand in both of his.

"I think," he said, "we forget, you and I, that gifts are *power*." Nodding, he smiled at her. "Together, we can be very powerful, I am thinking."

She stared at him. What was he suggesting? An alliance of some kind?

"E.S.P. cannot control us if we stand together," he said. "And the evil one also we can fight, yes?"

She frowned at him, still not sure of his intent. "And the police? And my cousins?"

Petrovsky took a deep breath. "They, too, are in danger from the same sources. But they, too, have gifts of power."

Rose wanted to argue. She was *not* powerful. Was she? She was—she was a telekinetic like Hannah, who had stopped a man from murdering his wife. And she was a precognitive who was likely to know when something bad was going to happen.

And he, obviously, was a spell-caster of some ability.

Rose breathed deeply. *Time to try a new story about yourself, Rosie.* "You're right," she said softly, then turned to Sadie, who was now buried in her mother's arms. "Sorry, Sadie. Sometimes, I get scared, too. It's okay. We'll figure it out and make everything safe again." *Please, God, let it be so.*

Chapter 30
Tuesday

Laughing at herself had never been Hannah's strength. She knew that much about herself. But she could admit her fear earlier at school had been ridiculous. Vampires? Dragons? Werewolves? Seriously?

If anyone else had told her she was being foolish, she'd have taken serious offence. But she was the one saying she'd been silly. She shook her head, sighed, and decided to consider the courtyard.

She had to turn on the courtyard lights, but she could see her results. Daffodils had appeared, sparse this year, but they would spread, and the vinca she'd planted as groundcover was perking up already. Tulip foliage showed against the back wall, early because the wind couldn't penetrate the courtyard, so the ground was a little warmer.

Everything would be thin this first summer, but next year the bulbs would spread, the foliage would start to thicken—A knock on the outer door interrupted her survey. It was late for visitors.

Another knock was followed by a male voice announcing, "Wethersfield Police."

"Coming," Hannah called. She assumed it was someone following up on the vandalism investigation or maybe the incident with the neighbor. She opened the door. "How can I help you, officer?"

"Hannah Levine?" The officer asked. He was a young man, face arranged in a polite smile, wearing the WPD uniform. He looked almost too young to be a policeman.

"That's me. What can I do for you?"

"We've been asked to make sure you're all right, ma'am?"

Surprised, all Hannah could think of to say was, "Excuse me?"

"Hartford PD has asked us to make sure you're all right, ma'am. They're worried that someone is following members of your extended family."

"What?"

"Have you seen any odd persons? Have you received any phone calls that—"

"Did Sergeant Downs send you? Or Detective Fine?" Trust Miriam to push in where she wasn't wanted or convince her partner to do the pushing for her.

"No, ma'am. It was a lieutenant." He pulled a notebook from his chest pocket and flipped through it to find something. "Lieutenant Winkoski? Winewski? I can't read my own writing. But I can tell you that someone made an attempt of some kind on your cousin and…"

Hannah frowned and tuned the man out. "Winewski?" She'd seen or heard that name somewhere recently. It would come to her eventually. "What kind of attack?

"Ma'am, I can check your house if you like."

Obviously, he wasn't going to answer her questions. "I'm fine. I've been here all day, and I haven't had any peculiar phone calls, and the only stranger I've seen is you." She shook her head and frowned at the man. "I'm fine," she repeated.

"If you're sure, ma'am."

Hannah breathed loudly. "I'm quite sure, thank you."

The officer nodded. "Yes, ma'am," he said and walked up the driveway toward his patrol car parked on the street.

Hannah waited until the man seated himself in the car before she closed the door to the courtyard.

Of all the officious things Miriam had done, this was the worst. She had no doubt, whatever the cop said, that Miriam was behind the welfare check. She'd been right to cut Miriam off—

Winewski. She remembered where she'd seen the name. At Vito's, the call that had taken David away that had been Mike Winewski. But that Winewski was a doctor, not a cop. Hadn't David said so?

She was sure David had said so.

Wasn't she?

Hannah walked slowly across the courtyard and let herself into the house. She would ask David when he came home. And in the meanwhile, she would play her beautiful piano, then make supper.

And she would talk to David when he came home.

Chapter 31
Wednesday

━━━━━━━━ ◆ ━━━━━━━━

Sitting in Downie's car across the street from 660 Farmington Avenue, Miriam couldn't stop her yawns. It had been a long, frightening night for her, and only her ability to compartmentalize let her sit here next to Downie and watch the building. Of course, it was her ability to compartmentalize that had created the worst of her problems, the fact that her children hadn't shared their fear and their abilities, if that's what—

"There they are," Downie murmured.

Just in time to distract her from her line of thought, the feds, three of them, strode out of the building toward their black Lincoln Navigator, those walking clichés and their driving clichés. They got into the car using the passenger doors, which meant there was a fourth man driving, possibly Ironed Blue Jeans.

Downie waited for them to pull onto Prospect Avenue before he put his car in gear and eased into the late morning traffic.

"Wethersfield?" Miriam wondered out loud.

"That's where the burned-out car was found, at the start of the Berlin Turnpike."

"Not to mention where Hannah, Rose and my daughter live."

"They don't know Maddy has inherited the whatchamacallit, Mir." He glanced quickly at her. "But there was a nasty bit of vandalism at the high school a few days ago. Blood in the pool and 'We know what you did' painted on the deck, also in blood. Animal blood, but still scary."

"Hannah teaches—"

"Has she done something interesting?"

"She lived in Europe most of our adult lives. Paris, I think. I don't know. Rose might." Miriam shrugged. "Assuming it's not aimed at the jocks on the swim team." Those spoiled punks had always gotten away with bullying and God knew what else. They had tried some of their punk shit on her David but his mother had taught him a few little tricks. It took only one minor demonstration for them to leave him alone.

Downie nodded, then frowned at the Navigator six or seven cars ahead. The SUV made the light at New Britain Avenue, which had just turned yellow, and turned east, toward Wethersfield, as assumed. But Downie had to stop for the red light.

"You can go down the turnpike and then up Nott anyway," she suggested for no reason. He did know what he was doing.

"Yep," he said and was quiet while they sat at the light.

When he turned onto New Britain, he nodded. "I think that's them up there—If Hannah lived in Paris, I can probably find out what she did there."

"I think she did, but Rose got a birthday card every year from wherever it was."

"You didn't?"

"Nope." Hannah had cut Miriam off there for a long while because Miriam had done a silly thing. She'd caught Hannah in a minor, unnecessary lie that hadn't hurt anyone or anything, but being in her self-righteous phase, Miriam just had to say something. Now she knew she could be a smug so-and-so and had learned the lesson, though she suspected that Hannah still lied a lot. Miriam didn't feel the need to repeat the story twenty plus years later.

"I have a friend in the U.S. Embassy in Paris," Downie said.

His roommate in college? No. Another seminarian who'd realized his so-called vocation was the product of a romanticized imagination. "Teddy...Peeler?"

"Pendergast," he corrected, then grinned. "Look at that, they got stuck at the light."

Everybody got stuck somewhere on this stretch of New Britain Avenue. The street carried too much traffic for its design, but it was definitely the most direct route from Hartford's West End and West Hartford to Wethersfield and the Berlin Turnpike.

The feds had taken the direct route, and now they sat at the light at Hillside Avenue, while a big semi slowly turned from Hillside onto New Britain Avenue. Cars were parked on both sides of the street, which was narrow even without them, so the truck driver would take a while to maneuver through the turn.

Downie let himself get stuck four cars back. "I'll call Teddy. What last name did Hannah use before she married Dr. Levine?"

"Fried. But she used Winkler sometimes. Especially after her father left."

"Spell Fried, please."

That Miriam could do. "I think once she left the country, she used Winkler. She said she wouldn't give her father credit for anything she accomplished."

Downie grunted as traffic resumed its flow, then seemed to concentrate on his tailing. Miriam watched the black Navigator move up White Street to Fairfield Avenue.

"They missed the shortcuts," she said. "You think they know we're following them?"

"Always possible," Downie said. "But it is nice and straight, and they're in the right lane. Berlin Turnpike for them. Let's go see Prentice, okay?"

Since Prentice was at Maddy's, and Sadie had been kept home from school, Miriam nodded. "That would be good, yes."

It was Prentice, in jeans and a blue oxford shirt, pistol discreetly in hand, who answered the door. "Sergeant. Detective." He let them in and shut the door before stowing his weapon in a belt holster that his shirt tail covered. "Everything is fine here."

Semi-fine anyway. The baby was protesting something, and Maddy was cooing at him, their noises coming from upstairs. Sadie sat on the bottom step, chin in hands, elbows on knees, and she rolled her eyes as Miriam walked toward her.

"That baby makes a lot of noise," Sadie pronounced. "I think we need a different one."

Miriam chuckled. "I think if you give Mark a chance to grow a little, he might be fun to play with."

"But, Gramma. It took *forever* for him to get this big. An' he can't even roll over yet. An' I can't go outside because Mommy has to take care of him. No going out alone, Detective Prentice says."

"Then it's a good thing I'm here, isn't it?"

Sadie raised her head from her hands. "Can we go on the swings?"

"Let me tell Detective Prentice we're going out, okay? Go put on your sneakers."

"'Kay." Sadie jumped up and ran up the stairs. "Mommy, Mommy, guess what!"

Miriam chuckled after Sadie, then went into the kitchen where the two men were standing, mugs of coffee in hand.

"Coffee?" Prentice offered.

"No. Thanks. I'm going to take Sadie out to play for a little while. I've got this." She opened her jacket to expose her belt holster.

"It's been quiet," Prentice said. "But I couldn't let her out alone. The yard is an open invitation."

"No. You're doing the right thing."

He nodded. "Oh, by the way, the, ah, invisible person left fingerprints on the doorknob at 660, but they're not in any database we can access."

"Figures." Had she expected easy results? Why would it be easy? Nothing about this case was easy. Or rational, for God's sake.

They stood quietly until Sadie bounced into the kitchen.

"'Kay, Gramma, I'm ready. Mommy says I hafta do 'zactly what you tell me to do."

"I'll try not to be too bossy, Sweet Pea."

"'Kay." Sadie led the way to the back door and straight to the swing set, where she perched herself on a swing and kicked off. "You don't have to push anymore. I know how to swing."

And she did, kicking herself higher and higher. After getting fairly high, she shut her eyes, looking blissful as she sailed back and forth, back and forth.

Miriam watched and tried to relax. But that was impossible here where all the yards were unfenced and backed by a narrow stream lined with trees on both sides.. Nearly everyone worked away from home, so almost every house on the street was empty most of the day. Anyone could walk down a driveway and through the back yards into Madie's. Prentice was right. These yards were an invitation to anyone planning anything, good or bad.

Petrovsky had explained last night after Sadie had finally been calmed down and put to bed that the woman coming after them could invoke a prepared spell attached to a charm and make the chain on the swing break or attach the charm to the back steps to make them collapse or cause any one of dozens of kinds of accidents. There were no fences to stop her. Of course, he'd also said that this spell-caster seemed powerful but ignorant. She performed the blood curse incorrectly, and she didn't seem to know certain basic spells that a well-trained caster learned as a matter of basic practice. His own teacher had made him perform what he called the ABC spells over and over until he could perform them without thinking first.

For instance, he said, she could have jammed car doors or house doors, making it impossible for Maddy and the kids to hide from her. Or she could have produced a spell to freeze Downie after he threw the rock at her. That sort of spell didn't last long, but a few seconds would have been to her advantage, giving her time to perform a more advanced spell or escape without having to run. She had done none of those things. She likely didn't know how. If she were self-taught, she might have dismissed such spells as unimportant, a waste of time, even foolish.

That information didn't seem to relax anyone in the room, including Petrovsky himself. An untrained spell-caster, like a novice robber, nervous, maybe angry that her spells weren't having the desired effect, might lash out, do something accidentally...

Miriam smiled at her granddaughter, who was now singing "Yankee Doodle" as she swung herself.

At least Sadie was relaxed.

"Sadie. Lunch," Maddy called from the back door. "You, too, Ma."

"Come on, Gramma. It's peanut butter on a bagel again. With apple slices. 'Cause Detective Prentice likes that." Using her formerly white sneakers as a brake, Sadie stopped the swing and jumped off. "C'mon."

Miriam followed Sadie to the door, where Maddy waited.

"Hi, Ma."

"You okay?" Miriam asked as she walked into the kitchen. Maddy looked like Miriam felt: exhausted.

But Maddy smiled. "Detective Prentice is terrific with the kids. He even diapered Mark when I was in the shower. Apples and peanut butter on a bagel is a small price to pay."

Unconvinced of the virtues of apple slices on a bagel with peanut butter, Miriam winced. "May I have cream cheese and tomato on my bagel?"

"So conventional," Maddy said.

Miriam smiled. Maddy might look awful, but the dry wit was back.

Lunch conversation revolved around the virtues of apples over bananas, *The Princess in Black*, which Sadie was reading aloud to anyone who would listen, and the matter of when Sadie could go back to school.

After she finished her bagel, Sadie was sent to wash up, and Miriam stood up to do the dishes.

"Any advances?" Maddy asked.

"We need to figure out why someone is after your mother and her cousins," Downie said. "If it were a case—"

"Then she'd be after me alone, not Rose and Hannah," Miriam said. They'd been over this ground last night. But they had no leads. "Rose got married right after college. She taught, had her babies, went back to school, and got a college job. Then there's me. Right after college, I joined HPD, got married, had babies, and kept working." She shrugged. " Hannah went to Europe—" She shrugged. "She might have done something in Europe that followed her here, but we don't know."

"Well, if there's anything in Hannah's European history, Teddy will find it," Downie said.

"You spoke to him?" Miriam asked.

"Left a message," Downie explained to Prentice and Maddy. "He's an old friend of mine from the seminary attached to the U.S. embassy in Paris. He's, ah…call him an agent."

"A spy?" Maddy said. "Really? That's interesting. Does he—"

"Agent," Downie repeated. "And an excellent investigator."

Prentice smiled. "A lead would be good," he said and stood. "If you're staying, I'll take Sadie outside again, let her burn off some energy."

Miriam looked over her shoulder at the clock on the wall. "Rose's class is almost over, so she and Dr. Petrovsky should be here soon. Rose was in touch with Hannah while Hannah was in Europe. Maybe she'll remember something."

"You think?" Maddy asked.

"It doesn't take much sometimes," Downie pointed out. "Just a suggestion of something can start us on the right path."

Miriam nodded. Downie's intuition worked better than hers did. He could see *something* in a hint and follow it to real leads and the making of a case. But she had a worry.

"What if we're dealing with someone like Rose's mother, a paranoid who sees insult where other people would see an accident? Or stupidity," Miriam wondered out loud. "None of us would have a clue."

"True." Downie cocked his head to one side. "On the other hand, you've told me that Hannah was pretty wild."

Miriam had to nod. "I know there was an affair with a married professor her senior year of college. And she did a lot of other sh—stuff. Rose had always been, not envious, but admiring. Because she didn't have the nerve to do those things, she said."

"Weird. Cousin Rose is no shrinking violet." Maddy said, then cleared her throat as Prentice and Sadie appeared in the backyard. "He's really good with Sadie."

"He does have those nephews and a niece," Downie said, raising his eyebrows at Miriam.

It wasn't her story to tell, the fact that Maddy and Big Mark had not been particularly happy. They had married far too young, blinded by a serious physical attraction, already ebbing when Mark died. The baby was the result of a vacation meant to rekindle the flame. It hadn't worked, and they'd been headed for an amicable divorce. Only Miriam knew about it, but the accident had been both an awful shock and a release for her daughter.

Maddy nodded. "Sadie really likes him. He says your boss told him to stay until you catch whoever it is. And that his partner has quit."

Miriam blinked at that. "Garber quit?"

Downie shrugged. "I'm not surprised. The, ah, supernatural stuff really upset him that morning."

"According to Detective Prentice, Garber totally freaked out. He was yelling about crazy people," Maddy said. "Speaking of paranoia."

"But he knows about Jones and the inside out bodies," Miriam pointed out. "How is he going to explain that business?

He *knows* there's magic." *She had just said those words. She wanted to deny them, but she had said them out loud. Damn.*

"Not my problem," Downie said, smiling. "Garber is Mike's business. So let's see what Teddy finds in Hannah's history, and we'll go from there."

Easy for him to say. His daughter and granddaughter couldn't do magical things that would have gotten them stoned, hanged, or burned at the stake a couple of hundred years ago—and in some countries even now. Not that he had a daughter or granddaughter. But the principle was the same.

On the other hand, they had to start somewhere. The feds had their approach, whatever it was. She and Downie had theirs. "Okay. We'll wait for Teddy. One question. Should we tell Rose about Garber and the yelling?"

"God," Downie looked at her. "Rose is a woman on the edge. But she ought to know. Part of the trouble here, I think, is so many secrets."

Chapter 32
Wednesday

◆ ◆ ◆

Rose stared at Miriam. She couldn't speak because she had stopped breathing. She stood on the edge of a steep cliff—

"Rosie?" Miriam said.

"Dr. Sherman?" Prentice said.

Petrovsky leaned over and whispered in Rose's ear, "I am here with you."

Those words reminded her to breathe. "But Detective Garber will complain to people and—"

"No," Petrovsky pronounced. "This is a story you tell yourself. Young Mr. Garber is afraid, I think. Suddenly, he sees what he has feared all his life, the magic, the supernatural—" he wiggled his fingers in the air as if to suggest mystical waves—"and now he does not know what to do. If he tells anyone, perhaps people will not believe him. Then what will he do? And if people do believe him? What will happen? He will lose control of his situation. Oh, no. Mr. Garber will keep this to himself for a while."

Rose turned to look at him. "You sound so sure."

"Because I have seen this. Truly, Dr. Sherman. I am more worried about the federal men who are not afraid and who are very sure that they know what goes on and what to do about it. And we do not know why they do anything. *They* make me very worried."

Rose studied his face, so concerned. He'd escorted her to work and class, bought her a meat pasty and tea at Tangier for lunch, and then come to Maddy's with her, all the while apparently enjoying himself. She certainly enjoyed his company, not to mention his sharing of information. He knew a lot about the gifts. But he didn't know much about the Feds, or, oddly, about Cal Jones. Cal had recommended him to Rose, true, but it turned out that he'd known her mother, Peony, who helped him when he first came to the States.

Calla Lilly Jones had spent her childhood at boarding school—visions of Hogwarts danced through Rose's head—so Petrovsky met her for the first time at her mother's funeral. And then he went to grad school in Washington while Cal went to Yale. Entirely separate directions except for the occasional conference.

Way off the point, Rosie. "Okay." She breathed. "Okay. So what do we do now? There's a limit to how long we can hide, right? Sadie has to go back to school sooner or later."

Miriam grimaced. "Without leads to that woman's identity, we're stuck. Sorry, Rose."

"No. There's got to be—" Rose suddenly remembered. "Didn't she follow a ritual?" She nodded. "She followed a ritual. She used paint and candles, right? Things she had to buy. She couldn't conjure them out of thin air, could she?"

Petrovsky shook his head as Miriam's eyes widened.

"Oh, God." Miriam said. "Of course she did. The white paint will be hard to trace, given how many hardware stores there are in Hartford County. But, Downie, she used black candles. Thick black candles. Button says they're tallow, not wax. It's not as if you can buy those candles at iParty."

"There is a trusted *botanica* in the South End of Hartford," Petrovsky said. "If she wanted to be sure of quality, she would buy them there. On Park Street."

Looking guilt-stricken, Detective Prentice nodded. "Garber and I were supposed to check the place out, but he walked out, and then—"

"Go now," Sergeant Downs ordered. "We'll wait for you."

Prentice snatched up his jacket off the back of the chair and strode out. "I'll get security tape if they have it."

"I thought we'd covered that," Sergeant Downs said by way of apology. "It's pretty obvious. But I never noticed the report wasn't in the book."

"We've all been shaken up," Miriam said.

It was obvious to Rose, even in the middle of being shaken up, that Miriam felt more than a partner's concern for the Sergeant. But she refused to even talk about him. Weird. *And once again off the point, Rose. Come back.* "There might be pictures of her buying the candles, is that the idea? Did you see her long enough when she was here to identify her?"

"Yes," Maddy and Miriam said together.

Sergeant Downs grimaced. "Assuming the shop has security cameras that work and she bought her candles at that *botanica*—"

"Aren't you a little ray of sunshine?" Miriam snarled.

Petrovsky shook his head. "This *botanica* is the place to buy true magical supplies. Other places pretend, but *la Señora* Navarro has the things required for real spells."

Rose had to smile. *Thank God for people who can pretend everything is normal, ordinary, regular. You have to buy supplies for spells, and here's the* botanica *where everyone who's anyone in the magical community buys their supplies—*

Sergeant Downs's phone rang—*The X Files theme song? Seriously?*—"This could be Teddy," he said, pulling the phone out of his shirt pocket. "It is. Teddy, you're on speaker, so keep it clean."

"Downie? Good to hear from you, you son of a gun."

"How are you?"

"If I told you, I'd have to kill you. And you?"

Both men chuckled. Rose rolled her eyes in Miriam's direction.

"I'm fine. You coming to the States this year?"

"Not till Thanksgiving. And I'll be in D.C. probably until Christmas—But that's not why you called."

At last.

"No. I need some information on a woman. We know she was in France in '82." The Sergeant looked at Miriam and Rose. "'Eighty-two?"

"'Eighty-four," Rose corrected. "Hannah graduated in '84." Later than she should have, because she'd been busy with her little adventures and almost flunked out of school. She had to make up at least one semester's worth of classes, possibly more.

"Eighty-four," Sergeant Downs repeated. "Hannah Fried, F-R-I-E-D, or Hannah Winkler. We're not sure which name she'd have—"

"Winkler," Teddy said. "She was calling herself Hannah Winkler."

Rose stared at Miriam, who stared right back at her. It was too easy, wasn't it?

"You knew her?" the Sergeant asked, raising an eyebrow in Miriam's direction.

"I was here at the embassy pretending to be useful, you know how it is. And she came in asking for help in placing her baby."

"Wrong Hannah," Rose said without thinking.

"Hannah never had a baby," Miriam added, frowning at her partner.

"This Hannah Winkler was about five-seven, slender, with brown curly hair, blue eyes, only about three months along when she came in, not showing."

It certainly sounded like their Hannah, but their Hannah had never had a child. Rose shook her head.

"You remember after all this time?" the Sergeant asked.

"Well," Teddy said, "she was very attractive and very insistent that we find a Jewish-American family to adopt the baby, and they had to take the baby as soon as she was born. A French family would not do. Very sure about that. And very demanding. Was this doctor any good, and what about that hospital, and so on. She called or came in every couple of weeks until the baby was born. And she always called the baby 'it.' No cute little nicknames for babies, the way people do, you know? Not even 'Bump' or 'Bèbè.' Nothing. And then, she refused to see the baby after she was born. That made her stick in my memory."

That sounded like Hannah. Miriam nodded with Rose. They knew.

Hannah had a baby?

"You say the baby was a girl?"

Hannah had a daughter?

"Yes. A wealthy, well connected couple took her. We checked them thoroughly." Silence. "Is there a problem, Downie?"

Hannah had a daughter.

"Might be. Do you have contact information for the family?"

Not a baby anymore. Somewhere in her late twenties now.

"You know better."

"They won't know where the info came from, Teddy. Unless it becomes absolutely necessary. This touches on a murder investigation. Unfortunately."

The sound of the deep breath carried clearly over the cell phone. "Fine. Hang on a sec."

It was more than a second before the man's voice came back to them. "Okay. Here it is. Berman. I've got a phone number in Portland, Maine, that's the summer residence, and then a primary residence in Manhattan. You ready?"

A daughter with multiple residences. How Hannah-like.

The Sergeant jotted the full names of both parents and the addresses and phone numbers on a piece of paper quickly supplied by Maddy.

"This might help. Thanks, Teddy. When I can, I'll let you know why the info is needed. By the way," the Sergeant said as if he'd just thought of it, "yyou wouldn't have kept tabs on Hannah Winkler after the baby was born, would you?"

Rose stared at Miriam. *If Hannah had a daughter, then she and Miriam had another first cousin once removed. Last name Berman. Late twenties, around Maddy's age, so of that generation. One could ask what gift or gifts Ms. Berman had. Interesting question. One could hope those gifts didn't extend to turning people inside-out with a spell. One could also hope Ms. Berman wasn't a paranoid. One could only hope.*

Teddy chuckled. "Like I said, she was an attractive woman, Downie, but awfully selfish. Extremely high maintenance, as they say nowadays. Definitely not my type."

"Not that way, Teddy, c'mon. Did she ever come to the embassy's attention again? Did she run into any trouble that you know of?" Downie had turned away so Rose couldn't see his face, but Miriam looked like she felt. Not really surprised, almost disappointed in herself because she should have known.

Who would Hannah's daughter look like?

"I'm looking at the contact list, actually. She came in for her passport renewals, other citizenship business. Nothing else except her boss died in a car accident in 2002, and she was questioned by the Procurator's office. She requested an embassy official be present, but it was just routine questions. Are you looking for anything in particular?"

"Well, it would be...odd things. Odd deaths. Unexpected manner of death, that sort of thing."

Odd things. Hannah having a daughter wasn't odd enough?

"She didn't strike me as mysterious. Cold, selfish, very high maintenance, like I said, but not mysterious."

Is that a fair description of Hannah? Yes, it is. Fair and accurate. But then, there were times it could have described any of them, couldn't it?

After all, they'd all...ah, yes, making excuses for Hannah, Rose. Yes, you are. But there Hannah is, with a major secret that she'd never shared with her family, and God knows what else Hannah knew that could affect all of them. Hannah was selfish, above all else.

Downie turned back, face arranged in a question. Because he didn't know Hannah, not really. "Yeah, well, we need to know, and we can't ask her directly without setting off a raft of trouble. So anything you can do."

"I'll look into it. I know where she lived, so I know where to start asking. Give me a day or two. Same number?"

A day or two until they knew whether they were dealing with more "oddities." Odd to call horrific murders oddities, wasn't it?

"Day or night, Teddy. This might become urgent."

"Got it. Talk to you soon."

"Bye, Teddy."

"*Adieu, mon ami.*"

Downie set his phone down on the table, grimacing at it. "She kept her secret all these years."

Rose shrugged. "Secret keeping does run in the family. You know that, Sergeant. We're better than the NSA at keeping secrets." Her own daughters, for instance, hadn't shared information about their gifts. Neither had she, of course—but a baby? "A baby. My God."

"Never so much as a hint," Miriam said, nodding. She turned to Maddy. "Did you ever hear her say *anything* that suggested—"

"Ma." Maddy laughed. "Hannah doesn't even like to be around Sadie and Mark. So I just always assumed no babies for Cousin Hannah."

Rose shook her head. "Except she didn't have a child. She did give birth. But she walked away." How could she have walked away? The minute Rose knew she was pregnant with Pena, she was in love with the baby and knew she would be named for Nana Pearl. She had loved Tava that way, too, the minute she knew she carried a child. And the whole time she was pregnant, through the morning-noon-and-night sickness with both of them, she was entirely in love with those babies. They were, in her mind, fully formed children to be cherished. But then, she had a job and could have taken care of them even if Harry didn't. She had Aunt Fanny and her cousins to turn to if she needed help. She had resources, and she wanted those babies.

"It's shocking," Miriam said. "I don't understand."

Miriam didn't look shocked, more bemused, maybe. But then, Miriam had never admired Hannah. Rose was the one who'd put Hannah on a pedestal. Miriam had had the right idea.

Rose grimaced. "It turns out, Hannah did a really conventional and fearful thing for those days, didn't she? Went away and had the baby in secret. After teasing me constantly for being so conventional and fearful." Rose grimaced. "I got a few things wrong."

"You're not the only one, Rosie." Miriam shrugged. "I *knew* something was wrong with her; she's a habitual liar, but— it's an amazing secret to keep all these years. Amazing."

"Do you suppose she told her David?" *As secrets went, a baby was a doozy. Harder to keep than the run-of-the-mill, my-mother-was-a-paranoid-who-beat-me-regularly secret. The need to share must have been overwhelming sometimes. Or is that projecting your own needs onto Hannah? Hannah the Cold and Selfish. Hard to come to terms with,*

Miriam chuckled dryly. "Told David? How likely—" She straightened up and smiled. "It's after three, right? Hannah gets out of school about now. And we should tell her about the threat."

"We did a welfare check, Mir. Or Wethersfield PD did yesterday evening. She wouldn't let the officer in, but she told him she was fine. And Wethersfield High School is closed for the rest of the week because of the vandalism I told you about." The Sergeant clearly didn't like the idea of approaching Hannah until they had more information.

"If she's home, she won't let us in, Mir. She won't take our calls. How can we tell her about the threat?" Not that Rose planned to go with Miriam, but "we" came naturally to her. They used to do everything together, the three of them.

Grimacing, Miriam pulled her cell phone out of her jacket pocket and tapped a number.

"Hello, David, it's Miriam....Yes, But I need to talk to Hannah. Is she there?...Really?...So do they know who did it?...Really?...Amazing what kids can manage....Yeah, no, I'll try again later. Take care....Yeah, bye."

Eyebrows raised, Miriam ended the call. "Hannah is at school for a meeting about the vandals. Who turn out to be a couple of freshmen who didn't make the team and got pushed around for their audacity in trying out. So we'll wait at her car in the parking lot at school." Miriam's smile took on a nasty twist. "Where's she going to go?"

The Sergeant was shaking his head as Maddy said, "Is that a good idea, Ma? That woman is still out there, whoever she is."

"We can't hide forever, Mad. And I am armed."

Would a gun stop a magician? A practitioner? Whatever we're calling them today?

"But, Ma—"

The Sergeant's *X Files* theme played.

"It's Prentice," he announced. "You're on speaker, Detective."

"Yes, sir. I'm at the *botanica* waiting on a warrant for the security tapes. The proprietor is happy to help, but the warrant makes it all official."

"Good. We'll meet you back at the station."

So much for confronting Hannah.

"It'll be a while. We have to sift through more records."

"Okay, John."

Miriam stood up as the Sergeant ended the call. "Maddy, you'll have to come to the station."

Maddy shrugged as she left the kitchen, going to get the children, Rose assumed.

"You don't need me," Rose said. Maybe she could just go home, set the alarm, and sleep for a couple of hours. *Doesn't that sound good? A nap.* She let a smile take over her face.

"You and I are going over to the school, Rosie," Miriam pronounced.

"But—"

"This woman may have spells to avert your bullets," Dr. Petrovsky said.

"But the rock Downie threw—"

"This she did not expect. Startlement—what is the word I mean? Surprise. She was surprised."

"I need to do this. I need to confront Hannah. And David won't be at school, so she can't use that excuse."

Rose understood. At this point, Miriam must have been aching for control.

"Mir," Rose said softly. "She might not matter. The baby, I mean. And Hannah is just…done with being part of the family." As she spoke, Rose felt tears threaten. But they didn't matter, either. "Maybe we should just leave Hannah out of this."

"She could be in danger." Miriam's protest sounded half-hearted at best.

"She's made it pretty clear she doesn't give a rat's patoot about us." Rose shrugged. "I miss her, but I don't think talking to her is going to make any difference."

Miriam glared.

That tactic used to work. But all the emotional yanking and twisting, fear, then anger, back to fear, then back to anger, and whatever the hell she felt about the good Dr. Petrovsky had exhausted her. "You can go if you want to," Rose decided and turned to the Sergeant. "If you don't need me, I'm going home. I'm just fried."

"But I need Dr. Petrovsky down at the station to help review the tapes with us." The Sergeant was shaking his head. "And you shouldn't be alone, even with your alarm system."

"We'll find a place for you to sleep," Miriam said as she walked over to Rose. "*Please*, Rosie. A stop at the station and then to the high school."

Rose sighed as dramatically as she could manage. "Now I know how my kids used to feel." But she followed Miriam out to her car.

Chapter 33
Wednesday

"That's her. Without a doubt." Maddy agreed with her mother, who nodded again and tapped the still printed from the *botanica*'s security tape.

"Absolutely." Miriam smiled. They knew the perp. They could name her, trace her, find and grab her. They could work the case one logical step at a time. All sweetly calm and rational.

"She looks...familiar to me," Rose added. "I didn't see her yesterday, but..." She stared at the print in front of her on the conference table, frowning. "I don't know where I've seen her, but she really looks familiar."

"How so?" Downie asked. He'd more or less taken over since Prentice came back from the *botanica* with the disc of recordings. It turned out the owner of the place knew both the alternate physics—she had laughed, Prentice said, when he used the term and told him it was magic—*and* the use of modern technology, and so *la Señora* Navarro had digital cameras throughout her store. Plenty of material that could have been overwhelming, except the woman also kept notes of who bought items for what she called "dark uses." So she was able to help Prentice winnow the recordings down to those for three afternoons, when a young woman had purchased "certain items," including black candles."

Now, prints of the young woman in question sat on the table, and everyone stared at them.

"She does look...kind of like you, Detective Fine," Prentice said. "A little."

Startled, Miriam began an automatic denial. "She couldn't possibly—" But she could possibly. Something about the eyes.

"Uncle Moe's chin," Rose muttered. "And maybe his eyes. Your eyes, too."

Hannah's father, Rose and Miriam's Uncle Moe, had left when the girls were preteens, but they remembered their favorite uncle, the rides to Wall's Dairy in East Hampton for ice cream, the free bicycle repairs, and the awful dad jokes.

"She looks like Hannah, really, Ma," Maddy said. "She does."

"She does." Rose sounded sad, and she sighed. "She could be one of the family."

Miriam frowned at the picture in front of her, then looked over at her partner. "You have the contact info on the adoptive parents?" Were they looking too hard for resemblance, seeing it where none existed because they wanted an answer, and Hannah's daughter was a convenient scapegoat? But even Prentice, who had no reason to scapegoat anyone, saw the family in the woman's face.

Downie nodded, fished in his pocket for his notebook, pulled a piece of paper out, and slid it across the table to her.

Miriam outlined the tasks. "While you make copies of the picture for a canvas, and John lets Mike know what's going on—and someone could call the New York DMV and get a driver's license photo—I'll call the parents and get a photo of her. If she's not sitting cheerfully knitting with her mother." Not that she wanted to make the call. Well. No. She did want to make the call. It was the logical investigative step. It was. But to confirm that the woman in those prints, the woman who thought a blood curse was a good idea, who thought—

"Wait a minute, wait a minute." Rose sounded puzzled and excited. "It can't be Hannah's daughter. It can't. Because if she is Hannah's daughter and she performs a blood curse that actually works, she dies, too." Rose turned to Petrovsky, sitting there at the end of the long table. "Wouldn't she? If she's part of the family?"

"*Da*. Yes," he said. "Absolutely."

Miriam let herself smile. It couldn't be Hannah's daughter.

Rose chuckled and turned back to Miriam. "So she can't possibly be Hannah's dau—oh. Damn. Oops, sorry, Maddy, I just realized—"

Miriam frowned, not quite keeping pace with Rose's thinking. And then she understood. "Oh, sh—sugar." Because there was more than one family inheritance, wasn't there? Yes, there was.

"Not to put too fine a point on it, but she might not be entirely rational," Rose explained to Prentice, who couldn't know what was going on. "There's a streak of paranoia, the real thing, not the metaphor, in the family. So she might not be thinking clearly at all."

Nodding, Miriam stared down at her hands. The other family inheritance, the one everyone wanted to ignore, demonstrated its ugliness again.

"You'd better make the phone call, Mir," Downie said. "We'll get the rest of the investigation going."

Miriam watched Downie leave the conference room, Prentice behind him. Then she checked Sadie, sitting happily under the conference table with crayons, paper, a baggie of raisins and dried apricots, and her water bottle. One happy kid. Not crazy.

So far. "Okay," Miriam said. "Calling now." Out came the cell, and in went the New York number Teddy had given them for the Bermans. She also tapped the Speaker button.

Two rings and a calm, icy female voice answered the phone. "Berman residence," it said, as if someone would challenge her claim.

"Am I speaking with Mrs. Berman?"

"This is Mrs. Kraft. The housekeeper." The words were spoken as if Miriam should have known.

"Ah. Hello, Mrs. Kraft." Miriam moved into investigative mode. "My name is Detective Miriam Fine. I'm calling from the Hartford, Connecticut, Police Department to speak to Mr. or Mrs. Berman."

Not a moment's hesitation or even a sharp intake of breath at a call from the police. "In regard to what are you calling?"

Either the woman was trained to ignore any emotion, or she was used to phone calls from the police. "It's a personal matter I'd rather not discuss except with Mr. or Mrs. Berman. Privacy concerns."

"I see." The woman sniffed. "Very well. If you will give me your name, badge number, and telephone number, Mrs. Berman will return your call within ten minutes."

"Of course." Exactly what Miriam herself would have done had someone claiming to be from the police called her. Take the information and confirm that the cop who called was, in fact, a cop calling from the department she said she was calling from.

Most people didn't know they should do that. Most people didn't have experience with police investigations. Mrs. Kraft apparently did, or she was well trained. Possibly both.

Miriam spelled her name and listed out her badge and phone numbers. "Thank you."

No response except a huff from Rose as Miriam ended the call. "She makes Mrs. Danvers look cuddly."

"Who's Mrs. Danvers?" Maddy asked.

"*Rebecca?*" Rose asked, laughing. "No?"

Maddy continued to look blank.

"You never saw the movie or read the book? Daphne de Maurier?"

Miriam took pity on her daughter, welcoming the distraction. "Mrs. Danvers was the housekeeper. Nasty bit."

"The villain, actually," Rose said. "She was the villain. You ought to watch the movie. In your spare time." She chuckled.

Watching Rose, Miriam could only wonder how she did it. Well, no. She did understand, really. When Rosie was a child, her mother had given her very few choices, all of them bad. And Rosie had refused all of those choices and survived the nasty childhood. She'd left home as soon as she could and made a decent life for herself, one careful step after another. She'd married a quiet man, so unlike her mother, he might as well have come from a different planet. She went to school—people thought Miriam's insistence on rationality was obsessive, but Rose went to school, where she could intellectualize everything. And she managed her contacts with her unpredictable mother, too, until the accident that killed the three sisters, the cousins' mothers. It had taken some therapy, but Rosie's strength had carried her through. So the emotional roller coaster wasn't a foreign environment to her. She recovered quickly or had a calm façade. Maybe both. And maybe the meditation she'd taken up a couple of years ago helped, too. Maybe Miriam should learn to meditate. *Fat chance.*

Miriam's phone rang. "It's the Berman number."

"Not ten minutes," Rose said.

It wouldn't take Miriam ten minutes to check a name and number. And she didn't have people to do the check for her. It was a safe bet Mr. and Mrs. Berman did. As she answered the phone, she dropped any emotion, sounded cool and professional. "Detective Fine."

"Detective Fine, I am Roberta Berman."

"Mrs. Berman. I'm sorry to bother you like this, but I'm inquiring about a baby girl you adopted in France in 1984 or '85. I'm sorry, I don't know the exact date."

Two or three seconds elapsed before the woman responded, and not as Miriam expected. "I see," Mrs. Berman said. "Is Sara-- ah. Is she all right?"

The woman wasn't entirely in control. Concerned, definitely. Maybe frightened for her daughter. "We're trying to trace her recent movements."

"But she's all right. She's not—" Another pause. "She's all right, yes?"

"She's…possibly a witness in a series of crimes here in central Connecticut. She's been seen. But the identification is tentative."

"I see." Sudden coolness.

"I'm sorry, but I have to ask. You don't seem surprised that your daughter is even tangentially involved in possible criminal activity. Is there—"

"Oh, Detective." A sigh. "Sara…has been difficult almost from the time she could walk and talk. As she got older, it…became obvious to us that she was developing symptoms of psychological difficulties. Paranoid thinking…and other things. We tried to get her help—but she came into a trust fund on her eighteenth birthday and cut off all contact with us and her brothers and sisters and her friends." Another sigh. "I'm sure I shouldn't say this to you, but I'm simply glad to know she's alive."

A mother's worst nightmare, the disappearing child. "Does Sara know the circumstances of her adoption?"

"Not—What does that have to do with—Has she done something to her birth mother?"

"There have been attempts on the woman's life." A small lie in the service of good.

"Oh. God. No. I…I can't say anything more. I have to talk to my husband, get her a lawyer—"

"She's not under arrest, Mrs. Berman. We're not even sure it's she who's been seen. A photo would help us to determine—"

"Oh, Sara. Sara. No. I'm sorry, Detective. I've said too much. I'm ending this call now."

And she did. "Damn," was all Miriam could think to say. "I didn't handle that well."

Rose shook her head. "But we know Hannah's daughter inherited the *other* family gift, right? And since she's part of Maddy's generation, we're reasonably sure that Sara has some gifts—"

"She is a talented spell-caster," Petrovsky said, tapping a finger on the photo in front of him. "Assuming this person is Sara Berman. Family resemblance is strong, and believing it is someone other than her requires believing in great coincidence. *Great* coincidence."

Coincidences like that don't happen. They do not. "I can probably track down a driver's license photo. Or Prentice can."

"I can, Ma." Maddy smiled. "The law firm pays me to research stuff, you remember that, right?" She chuckled. "You know? This is the first time I've ever seen or heard anything to do with your work. And it's interesting to see you work to build the logic. I do something like that, too. And so, really, does Cousin Rose when she writes her papers, right?"

Rose nodded. "It's true. We build trails of logic."

"That's a lot of what we do. Not like on TV at all." Not very dramatic, going to every door of every residence and shop on a block, or calling every single person on a contact list, hour after hour. But bits of information build the case, inch by inch. "I'm glad you're seeing it. I just wish we didn't have to put an armed guard on you while you're seeing it."

"It's okay, Ma. He's…nice, and Sadie behaves for him. She likes him."

Nice? What did that mean? Decent, kind, good. *Maddy needed nice.* "Okay. There's the computer. Here's my ID and password. Do *not* share them with anyone or tell anyone I gave them to you, but see what you can do. Rose and I are going to see Hannah, and you are not to leave here without Detective Prentice."

Smiling, Maddy sat back in her chair. "Yes, Ma."

"Humoring me?"

"Of course not, Ma."

"As long as the three of you are safe, you can use my picture for dart practice." Miriam stood up. "I'll see you later. C'mon, Rosie."

"Are you sure, Mir? The three of us together would be an easy target."

Rose had a point, but—

"She insists on using spells," Dr. Petrovsky said, standing up. "So I will accompany you. To be sure, yes?"

Miriam saw the smile Rosie bestowed on him, and the smile he answered her with. *More than consulting going on there.*

"Tell Downie we're in the Wethersfield High School parking lot, would you, Mad?"

"Be careful, Ma."

"Always, Mad. See you for supper."

"I'll cook," Rose offered, sounding almost cheerful.

What difference did it make how cheerful Rose sounded? They were actually going to *do* something.

Chapter 34
Wednesday

◆

Rose stared out the windshield of Miriam's car at the blank brick wall of the pool house, the annex in the rear of the Wethersfield High School building. She'd been happy teaching in that school, even with the usual garbage from parents, the weaseling, the begging, and the occasional threat to her career. But life had been...what?

Less lonely, definitely, with Tava still in college and coming home for holidays. That had been a while ago, and nothing to do with teaching.

Still, she had enjoyed the work here, the same way she enjoyed teaching at UHart, the way she learned from the kids and shared ideas. *Does Hannah feel like that? Is she open with the kids in her classes? Does she do the exercises with them to show them how a person with more practice would respond to the assignment? Does she worry about them, especially the ones who don't seem to grasp the basics? Does she agonize over the possible results of a D as opposed to a C– on a paper?* "Remind me why I thought this was a good idea?" she asked.

"Hannah has to know what's going on, for one thing. She's still a Winkler. And one of Nana Pearl's granddaughters."

"But couldn't a local police officer tell her?" Rose chuckled suddenly. "Can you imagine?" She lowered her voice to mock male depths. "Pardon me, Madam, but I'm here to tell you that your daughter is a witch and—" The mockery fell away. "There she is."

Hannah came strolling around the corner of the pool house, wearing the middle-aged-lady uniform of dark trousers, light-colored tailored shirt, a blazer with an appliquéd parrot on the lapel where Rose wore a lion's face pin and Miriam wore *Tannah*. She carried a black leather tote, obviously full of papers and books. Just like Rose's red leather tote, always full of papers and books.

Hannah was frowning, but Hannah usually frowned, so—

"Shall we?" Miriam said, releasing her seatbelt.

"'We?' You mean me, too?" Rose hadn't thought as far as actually talking to Hannah. Wasn't Miriam the logical one to do the talking? Yes, she was. *An easy decision.*

"You, too, Rosie."

C'mon, Rosie. You're an adult now.

"Okay." She heard the doubt in her voice, knew Miriam did, too, but she got out of the car anyway.

Hannah saw them and stopped.

"Miriam," she said. "Rose."

So that's what ice sounds like. Rose nodded.

"Hannah, we have to talk," Miriam said. "It's—"

"I know I was clear," Hannah began, then looked around and stepped closer to them. When she spoke again, her voice was a harsh whisper. "I do not want to speak to you or—"

"You're in danger," Miriam said in a normal speaking voice. "We all are. The three of us are being stalked—"

Grimacing, Hannah shook her head. "Lower your voice, please. People will—"

"Someone is trying to kill us." Miriam tried again.

Hannah laughed. "Of all the ridiculous—I think I'd know if someone were try—"

Rose clicked her tongue impatiently. "It's probably your daughter, Hannah."

For a second, Rose saw panic on Hannah's face. Her eyes widened, her jaw sagged, her cheeks paled. But she collected herself almost instantly. "I don't have a —"

"Liar," Rose hissed.

Hannah glared, but before she could say anything, Miriam shook her head. "Hannah." She sounded disappointed. "We *know*. We *know* you gave birth to a baby girl just after college. In France. We—"

"How *dare* you?" Hannah spoke through her teeth. "My personal life is none of your bus—"

"It's our business when someone has committed three murders and possibly more. All around the three of us."

"It has nothing to do with me. Now leave me alone." Hannah stepped around Miriam, heading toward her car.

"Hannah." Rose was stunned at how wrong she'd been about her cousin. "She's using spells to commit her murders."

That stopped Hannah. And when she turned around, she no longer hid her upset. "No," she whispered. "There's no such thing as spells. Or witches. No such thing."

If Hannah got any paler, she'd pass out. *Who would catch her? Not me. Not a kind thought, the consequences will be bad, but I would not catch her.*

"Oh, yes," Miriam said. "Turns out your daughter is a powerful spell-caster with a serious grudge against us."

That, Rose knew, was serious theorizing ahead of the evidence, but if it got them closer to the truth, what the hell.

"No," Hannah repeated. "She—No."

"Hannah?" Miriam reached out.

Hannah stepped back. "No! Leave me alone. Go away. Now." She turned away again.

Heat rushed up Rose's face with anger. "You know what, Hannah? You're a selfish, paranoid liar. Just like my mother. And the only reason I don't smack you silly is that I've never hit anyone. But you deserve it. You are—"

She stopped only because Miriam laid a hand on her arm and pointed at Hannah with her chin.

Their cousin had made it to her car, but that was as far as she got. She set the tote bag on the hood of her car, and now she just stood there, back to them, her shoulders hunched.

Was she crying?

Who cares if she's crying? Look at the trouble she's probably caused. Rose cleared her throat. "What should we do, Mir?"

Miriam shrugged. "Talk to her. What else? Stay here."

Not a problem. Leave it to Miriam. "Okay."

Miriam walked over to Hannah and started talking, too softly for Rose to hear. Hannah did look at Miriam and respond to her, but what she was saying, Rose couldn't figure out.

Petrovsky came up beside Rose. "She is badly frightened, your cousin."

"It's her own fault," Rose said, then shook her head. "Listen to me, talking as if I've never done anything selfish or—"

"I am thinking you do not turn your back on family."

"I'm about to turn my back on her. She's too much like my—like other people I don't want to be around. So what does that make me?"

"It is to protect yourself from her damage, yes? But what is happening?"

Rose's gut had begun to tingle as he spoke to her, and her hand drifted down to cover the sensation. But—"I'm not sure." The feeling didn't really rise to the level of premonition. It wasn't butterfly-fluttering anticipation, either. "I think we're being watched. But I don't—"

"Close your eyes, please."

After a quick glance sideways at his concerned face, Rose closed her eyes.

"Breathe and set your focus on your belly."

She did as he said, breathing deeply and concentrating on the tingling. Almost instantly, the tingling changed to a sense of awareness. Knowing.

"It's...two people. Two different people." Her eyes opened, focused on his face. "Sara and Ironed Blue Jeans. And I think Ironed Blue Jeans is trying to listen to us, too, but *Tannah* is interfering with his equipment. This isn't precognition, is it?"

"Clairvoyance," he said, already walking toward Miriam. "We must not stay here, Detective Fine," he called.

Where is the panic? Why don't I feel panic? To hell with panic. Where is Sara Berman hiding? And where is Ironed Blue Jeans? Rose squinted down the parking lot, seeing nothing but empty cars. Somewhere down that way, though, toward Jay Street, that's where the sensation was strongest. Cars always came and went from the back entrance to the school parking lots, and people waited for kids to walk down to meet them there on the little side street lined with Cape Cods and neatly kept lawns. Anyone could just park on Jay Street and look like a waiting parent or friend. Who could say you didn't belong there?

Rose turned back toward Hannah's car to see Miriam and Petrovsky hustling toward her. Hannah had already gotten into her car.

"Come on, Rosie, get in. We're going. Now."

"Don't go down Jay Street, Mir. Go out the Wolcott Hill exit."

Miriam stared at her for a second before nodding. "You're getting just a little scary, Rose."

Rose fastened her seatbelt as Miriam pulled out of the parking space. "You should try it from the inside," she said. *Scary. And exciting, if she was being honest. Admit it, Rosie, it's exciting to know things and move things and be more than safe little Rosie.*

"Are they following us? Can you tell?" Miriam glanced in her rearview mirror.

Before she could answer, Petrovsky muttered something and waved his hand in the air. "I have made an illusion. It will last only for a short time, but long enough." He smiled.

"An illusion?" Miriam asked.

"*Da.* We are still in the parking lot arguing with Mrs. Levine."

That was a little scary, and Rose frowned at him. He was a powerful spell-caster, wasn't he? And well trained. *Oh, Sweetie, you do* not *have to ask about his abilities, do you?*

He fished something out of his jacket pocket. A chocolate bar.

"Jonesing for a fix?" she asked.

Speaking around a mouthful of chocolate, he said, "Making spells uses energy," and went back to chewing the chocolate.

"I can live with that." *A great excuse to eat chocolate. Who would argue with that? Aside from the hot flashes, of course.*

"A reason to love the gifts," Miriam chuckled as they started up the ramp to 91 North.

Really, though, Rosie? Did chocolate offset the loss of Hannah, those jerks from E.S.P., the fear, the—Stop, stop. That way only leads to tears. Smile and consider an investment in Ghirardelli.

But she was quiet all the way back to Hartford PD.

Chapter 35
Wednesday

Sara felt power ripple along her scalp. A very powerful casting, the kind of power used to create the wards at Jones's house. If she had to be honest, it was the kind of power she wanted for herself, true and straight and—

She sat up and smacked a hand against the steering wheel of the car she'd stolen from the parking lot behind Nordstrom's at West Farms Mall. So easy when all it took was a whispered word to undo the lock and another to start the engine. Not so easy to determine what kind of spell had just been cast or why it felt as though it had been directed at her. Someone would have had to know she was there. Someone would have wanted to do something about her watching.

But nothing seemed to have changed as a result of the spell. The Winklers all still stood and argued there in the lot.

Did they? Did they? As far as she could tell, her birth mother's car was now leaving the parking lot and driving past her. The other two were getting into their car. Why did it matter? As long as they stayed there, she would stay there. Her mother would die with the others, but it was the cop who was the key. She was the strong one. If she died—

Sara realized that the two women in the car there in the lot didn't move or speak. It was an illusion. Which meant that one of the Winklers had cast the spell. One of them was a powerful caster.

Which one was unimportant.. She had to undo it, a matter of a counter-spell followed by two chocolate bars before she had the strength to open her eyes and see what was really there.

Both cars were gone. None of the Winkler bitches were in the parking lot. All three of them were gone.

She needed another candy bar. Maintaining her own illusion that her car was empty, and seeing through the other illusion at the same time had taken more energy than she'd expected.

Some of the books did warn about blood magic, using the caster's body to power spells. A caster could tax her body beyond its ability to power spells, but she had to do it. How much longer she could manage was the question, one she'd never had to ask before. She'd also never had to maintain so many spells for so long without results. So she had to do something about her situation, and she had to do it soon.

Fine. No blood curse. It hadn't worked, and now she knew why. One of the Winklers was a spell-caster of enormous power, counter-spelling her efforts.

A head-on, face-to-face strangulation spell would have to do. There was no finesse in that kind of spell, but the time for finesse was gone. The objective was to see her mother and the cousins dead. A strangulation spell would do it. One at a time. And there would be no evidence linking her to the deaths. She'd approach invisibly, cast the spell, and go. No one would know.

Sara smiled. It would be done.

Good. She'd decided. Another candy bar would hold her until she could get to a restaurant, eat, and start planning. There were plenty of restaurants down the Silas Deane Highway, any of which would do, and she'd leave the car in the lot of whatever place she ended up in. No one would notice a car sitting in the lot until the place closed and the lot emptied out, and by then, she'd have found another car to use. And she'd have a solid plan to take care of the Winklers. Very nice.

Sara dropped the empty car illusion and laughed at the startled look she got from the woman walking her dog toward her down the street. The woman would end up convincing herself she was crazy rather than say, even to herself, that magic exists. Very funny.

"Time to go, Sara. Eat and implement your plan."

Off she went.

Chapter 36
Wednesday

◆

Miriam hadn't said anything in the car, too busy making sure no one followed her, but she wanted to. No, she needed to. The urge to speak, to share, was nearly overwhelming.

Hannah—Hannah had spat a story at her, to make her go away, Miriam thought. A bad miscalculation on Hannah's part. Miriam had felt a cold fury settle on her that nothing shifted, not even Petrovsky's warning about being watched and listened to. She felt nothing but despite toward Hannah.

Nana Pearl's granddaughter or not, her cousin could die in front of her for all she cared. Miriam wouldn't lift a finger to save her, and the hell with a police officer's duty. Miriam Fine was done with Cousin Hannah.

But Rose had gone quiet, totally quiet. *That* concerned her.

Still, she had to tell Rose the story. As soon as they were out of the parking garage, climbing the stairs, she needed to talk. "Rose."

"Hmm?"

Whatever distracted Rose had to be serious, but this story had to be told. "Hannah told me something you should know, too. It explains why Sara Berman, if it is her, would want to hurt all three of us."

"Hannah knows why?" No one could blame Rose for her skepticism.

"I don't think she's put everything together. But *I* think it explains everything."

"Tell me then."

"When Hannah signed away her parental rights to the baby, she told the Bermans that the reason she'd left home and couldn't keep the baby was that her parents had told her to leave and never come back, that she was a disgrace to the family. And we, you and I, her cousins, who used to be so close to her, had agreed with her parents and turned our backs on her. So she had nothing and no one." After hearing that story, Miriam had wanted to smash Hannah's face against her car to clean the smirk off her face.

Rose stopped climbing the stairs, her face—no one had ever accused her of having a poker face—a study in wide-eyed shock. "*We* turned our backs on *her?* She said that out loud? Seriously?"

Miriam nodded.

"Miriam. Seriously."

Miriam nodded again and started climbing the stairs. "That's what she said."

"But, Mir, we didn't even know she was pregnant. And Aunt Fanny gave her the money to go to France. I was there when Fanny handed her the envelope. And I would have helped her—oh."

Miriam stopped to look behind her at Rose. Rose had stopped, too.

Rose's mouth set in a thin line as she nodded. "Just like my mother." She nodded again. "I said it before, I know, but I didn't really believe it until now."

"No argument here."

They went up the last few steps and into the hall quietly. She'd have to tell Downie and Maddy, too.

What a mess. One lie. Just one more lie in a family of secrets and gifts and paranoia, and look what a mess of rage and—

"Mir." Rose's panicked whisper stopped her. "Mir, did you see that?"

Mir looked back. They were past the Cold Case office and Robbery-Homicide, but she hadn't been paying attention. "See what?"

Rose gestured for her to lower her voice. "Back there." She pointed to the Robbery-Homicide door.

"What?"

Her eyes widened, Rose whispered. "Those Men in Black. And David Levine, I think. Hannah's David."

Hannah's David? Who supposedly didn't know about the gift and who wasn't ever going to know about the gift because he'd leave his wife if he knew? That David?

Miriam decided she needed a file from the Cold Case office. "Wait here," she whispered to Rose and Petrovsky and walked back to that door with a quick glance toward the office across the hall.

Yep. David Levine stood there with the same men, still wearing their dark glasses, *for God's sake,* who'd been at the Farmington Avenue scene. No Ironed Blue Jeans, but the other three in their black suits and skinny ties stood just outside Mike's office, talking as if they were all old friends.

She left the door to the office open while she rifled through the file cabinet for something to excuse her presence—a copy of the book on the first scene, the first inside-out body would do—found it, and turned around. Miraculously, the group of men, who she would swear under oath included David Levine, had vanished.

What the hell was going on?

And here came the hot flash, *Damn it.*

At least *that* family inheritance was reasonable. She really didn't suffer too badly. Rose had read that caffeine aggravated the flashes and the other symptoms, so they'd decaffeinated together, and really, if she wasn't at the point of enjoying a private tropical vacation like Rose, at least it wasn't awful. But when she got upset—

And why should seeing David Levine talking to the feds upset her?

Excellent question. Just excellent. The fact that he betrayed his wife by letting her think he didn't know something important shouldn't matter anymore. If Hannah didn't matter, then what her husband did or didn't do shouldn't matter either.

Damn it.

She tucked the binder under her arm and rejoined Rose in the hall. Petrovsky wasn't there.

"Where's Dr. Petrovsky?"

Her eyebrows practically in her hair, Rose pointed to the conference room. "With Sergeant Downs."

Taking pity on her cousin, Miriam nodded and beckoned Rose into the conference room.

Rose shut the door. "Well? What is David Levine, for God's sake, doing talking to *them?*"

Miriam turned to Downie. "Good question, isn't it?"

Downie raised his hands in surrender. "Mike kicked me out when the suits showed up, so—" He shrugged.

This time, the fury came on hot. Sweaty and furious, Miriam flung open the door and marched down the hall to Robbery-Homicide.

If anyone sitting in any of the cubicles said anything to her, she didn't hear them. Mike's door was closed.

Too *fucking* bad. That door flung open, too, revealing—

Mike, sitting there staring up at her like an innocent choir boy. "Miriam—"

"That's Detective Fine, Lieutenant. This is not a friendly visit. I need to know what those bastards from E.S.P. and David Levine were doing here."

"Miriam." Mike got up from his desk, walked around her, and shut the door. "Miriam. Did it ever occur to you that having a bunch of people running around loose who can do things like make you see things that aren't there could be dangerous?" He sat back down behind his desk. "There has to be someone–"

"A bunch of people?" Her hand rose to *Tannah* on the lapel of her jacket. "A bunch of people? Like my family, you mean?"

Which includes Hannah, don't forget.

And Rose. And Maddy. And Sadie. And David, Pena, and Tava. And Aunt Fanny, the amazing Aunt Fanny—"My family," she repeated. "Not some 'bunch of people,' Lieutenant. So." She reached into her pocket for the small leather folder with the ID and shield, laid it carefully on his desk, then unclipped the holster from her waistband and set that next to the folder. "Do you need a letter?"

"Miriam. Maybe I misspoke. Let's sit down and—"

"No, maybe about it, Lieutenant."

She strode out of the office and down to the conference room. "I don't work here anymore," she announced.

"Miriam?" Downie did sound upset, give him that. "What happened?"

"Mike drank the Kool-Ade is what happened."

When he looked confused, she relented. "Those Men in Black? Convinced him that it isn't safe to have a—" she made finger quotes in the air—"'bunch of people who can do things' running around loose."

As Petrovsky muttered in Russian, she finished. "Like my family. C'mon, Rose. You and I are done here. Dr. Petrovsky?"

"Yes, I come with you. This is what I feared. We meet somewhere?"

"My daughter's house. She needs to know about this. And we have to decide what to do."

"What about Sara Berman, Mir? It is her. Maddy got her New York driver's license photo." Downie held up an enlargement of the license.

"I have to protect my family." She turned, leaving Rose and Petrovsky to follow her out.

Rose caught up with her halfway down the stairs. "What about David Levine? Did the Lieutenant tell you what David Levine was doing there?"

"I didn't get that far, Rose. Honestly, I was so angry when he talked about 'a bunch of people' like that—I mean that kind of language is the first step, right?"

Rose sighed. "It is. Then they make laws. And then—"

"In Soviet Union, they killed families of those of us who would not do as they wanted."

Mindful of the cameras where they stood in the parking garage, Miriam shook her head. "We can't talk here. At Maddy's."

Clearly, he understood. "Dr. Sherman and I will follow you."

Nodding, Miriam watched him and Rose walk toward his black Chevy pickup truck. She smiled at the idea of a college professor driving a big Silverado, but he wasn't your typical college professor, was he? Nope. He was not, and good for Rose.

Maybe good for the family, too. Since he knew a lot about the gifts—*Gifts, my ass.*

But okay, if she was going to protect Maddy, Sadie and Mark and maybe get her son back, she had to focus and make everything right. She'd messed up when the kids were younger, but now she had the chance to make everything right, and she would. The hell with the police. She'd figure out a way to protect everyone and make things right herself.

Chapter 37
Wednesday

<hr>

Not only did Dr. Petrovsky help her up into the truck, but he looked believable behind the wheel. On the negative side, he seemed to be an extremely powerful spell-caster, *which, really, if you think about it, is just another way of saying "witch."* Still, in the midst of all the things she should have been thinking about, Rose had his elegant manners to consider, as well as the story he wanted to tell her and which he began before they'd even pulled out of the parking lot onto Morgan Street.

"The Soviets gathered many like me and you, removed us from our families, and, in my case, demanded that I cast spells to harm people deemed enemies. To force us, they threatened our families, you see?"

This part of the story she'd already heard, but she didn't want to interrupt, so she simply said, "Yes."

"There is still a bad part to this story."

"Bad" was one of those generalities her first-year students scattered through their papers like sesame seeds. It needed details to explain what the user meant—

"When I would not do as they asked, they killed my mother."

Words dried in her throat. She could only stare at his profile as he stared out the windshield.

"Not my mother only. Others refused, too. And they, too, lost beloved people. We rose up and killed guards and ran." He glanced over at her. "Bad."

In the broad scheme of the universe? In terms of karma? "Self-defense, wasn't it? They were abusing you. And they murdered people. I'm not sure you had a choice."

He seemed to concentrate on traffic around the highway entrance, which didn't need the level of concentration he was bestowing on it, since the exodus from Hartford was close to over. Besides, the merge onto 91 South from the Morgan Street ramp was easy, even when traffic was heavy. As they approached the first Wethersfield exit, he finally spoke. "You are concerned that E.S.P. would gather you up and perhaps force you to do things you do not wish to do. As the Soviets did."

What would you do if Pena were threatened, or Tava? What would you do, Rosie? "I *am* worried about it. More than worried. I'm frightened. But I think we have a more immediate problem."

He huffed a small chuckle. "A more immediate problem. Interesting words, considering the problem is a young woman who wishes to kill you and your cousins."

"Can you counter-spell her? Is that what you call it?"

He chuckled again, then sobered. "I can protect in various ways, yes. I will lay wards in your house and also Detective Fine's, and strengthen the ones for Madelyn and her children. But this young woman is...unpredictable, you see? Because she is self-taught, she follows no system. I do not know the pattern. Is that the word? Yes. I do not know the pattern of her spelling. It is odd to consider that this results in her being difficult to counter, as I do not think she understands what she does. Not truly. So..." He shrugged. "I do not know what to counter until I have felt her spells. This means you could face danger until I determine what she does."

Rose sighed, just as her belly signaled a cell phone call. Pena. At last. "My daughter is going to call. Will you excuse me, please?"

"Of course," he said.

He also nodded when she let it ring three times before she took the call. "Pena, hi. How are you?"

"I'm fine, Mom. Sorry, I haven't been calling. Tav and I...well, Maddy says you know about...ah…"

Oh, yes, the three younger cousins talked all the time. Just like their mothers.

"The gifts? Sweetheart, I'm sorry I didn't know about them when you were younger. When *I* was younger—" This needed to be a face-to-face conversation. The phone made it so difficult. Rose could hear sirens behind Pena's voice.

"Damn. Mom. I'm sorry, but I've got two ambulances coming in right now. Bad car accident. I'll call later."

Rose could hear the sirens. "But, Pena—"

The call went dead.

"Damn it. I need to talk to them." But Tava was finishing medical school, Pena was a nurse in the Emergency Department, and phone calls always seemed to go the way that one had gone. She just wanted to have an honest conversation. "Damn it."

"It is hard," he said softly.

She sighed loudly. "Impossible sometimes."

He said nothing until they parked on the street in front of Maddy's house. "That is young Detective Prentice's car."

When they walked into the house, they both heard voices raised in an obvious argument. Miriam and Sergeant Downs— *The Sergeant?* Yes, Miriam could argue about anything, but the Sergeant never raised his voice.

"You permit?" Petrovsky took Rose's hand and tucked it into the crook of his arm. "I say a small protection." He muttered a couple of words in Aramaic, making her scalp and back tingle for a second.

She smiled over her hand, said nothing, just walked with him into Maddy's living room. There stood Miriam and Sergeant Downs, almost nose to nose.

"He could be working for them—and so could you, for that matter, *Sergeant*," Miriam snarled.

"Miriam. It's me, for God's sake."

Prentice, whom Rose hadn't seen until now, spoke up. "I wouldn't. I wouldn't spy for those bastards. None of us would. They're—"

"You can say whatever you want, can't you? How do I know I can actually trust you? My daughter—my grandchildren—you—"

"Miriam?" Rose said quietly. She felt herself on the verge of crying, because Miriam and the Sergeant had always been so *solid*, but really, how would crying help? Miriam had panicked, obviously. She had cause, but panic was supposed to be Rose's job. "Miriam. We need to talk."

Miriam whirled on Rose, hand raised as if she were going to hit her. *Like Mother. Oh, God, Miriam is going to hit me.* Rose half-turned into Petrovsky's arm, wincing.

But the smack never came.

Instead, Miriam gasped. "Oh, God. Oh, God, Rosie. I'm so sorry. I would never—I would never hit anyone. Oh, Rosie."

Heart thudding away, Rose pushed herself off that solid, comforting arm and straightened herself up. *Nothing like a little flashback to get the blood flowing and the hot flash flashing.* "Miriam, I know you wouldn't, but you can't go paranoid on me. Please."

"They're still cops, they still work for that bastard Winewski, who is shilling for E.S.P. They could be—I don't know, they could be the people set to keep track of us."

"Never," Prentice said firmly, while Downie just stood staring at his partner.

"Detective Prentice has a gift. Unrealized," Petrovsky said, "but he is one of us."

"And I'm—" Sergeant Downs started, then sighed, his face suddenly the very illustration of sadness. "Miriam, we've been partners since you made detective. And I've been in love with you for I don't know how long. At least since Martha died. You know that. And if you seriously think I would betray you...you've betrayed me."

Rose held her breath as Miriam shut her eyes. "Miriam Fine!" she wanted to scream. "Listen to the man!" But she didn't say a word, not so much as a whisper. Because Miriam would only continue to argue. All she could do was watch as the Sergeant, *poor man,* nodded, then turned to Prentice.

"If you need me, call my cell."

He walked out past Miriam, whose eyes stayed shut.

"Rose," the Sergeant said softly, "Dr. Petrovsky." And he was gone, out the front door, which did *not* slam.

"Miriam," Rose whispered.

Miriam shook her head and opened her eyes. "He wants me to see things from Winewski's point of view. 'He's just scared,'" she said in a mocking tone, then raised her voice. "Too fucking bad." She stepped around Rose and walked to the bottom of the stairs, looked back at Rose, shook her head, and started up.

"Madelyn and the kids are upstairs," Detective Prentice said. "Detec—Mrs. Fine sent them upstairs and just—"

"Went off on you," Rose said.

"Yes, ma'am. And the Sergeant—"

"This situation is difficult for everyone," Petrovsky said. "Even I am upset. Afraid. E.S.P. is...unknown entity."

Rose walked to an armchair and sat. "Here's the thing. We saw David Levine talking to those men from E.S.P. and—"

"Mrs. Fine told us about that when she came in. That's what set it off." Prentice slapped his thigh. "Damn it. Sorry, but I only ever wanted to help people, and being a cop felt like the best way to do it. But you can't surveil people who haven't done anything. It's not right. So I guess I have to quit. It's the right thing to do."

"Will you be all right, though?" Rose asked. She didn't know whether the man had any money or family to fall back on. "If you quit?"

He grinned at her. "Yes, ma'am. A private security firm has been trying to recruit me for a while now. I guess I'll let them."

"Good for you," Rose said. "It's—"

Sadie bounced into the living room. "Cousin Rose, Gramma says to ask you to please make me a peanut butter 'n jelly samich. Please."

Time to pretend everything is okay. A handy skill picked up in childhood. "I'll be happy to, Sadie. Would anyone else like a sandwich?"

Both men decided to join Sadie in a PB and J feast. Rose, realizing it had been a long time since lunch, declared PB and J all around. Then, having settled everyone else with sandwiches and milk or tea, she was about to sit and eat when she realized her phone was going to ring. Hannah, panicky Hannah, was punching in the number.

The phone, in her purse, was on the floor in the living room. She excused herself and went to get the damned thing. When it rang, she made no pretense about needing caller ID.

"Hannah, what's the matter?"

"Rose, she called. My daughter called. She demanded that I meet her tomorrow morning at Elizabeth Park. But Miriam said—I can't go. Can I? Should I go? Will she listen if I try to explain? I'd like to explain. But I don't know—"

"Excuse me, Hannah. Why are you calling *me?*" A cold response, but could Hannah really have expected anything else? Considering that Hannah had cut ties with her and told monumental lies about her and Miriam and Aunt Fanny, who only ever helped the three of them—"I can't do anything to stop her. That's why there's a police officer watching Maddy and the kids and—"

"I don't know what to do, Rose. I can't talk to David about it—"

"Sure you can, Hannah. He's your husband. Better him than Miriam and me, right? Good-bye." *And if he had betrayed his wife, too damned bad. Hannah had betrayed the two people she grew up with. She'd lied about them, David had lied to her, and things came full circle. Too damned bad.*

For a second, maybe two, she actually felt good about letting Hannah stew in her own juices. The woman had lied and—

But, Rose. It's when people are at their most unlovable that they most need to be loved. Damn it. Besides. It's Hannah. A Winkler. One of Nana Pearl's granddaughters. Nana had just three: Miriam, Rose, and Hannah. Damn it.

Sighing, Rose punched Hannah's number into the phone, swearing softly so Sadie couldn't hear.

"Rose?"

"Yes. Give me the details. When and where?"

"Tomorrow morning at 7, by the gazebo in the Rose Garden in Elizabeth Park."

Away from any passing traffic and before the morning joggers would get that far into the park. "Okay. I'll talk to Miriam and get back to you."

"Thank you, Rose. I know I don't deserve help—"

"Don't. Just don't. We'll talk about what you deserve later." Would they ever. The bitch was going to grovel—*Rosie, Rosie, Rosie. You won't like yourself if you make Hannah grovel. The fantasy might be fun, but doing the right thing feels better in the long run. Besides, Nana Pearl is probably watching.*

Damn it.

Rose peeked into the kitchen, where Sadie and the two men were discussing peanut butter, chunky or smooth. Sadie already understood how adorable she was; clearly, she had both men convinced.

So it was safe for Rose to go upstairs, find Miriam, and figure out how to help Hannah, not to mention stop the woman who wanted to kill them all.

And maybe make some points with Nana Pearl. A bonus. Damn it.

Chapter 38
Wednesday

<hr>

Hannah's hands shook as she set the phone down on the counter. Her daughter, not some nameless random person, the child she'd given birth to, wanted to kill her. And Rose, who used to be so quiet and always followed along as if Hannah were Queen of the Universe, *that* Rose had pretty much told her to go get herself killed.

Yes, Rose had called back and offered help of sorts; she would talk to Miriam and see what Miriam wanted to do. But she'd been so cold. No more sweet little Rosie.

Did she honestly think Hannah had meant for this to happen? No one could honestly think that.

All right, yes, she'd told lies back when she gave up the baby. But they were just *stories* she'd told. How could anyone have believed *stories*? How could anyone hold her responsible for what was happening now?

It was all…ridiculous. Just ridiculous.

Nevertheless. The fact remained. The baby she'd given up years ago had grown up crazy *and* with powers and was now coming after her.

David could never know about any of this, not the baby, not the powers, not the threats, none of it. Thank God she was getting a headache. She could wait for Rose's call in bed, and David could eat leftovers or takeout.

As she took herself to the bedroom to start undressing for bed, an awful thought occurred to her. What if Miriam wouldn't help—no. Not possible. Miriam had told her Sara, that was her daughter's name after all, Sara was trying to kill Miriam and Rose, too. So they would help her if only to help themselves. Of course they would.

Miriam would arrest Sara or...something, and it would be done. And everything would be fine.

Everything had to be fine.

Chapter 39
Wednesday

◆ ◆ ◆

Last night had been...interesting, Peter decided. When he found their encampment, he knew the rogues had been smart about it. Of course they had. They were wolves, *Homo lupus,* highly intelligent. They had encroached on LeBeau territory, a foolish thing, but they had been smart about it. Not that Peter would say so aloud, but these rogues had done well. They found a natural clearing well away from human habitation and near a small pond. They buried all their waste, including the bones and clothing from their meals, carefully away from their camp. And they used the same scent trails to come *and* go. Smart.

Although that encampment had been abandoned, the rogues were still in the area. Fresh scent trails led up toward Simsbury. Martin and the rest of the LeBeau pack had to do something about them.

Martin had a tame vampire with excellent hearing and the ability to see in the dark, far better than any wolf.

So Peter and Emile sat in Emile's Subaru in the parking lot at the Big Y supermarket on North Main Street, waiting for instructions from Martin. The odors of the grocery store, particularly the bakery, distracted well from the aromas of the few humans shopping after dark. Peter closed his eyes to wait, but Emile insisted on watching traffic in the lot. At regular intervals, the wolf gasped or swore under his breath.

"Mon Dieu!" he shouted finally. "Where did these humans learn to drive?"

Peter opened one eye and looked at the wolf. "They *are* amateurs, Emile."

"Even an amateur knows to look before he backs out of a parking space. That...*fou* just got into his car and backed up. He missed that Taurus by an inch. Possibly less."

Peter shut his eyes. "You might be more comfortable if we leave the lot. A little drive along Simsbury Road to settle you?"

"I have my instructions. I am to wait here."

He had created awkwardness for the wolf. "Of course, Emile. Forgive me. I am perfectly content to wait here." That was the truth. He could rest here because the wolf watched.

"Thank you."

"I like shutting my eyes here." Peter waved a hand in the direction of the windshield. "It shuts out the human misbehavior."

"I don't want to be startled."

Peter opened both eyes now and straightened. "Of course you do not." A truly started wolf could lose control. "That would be most unfortunate."

"I thought so."

"It is good that one of us is thinking tonight, Emile."

"Thank you." The wolf almost smiled.

"I think of waiting as just waiting." Peter shrugged one shoulder. "Unless I am stalking, of course. Then it is something else altogether."

"It is." The wolf smiled now, openly the predator, perhaps remembering his last hunt. "It is."

Peter's phone rang. "Alpha," he said.

"Vampire. We have found several scent trails, all converging on Penwood Park."

Emile nodded and started the car before Peter answered. "We are on our way. I will locate the encampment."

"You will find us at the edge of the lake near the park entrance. Thank you, vampire." The call ended.

Having backed into the parking space, Emile now pulled out into the driving lane and exited the lot onto North Main Street. He drove at the speed limit on Simsbury Road and made the left turn.

Again, he maintained the vehicle at the speed limit until the road narrowed, resembling the country lane that was its origin. Then he slowed to 20 miles an hour. "We are approaching the park now."

Thank you, Emile. I am going invisible now."

"I will be with my Alpha."

"Of course. I am leaving the car now." Peter rose up through the roof of the car and hovered to survey his surroundings as he faced the park. The road lay in darkness, and the woods appeared uninterrupted. He was nowhere near the trails that made Penwood popular with hikers. Emile and he had agreed the rogues would avoid any regularly used trails and picnic spots, thinking that missing hikers, especially in a place like Penwood Park, in a wealthy community like Simsbury, would be noticed and bring exposure. He did not require reminding that the rogues were only foolish, not stupid.

Peter now entered the trees and listened. At first, he could still hear the buzz of Emile's car, but that was easy to ignore. He also heard various insects that had been fooled by the unusual warmth in the air. Somewhere to the west, five or six hundred feet away, a bobcat had frozen in place, perhaps scenting his presence.

Closer to him, to his east, an eastern screech owl sang its lovely tremolo. All the tiny prey animals that he could smell, particularly voles and rabbits, froze at the sound, or perhaps it was his presence, but he smiled at the song.

However, it was not his task to enjoy the dark forest or his invisible flight. He was supposed to be listening for the rogues. He heard nothing to suggest their presence, so he began to float around the trees, first a hundred feet farther away from the road, then a hundred feet to his left, startling that bobcat into running from him. He waited until he could not hear that creature before he turned to the east and moved diagonally along, stopping every now and then to listen.

Finally, he heard what he knew to be two feet walking through leaf litter. The sound was tiny, almost imperceptible, but it was unmistakable. Two feet, not four, took a few steps and stopped.

Now Peter had to take care. Even so, he smiled, fangs bared though no one could see them as he flew toward the noise. He had to stay downwind of his targets—not his prey. The ones he stalked were magicals, like him, and did not smell like prey. They were his targets, but targets with an extraordinary sense of smell. He could see in the dark and hear better than the owls and bobcats and wolves, but *Homo lupus* could detect him with their noses better than any bear or vulture could.

He therefore took a course oblique to the noise, avoiding any branches, noiseless except for the necessary sound of his breath. More than once, he stopped to make sure he was heading in the correct direction.

Because the trees were still bare, Peter saw them sooner than he would have later in the season. He stilled his breath and counted. Eight in human form, three in half-wolf, four in full wolf, all male, none obviously starving, but scrawny, all of them, even the young ones.

The smallest might have been a pup, too young to be away from his mother—a question for Martin, not the vampire. Peter also noted that one of the wolves in human form wore a makeshift sling in which his right arm rested. They shared the remains of two humans, and as Peter watched, two of the half-wolves gave the injured one a share of the flesh. Human flesh.

He could not stay there any longer, inhaling the aroma of that meat and blood. It was tempting, almost arousing.

Peter turned away, moved as quickly as he could, startled an owl, and did not linger to know whether the rogues heard the owl's displeasure. The aroma of human blood persisted in his memory, if not in reality, so he flew toward the lake where he knew he would find Martin. He forced himself to listen to the insects and little creatures prowling the forest for their nightly meals, and by the time he smelled familiar wolves, he was calm again, or perhaps only calmer. At least the temptation to hunt was gone.

He found Martin easily. The Alpha sat, looking quite human, on a stump just at the edge of the pretty little lake one saw in flashes through the trees if driving past the park in daylight. He was flanked by Jean-Claude and Jean-Marc in half form, and Emile behind him, now also in half. Martin's *tachi*, longer than a *katana*, honed and ready for killing, should it be necessary, lay across his lap.

Peter became visible and alit a few feet away from the wolves, none of whom smelled entirely calm, even to Peter's lesser nose. He bowed to the Alpha, and all four wolves bared their throats. He understood the daring, now, of that gesture— of all the predators in the park tonight, *he* was the one all the others had to fear, but they offered him their vulnerable throats. Peter realized, too, how easily Martin could swing that long sword and cut his head off when he bowed. Even so, he bowed: one predator honoring another.

"Alpha," he said. "There are fifteen rogue wolves in a clearing about two and a half miles from here. One is injured, but they are sharing food with him. Unfortunately, the food is two human bodies."

Martin grunted. "You are sure."

Peter stared at Martin. Who would ask a vampire whether he knew human blood? "Alpha," was all he said.

Now Martin huffed. "Of course, you are sure."

"I am also sure they are a coherent group," Peter said. "They are scrawny, not well fed, but they are taking care of one another. I suspect the blade will have its fill of blood tonight."

Frowning, Martin nodded. Peter knew he would have liked to recruit at least a few more wolves into the pack. He wanted to bring LeBeau to the numbers they had before World War Two. The pack did have the resources to support many more members, and a bigger pack meant he could negotiate with other packs to bring at least another female or two into the territory. The rogues were themselves a true pack, however, loyal to their own, making LeBeau's expansion unlikely tonight.

"Location?" the Alpha asked.

Peter closed his eyes to remember. "A mile northwest of the main park sign on the street. They are quiet and careful."

"You will start them running, please, and Emile will please watch for anyone who escapes the circle."

Emile nodded. Of course Emile nodded. His Alpha only sounded as if he were asking.

"I will lead Emile to the place now."

"Thank you."

Peter turned into the woods, hearing Emile's padded steps behind him. They moved quickly toward the spot Peter remembered, knowing Emile's nose would let them know if they were off the trail. He did not worry this time about staying downwind of the rogues, just went straight for them.

When Peter could see the other wolves, he gestured Emile behind a tree, then went invisible and waited for a signal that the rest of Martin's wolves were ready. Someone coughed behind him, not Emile, and Peter alit in the middle of the rogues' clearing and made himself visible.

"My friends," he said. "You are in the territory of—" He had to fly up a few feet to avoid the rush of half-wolves and their teeth.

Looking down on the angry rogues, he spoke again. "You are in the territory of the LeBeau pack without invitation or permission. You—"

"We don't require permission," one of the human-looking wolves said.

Peter ignored him. "You are killing humans in LeBeau territory. We do not permit—"

"We?" someone said. "You are not a wolf."

Now Peter grinned, showing the fools his fangs. "Nevertheless, we do not permit—"

Not so foolish, those wolves. They knew exactly what his fangs meant. They scattered. One of the half-wolves, he noticed, led the injured one away. Too bad they were likely going to die. They did take care of one another.

"Coming your way," Peter called and swooped down to snatch one of the human-looking wolves by the arm. He rose again. The wolf flailed wildly for a moment, which Peter had no patience for. He cuffed the fool's head, not too hard, not as hard as he would have liked to. The fool stilled.

Peter adjusted his grip to be sure he would not drop his burden until it was time and flew to the spot where Martin and the twins waited. When Peter lowered his captive to the ground, Martin nodded. "The others are running?"

"For some reason, my fangs frightened them." Peter raised his eyebrows. "This one was a little slower fleeing."

Martin's sense of humor had also apparently fled. "Will you check the others, please?"

Peter cocked his head. "You do not wish me to hold the sword." It fell to him, generally, to deliver the *phyle's* judgment.

"This is particularly the pack's business, vampire."

Peter bowed. "Of course, Alpha."

This time, Peter walked into the woods until he was sure the temptation to mutter "Your ever faithful pet vampire obeys" had passed. Peter *knew* this business belonged to the pack. Wolves defend their territory, no matter how much they look or behave like humans. He *knew* that the human form is camouflage, even if there was a real Picasso hanging opposite a real Mondrian in the Alpha's living room.

But to be excluded now confirmed that he had stayed too long. The pack would take care of its own. The casters would take care of themselves and the pack when needed. And he could just stop.

Not yet, however. He heard sounds of wolves fighting, lifted into the air, and flew to the melee. Three of Martin's wolves fought five of the rogues. Martin's wolves had the matter in hand, so to speak, but Peter's patience, already thin, snapped.

He grabbed one rogue and threw him into the nearest tree, snatched another, and started up. The wolf yelped, of course he did, and tried to claw himself free, so Peter dropped him. The fall did not kill the wolf, but the crack of bones satisfied the vampire.

He would have swooped at another, but the rogues were beginning to give themselves up. Ignoring the thanks of Martin's wolves, Peter snatched up the two he'd broken and carried them to Martin. He dropped them among the rogues now under watch by several of the pack members and flew back into the woods.

Behind him, he knew, were only fourteen rogues who would be given the choice of the discipline of the pack or the sword. Someone, he thought it might be the little one, had eluded the circle. Peter went back to the small clearing and breathed in all the scents. The human blood he set aside. He might have to do something...interesting later, but for now, he followed the scent of wolf overlaid with fear, not mingled with anger like the other trails.

This frightened wolf had somehow eluded all of the LeBeau wolves and run toward Simsbury Road, almost to the spot where Peter had left Emile's car. The stink of fear grew stronger the closer Peter got to the road, so he made himself invisible and went the last few feet to the street silently.

No wolf, but two Lincoln Navigators filled with humans sat idling across the street with their lights off. A bad choice on this stretch of narrow, winding road. Humans do not, after all, have night vision.

Vampires do. Despite the heavily tinted windows on the two SUVs, Peter could see men, ages hard to guess but young-looking, with military haircuts, white shirts, skinny black ties, and black suit jackets. A match for the vehicle that had been parked for two days behind the Little League field in West Hartford.

Peter considered ignoring the vehicles and just following the scent of the frightened wolf, but he wanted to see what these *salauds* would do. Within seconds of his decision, the driver of the first car took a call on his cell phone.

"Yes, we have one," the driver said.

"Bring the specimen in," he was told, "and then join the surveillance in Wethersfield."

"Yes, sir." As soon as the call ended, the driver appeared to set his phone aside and flashed his headlights twice. Without waiting for a response of some sort from the car behind him, he started his vehicle, turned on his headlights, and pulled away, closely followed by the second vehicle, toward West Hartford.

Peter had not eaten enough, he knew well, to follow them. He did not have time or energy to think about what or who might be in Wethersfield that merited surveillance. He had to follow the scent of the escaped wolf. Once the noise of the two Navigators faded away, and he could be reasonably sure they were not coming back, Peter alit and walked into the road. The wolf-and-fear stink vanished abruptly where the second vehicle had been parked.

He did not reproach himself for not having gotten close enough to look into either vehicle's cargo space. Single-handed, he could not have taken on eight military-trained human males.

Four in one vehicle, he could have managed, but he expected the four in the second vehicle would almost certainly have recovered their wits quickly. Even if he had remained invisible, they would have taken shots at him with who knew what sort of weapons.

One lucky hit would have stopped him, likely making it impossible for him to maintain his invisibility. And he would have been company for the kidnapped wolf. Or they would have missed him and escaped, but with confirmation of the existence of a creature that could turn invisible.

Was the invisible creature detectable with infrared vision? The invisible creature had no idea except that the time for speculation was later.

Now, the invisible creature—Peter did like that locution—had to report this incident to the Alpha of the LeBeau pack. This incident was interesting, but more than that, it was worrying.

No mistake. Peter the Vampire was worried for his *phyle* and his friends. He had to set aside thoughts of the sword on his neck until he knew the *phyle* was safe.

Chapter 40
Wednesday

Miriam sat on the double bed in the dark guest room and sniffled. Again.

Sniffling was better than the sobbing that had come earlier, but it was still crying, which she did not do. She hadn't cried on the job, she hadn't cried when Izzy left—she came close when David decided to go with Izzy, closer when she found out why he'd gone with his father. But seeing David Levine with those men and then hearing Mike say what he said, and then Downie said what he said, and—

She only wanted things to be calm and rational and simple again. That's all she wanted. No fancy gifts, no fear—

A soft tap on the door was followed by, "Miriam? Can I come in?"

That was Rose, who seemed to be handling all the changes fairly well, except for Hannah's lies. Rose was not taking Hannah's lies well at all. In fact, given Rose's recent behavior, if Hannah were to die in questionable circumstances, Rose would be the number one person of interest. No doubt about it. Aside from that, Rose was okay. Rose would listen and understand.

"Come in."

Rose walked in, shut the door behind her, and sat next to Miriam on the bed. She said nothing about the darkness.

"If you don't want to talk about it, that's okay," she said instead.

Miriam sniffled. "It just all got to be too much. Too damned much. It's all just so irrational. And those bastards from E.S.P. And the fucking lieutenant said that. I couldn't take anymore."

"It's scary, too."

"And then Downie—I owe him a major apology."

Rose didn't say anything, which generally meant she agreed. Downie was definitely due an apology, possibly involving groveling, a lot of groveling. Tonight would be best.

"He'll understand," Rose said suddenly. "You know how he feels about you."

She did. And that was part of the problem. She was definitely attracted to him. Hell, she really liked him—Okay, maybe she loved him. But she didn't know what to do about it. She hadn't dated anyone since Izzy left. She didn't know if she wanted to take the chance. And however much she resisted her father's religion, dating a Catholic man, even a non-practicing one, felt...odd. "Life used to be so much simpler," she said. "Why can't we go back to when life was simpler?"

"You mean when I had to deal with my crazy mother? Or when I didn't know Harry had a girlfriend? Or when we didn't know Hannah had told terrible lies about us? And herself? That simpler?"

Or that Izzy was scaring the kids? Or—"Yeah. Okay. I just want things to be...normal. Can I have something normal? Not telepathic or telekinetic or—just normal?"

"Oh, God, Mir. That was the dream of my childhood. Just to be like everyone else." Rose chuckled. "That did *not* happen."

Miriam sighed. "So, no normal, huh?"

"I can't offer normality, no. I'm not even sure I can define it. However, I can offer you news. I guess it's news. Maybe it's just new. Hannah called me."

Could Rose see her stare in the dark? Because that was all Miriam felt capable of doing. She stared at Rose as if her cousin had grown two heads, wings, and a tail. Which, given recent events, might actually be possible.

"She said Sara called her and demanded a face-to-face meeting tomorrow morning in Elizabeth Park. At seven by the gazebo."

"What?" Miriam couldn't believe Hannah had called. No. Of course she could believe it. Hannah was the embodiment of *chutzpah*, wasn't she? Oh, yes, she was. "And she wants our help, right?"

"I told her we'd get back to her. I'd really like to leave her to the consequences, but we can't. Can we?"

Miriam sighed. "Damn it. It's so tempting not to, but of course we have to help her. She's one of Nana Pearl's granddaughters, right? And Sara wants to kill us, too. We have to stop her. Damn it." She sighed again. "Okay. Let me call Downie and grovel. And then we'll talk to Hannah."

"I really don't think you'll have to grovel, Mir. But I'll be downstairs when you're ready."

"Thank you, Rose." And *God bless her good, not-so-naive-anymore cousin.*

"You're welcome, Mir." Rose stood up and walked to the door, where she stopped. "You know. If I could summon Godzilla to stomp on Hannah? I would. I know we're going to help her, but Hannah deserves to be toe dirt on Godzilla's left foot. Just so you know how I feel."

Toe dirt on Godzilla's left foot. Seriously? Miriam started to chuckle.

So did Rose.

The chuckle quickly escalated to laughter, roaring, belly-shaking, tears-rolling-down-the-cheeks laughter. Rose plunked herself down on the bed next to Miriam, and they just roared together.

The door was pushed open, and Maddy leaned into the room. "For God's sake, Ma. I just got Mark to sleep," she hissed.

"Sorry, sorry, my fault," Rose gasped.

"Me, too," Miriam managed to get out before she snorted at least once. "We'll go downstairs."

"And send Sadie up, please. And tell her to be quiet."

But Sadie was busy with Dr. Petrovsky, hiding crayons in corners and next to doors. Why? Miriam had to wait for the answer because Rose took a look at her face and sent her to the bathroom to put cold water on her eyes.

While she was in there, she called Downie.

"Miriam." He sounded concerned rather than angry.

"I lost it there, Downie. Just...overwhelmed. But taking it out on you was way over the line. It won't happen a—"

"It's okay, Mir. We're good. We're good."

"Thank you." His patience was a gift. "You should know. Hannah called Rose to say that Sara wants a face-to-face tomorrow morning by the gazebo in Elizabeth Park. Seven a.m."

"Hannah will end up dead."

"Not if we go with her." Her hand rose to touch *Tannah*. "We—"

"Got it. You still at Maddy's?"

"Yes."

"Give me 15 minutes."

"Thank you."

"See you in a few."

He might be the gift. Truly.

Better to find out what Sadie was doing with the good doctor. The two of them were now at the kitchen door, taping a pink crayon against the jamb near the floor.

"You say magic words now, please," Petrovsky said, squatting next to Sadie.

Sadie touched the crayon, closed her eyes, and said, "Please and thank you."

As she spoke, Petrovsky whispered a few words in Hebrew. A shiver ran up Miriam's spine and across her scalp at the same time. Damn, but that was creepy.

Petrovsky smiled as he straightened up. "Now, you see, badness cannot come into this house."

Sadie looked quite pleased with herself. "That's good. I don't like badness. It's scary."

Miriam could only agree and feel a little sad that Sadie knew about badness. "If you're all done, Mommy wants you upstairs."

Sadie sighed dramatically.

"Go on, Sweet Pea. Help Mommy."

"Fine." Sadie walked out of the kitchen, her head hanging down as if she were going to her doom. But she went.

"Are you serious?" Rose asked Petrovsky as soon as Sadie started up the stairs. "Can a bunch of crayons really keep bad people, which I assume means people with bad intentions, from coming into the house?"

"Not merely crayons," Petrovsky said with a small smile. "The child's favorite crayons. Used by her, enjoyed by her, suffused with a child's innocence. And her words, said with intention and reinforced by my words. It is a simple spell, but it is truly powerful. Only good people can come into this house now."

"Like a lie detector," Rose said, "but for intentions rather than lies. Very nice."

Petrovsky bowed in her direction.

Prentice, who had also been watching the performance, piped up. "You really think I can learn to do that?"

"*Da.* Yes. I know you are capable."

"And the private security firm? Can you do both?" Miriam asked.

"I hope so," Prentice said. "Dr. Petrovsky—"

The doorbell rang.

Prentice stood almost instantly, weapon in hand. "I'll get it. Please stay back," he said, leaving the kitchen before Miriam could even argue about the gun. If Petrovsky and Sadie's charms worked, he shouldn't need—*had she seriously just thought that?* She had. She was putting her faith, such as it was, in magic. *Dear God in Heaven.*

A moment later, Prentice came back into the room, followed by Downie.

So, Downie had passed through the charms, meaning he was a good man. Had she really needed that confirmation?

Besides, he carried two large pizzas from Vito's. A very good man.

"Supper and planning," he said.

"Shall I call Hannah?" Rose said.

Setting the pizzas down on the table, Downie nodded. "Tell her we'll be at the park at 6:30."

"The park doesn't open until sunrise," Rose pointed out.

"It'll be okay."

"He's a police officer, Rosie," Miriam said, smiling.

"Oh. Right. Okay." Rose walked out of the kitchen, phone in hand.

"Shall we plan?" Downie said.

Everyone agreed as Miriam pulled paper plates from a cabinet. "And eat." Suddenly starving, she settled herself at the table and passed around the plates. "I suppose we have to arrest Sara *before* she hurts Hannah?"

Downie grinned across the table at her. "As tempted as I know you and Rose are to let Hannah have a little taste of pain, I think we ought to stop her daughter before there's any physical damage, yes."

"Can we do it?" Prentice asked.

"I am thinking of a way," Petrovsky said and began to explain.

Miriam didn't argue, even when his explanation involved the use of spells.

Chapter 41
Thursday

<hr>

Rose pulled the scarf higher on her neck and checked the buttons of her short winter jacket again. The weather had reverted to cold, damp mid-March form, of course, on the morning she had agreed to help save Hannah. *No good deed goes unpunished. At least be grateful you're not standing in the middle of a March nor'easter. It's just cold. Okay, raw. But you won't be here for long. And there's chocolate waiting.*

Besides, she wasn't alone in the miserable dawn. Miriam stood about ten feet to her right, Downie stood about ten feet to her left, and Dr. Petrovsky stood about ten feet behind her. All of them breathed white plumes into the dark.

The real problem wasn't the cold, because not quite 30 degrees isn't that cold, not really. No, the trouble was that she couldn't babble. Talking would break Dr. Petrovsky's concentration as he chanted the words that would keep them hidden from the eyes of anyone passing by the park on Asylum Avenue or coming into the park, including Hannah Levine and Sara Berman.

Hannah had been told her cousins would be there, unseen; whether she would remember anything her cousin said was a question Rose didn't want to consider. She didn't feel capable of considering much at all. She felt capable only of wishing she had worn her long coat and hadn't given up caffeine. *Where are those hot flashes when you actually want them?*

As she listened to Petrovsky's barely audible Hebrew, she let her eyes sweep the area. To her right, illuminated by the safety lights, she saw the greenhouses and the parking lot, empty except for Sergeant Down's grey SUV.

Then she saw the line of trees that separated the lot from the great lawn and the rose garden, which she had to imagine in the dim morning light. She knew the plants were pruned almost to the ground, knew the gazebo, which stood on a small rise in the middle of the garden, was bare of the vines that covered it in summer. But she could barely see any of that. She could see the Pond House restaurant and the pond behind it to her left because of the security lights around the building, and she could make out the trees that lined the footpath and the beautiful stone bridge over the stream that fed the pond, but she was standing in the cold and the almost-dark, and she had to wonder whether they could have or should have handled this problem some other way.

She couldn't ask; she had to keep quiet while Petrovsky chanted, and when he finished his spell, she had to be quiet because his words made human eyes slide over people without registering their presence, but the spell didn't stop human ears from hearing.

So until Sara Berman came into the park, Rose had to swallow the urge to ask Miriam where she'd stashed the chocolate bars, whether she was carrying her gun, whether *Tannah* was secure, pinned as it was to Miriam's glove—absurd really, but those questions distracted her from her nervousness, she knew. She babbled when she was nervous and made other people crazy. It was her shtick.

When the mild tap dance, maybe a soft shoe, began in her belly. Rose knew it wasn't nervous butterflies. Focusing her attention on the sensation, she knew that Hannah was coming into the park. Precognition, the original gift, *if you want to call it a gift*. She carefully didn't snort.

Rose knew the car was coming in the Asylum Avenue entrance, behind them. She pointed that way and breathed to calm her nerves. The others would see Hannah as soon as she got out of the car, which logically she would park in the lot by the greenhouses, since she had to go to the gazebo, straight across the lawn, and through the rose garden.

Now, all Rose had to do, besides shivering to stay warm and keep quiet, was wait for Hannah's daughter to show up, and then she had to stay in place to help anchor the spell.

Okay, fine. She would do that, but it just gave her one more reason to be angry at Hannah, utterly, entirely, completely, thoroughly pissed.

****

Miriam watched Hannah get out of her car and turn on a flashlight. The woman shone the flashlight around as if she were looking for someone before she started walking toward the naked rose garden and the gazebo that sat on a small rise in the middle of the garden. Every few steps, she stopped and looked around.

Nervous. Definitely nervous.

Good. Hannah had caused this whole damned mess. Well, no, not entirely. She had lied, but the craziness was a family problem. Still, Hannah wasn't an innocent victim. Miriam had

313

never expected much from Hannah, so she wasn't particularly disappointed or even angry except about the fact that Hannah wouldn't acknowledge her very real part in this mess. She'd told a mean lie about her cousins when she didn't have to lie at all except to make herself look better and justify her selfishness. As if she didn't *want* to give up her daughter, she *had* to. Poor Hannah.

Miriam also felt a little stunned at her own willingness to help anchor a spell. She'd noticed last night that she was willing to let spells protect her child and grandchildren, but that was more or less passive. This? Not so passive. The handsome Russian Rosie had found could explain it all as a manipulation of quanta, nothing supernatural at all, but it looked like what witches and wizards performed in the old fairy tales. It looked like magic, and she was definitely helping a magician.

So she breathed deeply and concentrated on keeping her hands still. And she watched Hannah make her hesitant way to the gazebo where her daughter had told her to go.

As soon as they had arrived in the park, Petrovsky and Downie checked the place thoroughly to make sure Sara wasn't waiting, invisible, to murder her mother before anyone knew what she was doing. Then Petrovsky had led them onto the lawn and arranged the four of them at compass points, Rose to the north, himself to the south, her to the west, and Downie to the east. When he was satisfied that they were properly positioned, he began to chant softly in Hebrew, too softly for her to understand the words, though her scalp crawled with the wash of magic.

Miriam heaved a breath and considered what would happen when they stopped Sara Berman. What would they do with a paranoid spell-caster? What *could* they do with a paranoid spell-caster? They hadn't even talked about that part of the operation last night. They'd talked about stopping the woman and catching her, but no one had even asked about what they would do afterward. And it was too late to talk about it now.

Really, she and Downie should have just brought HPD in and arrested Sara Berman, even though Petrovsky didn't think they'd be able to do that. The young woman was all too willing to kill, and she threw power around wildly, as if it didn't cost her anything. It would take a spell-caster and other talents to capture her, he insisted.

But then what?

Miriam didn't like to plan too tightly because she knew nothing ever went strictly according to plan. But this was no plan at all. She didn't like it, but she had to stand there, quiet per orders, watching Hannah the Liar, who had reached the bottom of the steps leading up the little rise to the gazebo. She was doing a bad job of hiding her nerves, jiggling her hands in her pockets, bouncing on her toes. Not such a sophisticated woman now.

Okay, okay. Sara Berman had to be stopped. She had murdered at least three people that they knew of, she had to be stopped before she murdered more people, and Miriam Fine was going to help stop her and keep Maddy and little Sadie and Mark safe. *And Rose. And Downie. And everyone else she loved.*

She was a police officer, using the means she had at hand to stop a supernatural killer. What happened after that would happen. She'd just have to wait and see.

****

Why had she come here? Hannah couldn't answer the question. Truly. Her daughter wasn't her daughter, not really. Giving birth didn't confer motherhood on a woman. Raising the child, the thing she had not done, made a mother.

Still, she stood there, waiting to meet the child she'd given up in 1985 and feeling nervous, but not upset about it, as she'd been last night. She'd definitely been upset then. But not because she was convinced her daughter was trying to kill her. She didn't believe Miriam's story at all. That story was a lie meant to frighten Hannah into falling into line, the dutiful cousin following Miriam, ever so important Miriam, the cop, the Big Deal—

Who was supposed to be somewhere near the gazebo. Wasn't that what Rose said last night? Rose said she and Miriam would be near the gazebo. So where were they?

Not here. Probably home, sitting comfortably with tea and the morning paper, if they weren't still tucked up nice and warm in bed. Wherever they were, they were laughing at her. And if Sara Berman didn't show up soon, Hannah was going to go home and make a cup of tea and forget any of this had ever happened. This whole thing was ridiculous. Just ridiculous.

****

Rose glanced over her shoulder at Petrovsky, who had stopped chanting and smiled at her. He didn't seem bothered by the cold, just stood there calmly, waiting.

The morning was fairly quiet. Most of the migratory birds hadn't made their comeback yet, Rose thought. The morning commute hadn't started in earnest, so only a few cars passed the park on the Asylum Avenue side. Otherwise, nothing much was going on. Maybe—

An elephant stomped down hard in her gut. No dancing this time. A marching, breath-stealing elephant of pain doubled her over almost before she knew what was happening. Past the noise of her desperate gasps for breath and the bass-drum rhythm of her heart syncopating with the elephant, she heard someone mutter *"O gospodi"* and felt arms around her.

Petrovsky?

"She's...there." Rose could point, even if she could barely breathe. Across the park, on the other side of the lake, behind the Pond House. "Car. No lights. Coming in off Prospect. Very angry."

The pain eased. It was happening, so no more precognition. Rose simply knew now. Not quite with the other woman, not seeing directly over her shoulder, but "like a dream," she murmured, caught her breath, and straightened.

Petrovsky did not let her go. "Tell me," he whispered.

"She's furious. She wants Hannah dead *now*. She's past the park entrance, considering where to park. But what should we *do?* She doesn't have any weapons, just some charms and—I don't know how I know all of this. How do I know all of this?"

"A powerful emotional connection," he said. "You are a powerful woman." He squeezed her shoulders. And he let her go.

"Holy shit!" Miriam muttered.

Rose looked up and saw why. The trees on the other side of the lake, where Sara had parked her car, whipped around as if a strong wind were blowing. No other trees in the park moved, just the ones around the spot where Sara Berman sat waiting for 7 a.m. on the dot. The wind whined through the bare branches, and the trees creaked.

"It's her," Rose said, watching the trees move around in the gale of Sara Berman's emotional storm. "I don't think she knows she's doing it. Or she doesn't care. But it's her. Her anger."

****

The bitches were going to die this morning. First, her birth mother, who'd given her to those people who claimed to love her, and then the two cousins who had turned her birth mother away when she needed them.

Her mother's breath would freeze in her lungs. And she would know who was killing her. She would see her daughter, her flesh and blood, whom she had abandoned all those years ago to be unloved and unwanted.

She would suffocate slowly in great pain. And Sara would stand over her so she'd know, as she died, what her daughter looked like and the great power she possessed.

It was time.

****

In the dawn light, Miriam watched the wind whip the trees that stood across the lake as if they were caught in a hurricane. Starlings flew up, twittering in panic. And the wind began to travel.

"She's coming," Rose called.

Unnecessary. The trees calmed in one spot and began to lash against one another a little further up the road. More birds tore out of the branches, squawking and shrieking across the park.

It was terrifying to watch, knowing that one person made it happen. But Miriam kept watching.

She jumped when a loud crack carried across the pond and a branch, a big one by the sound of it, crashed to the ground.

Hannah had to be seeing it, too. The gazebo sat well to the left of the direct path the wind was taking, but the trees were tall and easily visible from everywhere in the rose garden and on the lawn. Anyone could hear the trees move. Anyone could smell the ozone, like the aftermath of a thunderstorm. Miriam did.

She knew they had to stop that storm before it reached Hannah.

Could they stop that storm?

Petrovsky said he could. He said that he could counter any spell the woman cast, once he understood what she was trying to do. He also said that bullets would stop her because she couldn't control too many spells at once. Besides, her shield wasn't that powerful, not if a rock had gotten through it.

Watching the wind, now on the path that cut through the trees alongside the lake and onto the stone bridge over the brook that fed it, Miriam decided that their plan was ridiculous, like dousing a house fire with a Dixie cup of water.

But they had to do something. It was her job: stopping people who did bad things. She had to do her job.

****

As Hannah watched, the trees moved impossibly over by the lake, as if there were a storm tossing them around, and then those trees calmed, and the trees closer to the stone bridge began to move as if the storm had shifted there. Then those trees calmed and—

That just wasn't possible.

Hannah had to get closer to see what was going on, what caused that impossible windstorm. Despite hearing branches break and thud to the ground, she had to know. She started walking down a path past rose bushes pruned nearly to the bare and lifeless ground. Like spokes of a wheel radiating from the gazebo, so many paths, all lined by brutally cut stems.

To her left, suddenly, she saw Rose, Miriam, Miriam's partner from the Police Department, and that man who'd been in the parking lot yesterday afternoon, all standing and watching on the lawn. How had they gotten there so suddenly?

But then, to her right, just stepping off the bridge, amid trees moving in a storm of wind, stood a young woman. Her daughter. *Her daughter.*

The woman's long hair swirled in a nimbus of static electricity that snapped and cracked in the wind, and her scarf flew away. Her face was twisted by strong emotion, but it was her daughter, tall like her grandfather, with the Winkler curly hair.

"Sara?" Hannah said. Suddenly, she wanted to know who this woman was. Suddenly, she needed to say something, anything to explain what she'd done all those years ago, why she'd given the child away. "Sara. I'm—"

The woman began to shout, not in English. Latin maybe. She pointed straight at Hannah. And Hannah couldn't breathe. Her breath simply stopped.

She couldn't breathe. *Oh, God, she was going to die. She was going to die, and her daughter was killing her.*

****

Rose saw Hannah stagger and fall to her knees, hands clawing out at the young woman who screamed in Latin. Sara's hair writhed in the wind like Medusa's snakes and sent arcs of light into the dark, and she was screaming a spell.

"Oh, God!" she shrieked. "Hannah!"

Downie ran past her—he thought faster than she did, obviously. He had a gun in one hand, and he ran toward Hannah, yelling something she couldn't understand.

Petrovsky followed him, walking, not running, muttering in Hebrew again, too fast for her to even catch words.

The woman—*Sara, your cousin Sara*—flung a hand in Downie's direction, and he lifted into the air, flew toward the lake, arms and legs flailing.

No. If he dropped into the shallow water, he would be hurt. But what could she do?

Catch him, Rose. If you can move your sofa, you can catch him. Do it now.

She reached out her arms and decided to grab the man out of the air. She would not allow him to fall into the lake. She would not.

Nothing happened. Downie simply flew—No. He stopped moving toward the water, just hung there above it, nine or ten feet in the air.

Rose staggered, aware of a terrible weight as if she were pulling on him against a strong opposing force and realized that that was exactly what she was doing. She was pulling against Sara's intention to drop him into the lake.

She could not let go. She had to keep him out of the water. But someone needed to stop Sara *soon*.

✳✳✳✳

Stunned, Miriam stood watching. Hannah had fallen to her knees, now clutching at her throat. And Downie—*oh, God, Downie*—hung in the air a few feet above the cold water of the lake. Petrovsky had calmed the trees and the woman's hair didn't whip around her face anymore, but Hannah's hands still clutched her throat. And Rose's arms, stretched out toward Downie, had started to shake, who knew why.

Miriam knew she had to do something—shoot Sara maybe. Yes, she had her weapon in her pocket. She could shoot Sara.

First, she rubbed *Tannah* for good luck. "Help me, *Tannah*," she whispered. "Let me be strong." She'd never killed anyone before, but she was, by God, going to kill that woman, even if that woman was her cousin.

Except that, suddenly dizzy, she couldn't reach her pocket. She tried to call out, couldn't speak, couldn't stand. Agony washed through her, but she couldn't scream.

She roared. She knew she roared, and she knew she had left her human body and she flew with sparkling wings that moved with no need of her thinking. She simply knew how to fly, so she flew and swooped down on the spell-caster who'd caused all this trouble. The troublemaker stared open-mouthed at the flying beast, and the other spell-caster shouted something to make the woman fall down. Roaring again, Miriam snatched the troublemaker up in her talons and flew back to her human body on the ground. She knew she had to do that, and then she had to set the troublemaker on the ground. Carefully, she uncurled her talons and let the unconscious woman roll onto the cold, sleeping grass.

As soon as she let go, agony pushed through her again, but this time she could scream, and she did.

****

Rose nearly lost her distant hold on Downie when the animal roared just behind her. She couldn't look to see what was happening either, or she'd drop him. This business wasn't going well. Petrovsky had obviously underestimated the power of Sara's anger, and it was taking him too long—

No. Hannah was able to scramble away from Sara on all fours, and Sara began to cry as Petrovsky chanted, and then she fell to the ground, unconscious or so spent she couldn't spell anymore.

A dragon flew past her. A dragon! Silvery and roaring, a small dragon swooped down and snatched Sara up in its talons and came flying back toward her.

Holy shit! A dragon was flying toward her. Not a gigantic thing, but still, it was a dragon, silver, red-eyed, and—It released Sara from its talons, then hopped once nearer to Miriam, who lay on the ground, eyes open. It—she shimmered, wavered, Miriam screamed, and the dragon vanished, leaving Miriam alone there on the ground.

Tannah was the dragon. The dragon was *Tannah*. So was Miriam.

Cousin Miriam was a dragon. Cousin Miriam was a *dragon*, and she, Rose Winkler Sherman, had saved Sergeant Downs. *Talk about magic. Holy God in Heaven. Miriam is a dragon and I'm a whatever I am, and we are magic. Holy God.*

323

Chapter 42
Thursday

ownie! Rose had to lower him to the ground. She'd forgotten about him—how often do you see a dragon, after all?—but when she turned back, he stood on solid ground, pale and shaken but otherwise unhurt, and Petrovsky stood next to him, already biting into a chocolate bar.

Hannah sat on her heels, not too far from the two men, sobbing loudly.

For a moment, Rose heard nothing but Hannah's painful sobs.

Really. Someone should take care of Cousin Hannah.

But it wasn't going to be Rose. He legs had turned to a not very firm aspic, her arms likewise. Sitting seemed more and more attractive, although she didn't quite know how she could sit down without falling down.

Hands seized her by the upper arms. A voice murmured into her ear, "You must sit and eat this."

And there she was, chocolate bar in hand, sitting on the cold ground, not caring that the ground was cold.

"Eat," the voice urged. "I will come back with more."

Rose managed to get the chocolate into her mouth and recognized cheap milk chocolate. That heavy, almost cloying sweetness started melting before she could chew, and she didn't care that a hot flash would follow as sure as she was sitting there.

She ate the whole bar and two more. Slowly, she began to notice the cold ground under her. Standing now struck her as possible and probably a good idea, so she stood, not gracefully. *God.* She had to get onto her hands and knees, then on her knees, then one knee, then up.

Like an old lady, Rosie. Good Lord.

Taking a deep breath, she discovered she'd missed a lot, all of it important. Two Men in Black, E.S.P. agents, stood arguing with Dr. Petrovsky. Ironed Blue Jeans argued with Downie, who stood between him and Miriam. Miriam lay there, and a small box of Hershey's chocolate bars, plain, not almonds, lay on the ground next to her.

That box looked good. Rose wanted more of the chocolate, even as the hot flash started at her neck and swept upward. The heat felt good, actually, and more would be better.

****

Miriam stared up at the sky. The astonishing pain had left her too weak to move. No, she understood somehow, it wasn't the pain, which had come and gone fast, it was the transformation that left her feeling like jelly. *Not the point, so not the point.* The point was, she had turned into *Tannah*. She had become the dragon.

She had turned into a dragon. She, Miriam Winkler Fine, had turned into the holy fucking shit dragon.

No rational explanation existed for that fact. Even asking for a rational explanation was absurd. *She* was magic. *Holy fucking shit.*

The cold began to seep through her heavy coat, but it didn't matter. She laughed at the thought of complaining about the cold when she had turned into a dragon and back to human again. She laughed at the thought of trying to explain *Tannah.* She laughed at the absurdity of asking for an explanation. It was magic.

"Mir?" Rose's face loomed over her.

Miriam laughed.

Rose's hand extended, holding something out to her. A candy bar. "Dr. Petrovsky says you have to eat this. There's a whole box of these bars right here, and we're supposed to eat as many as we need to."

Rose helped her sit up, unwrapped the bar, and handed it to her. "You know you turned into a dragon?"

Miriam began to laugh again and almost choked on the sweet chocolate in her mouth.

Rose looked puzzled, and Miriam felt bad about confusing Rose. "Yes. I know." She wanted to laugh again, but Rose must have been the one keeping Downie from falling into the lake, and she was good Cousin Rose, so brave and so strong, so it was time to be kind. "I was both. I knew what Tannah was doing, and I knew Miriam was on the ground." She began to chuckle again. "A real out-of-body experience."

Rose chuckled, too, then stopped, probably because Downie's argument with the Men in Black had become loud.

And Miriam could see that Downie held his .38 in his hand, pointed at the ground, but it was in his hand. Petrovsky stood between the argument and Miriam and Rose, and he watched intently as if he might need to cast a spell to keep them safe.

She could also see Sara Bloom lying very still and pale on the ground to everyone's right. She looked a little like Maddy, actually. Miriam suddenly felt sorry for the woman. The family inheritances had betrayed her.

Speaking of family, "Where's Hannah?" she asked Rose softly, under the noise of the argument.

Rose pointed to Hannah, still on the other side of the lawn, sitting on her heels and weeping. As Miriam nodded, David Levine walked out of the trees and crouched next to his wife.

****

"Hannah?"

Hannah recognized David's voice and wailed. "No, no, no."

"Hannah, it's all right. I'm here. Come away." He spoke softly.

"No," she sobbed. "You don't know. I—"

David put an arm around her shoulders. "I do know, Han. I've known all along. Not about your daughter, not until today, but about the telekinesis. I should have told you, but you didn't want—"

Stunned, Hannah stifled the sobs and straightened up. "What?"

"I've known about the telekinesis. I've known about the family...abilities, and—"

327

"No!" Hannah shrugged his arm away. "How could you know? I didn't know. *We* didn't know. How—"

"Not here, Han. Let me take you home, and we can talk. Come on."

"No. No." Hannah sniffed and got herself onto her feet, ignoring his outstretched hand. "Get away from me. Get away from me, you bastard. You bastard. You let me think—and I— Just get away."

"You're in no state to drive, Hannah, please."

Hannah just stumbled away from her husband onto the path leading away from the lawn. Her husband had betrayed her, her daughter had tried to kill her—She needed to go home and curl up in bed. That's what she was going to do. She would go home and go to bed, and no one could accuse her of anything.

"Hannah," David called behind her. "Please."

Hannah kept moving.

****

Rose frowned as Hannah disappeared, almost reeling, into the trees on the other side of the lawn, David trailing after her. "Should we do something?" She could lift David up and drop him, but that wouldn't actually help anything. It might soothe her urge to do *something*, but saving her energy for what she actually had to do would be better.

"No," Miriam said and pointed again, this time back to the Men in Black.

Two of them had lifted Sara Berman onto a stretcher. They strapped her down and walked her to the parking lot near the greenhouse, where an ambulance was now parked. Ironed Blue

Jeans followed them, talking on his cell phone to someone. Downie and Petrovsky stood side by side watching them go. Rose didn't see Downie's gun anymore.

"We're just letting them take her?" Rose asked.

"They showed me a federal warrant." Downie shrugged. "I'm not surprised."

"But she's family, and we—"

"The warrant trumps family, Rose," Miriam said. Her voice trembled as she spoke.

"But what will happen to her?" Rose's anger had dissolved in relief that the threat to her children, however remote, was gone. Now she saw her cousin, her first cousin once removed like Maddie, being tucked into the back of an unmarked ambulance to be taken God knew where for God knew what purpose. "Where are they taking her?"

Lips compressed, Petrovsky shook his head. "We do not know. I am sorry, Rosa."

Rose could only sigh. "It isn't right." That woman was a murderer, but she had a mother who raised her and loved her. It wasn't right to just let her disappear. "It isn't right."

"No, it is not, and Sergeant Downs says we can do nothing for now, but only for now." Petrovsky agreed. "Also, let us consider. You performed wonderfully. You saved Sergeant Downs. And you, Detective Fine." He grinned suddenly. "Who could have imagined? I did not believe it possible, but you are a dragon! It is magnificent! Splendid!"

As she reached for another chocolate bar, Miriam shut her eyes. Rose thought she saw tears under Miriam's lashes.

Miriam was badly shaken, Rose decided. Despite her laughter at the wonder of being a dragon, Miriam was going to need time.

"We will sit and talk about all of this," Petrovsky said. "But you must eat and rest first."

"And we have to figure out how to report all of this," Downie said. "Or maybe not. I don't know."

There was a lot to figure out, Rose could only agree. Not just whether to tell the Hartford Police Department how the three murders had been committed and how the case had been resolved. Besides the problem of what E.S.P. wanted with poor Sara, and David Levine, who might well turn out to be the viper at their bosom, so to speak, the kids, especially the little ones, needed protecting from E.S.P. And there was the question of Cal Jones, who had disappeared. Why had she gone, and where? And there was the whole question of E.S.P. What could they do about a federal agency that seemed to know more about them than they knew themselves?

Downie came over and squatted in front of Miriam. "Can you stand up, do you think?" He offered her a hand.

Miriam took it, and Rose smiled. Good for Miriam. Not just a dragon, but a woman who was loved. That was a good thing, maybe better than the dragon in the long run.

Rose stood up with another candy bar in her hand. "Next time, we need to bring better chocolate."

"Better chocolate does not have so much sugar, which is what we need to hold us until we eat," Petrovsky said. "Using gifts takes great energy, many, many calories of energy."

"Oh, food. I could definitely eat, even after all this chocolate. Come to my house, and we'll cook—"

"I will cook," Petrovsky announced.

"You cook?" Rose smiled at him. Completely inappropriate, but she had to smile.

"Oh, yes. I am a very good cook. You will taste." He smiled.

That smile was delicious.

But it was a distraction. E.S.P. was taking people now. Sara Berman was family, and E.S.P. was taking her away.

And Miriam suddenly was crying against Downie's chest. Miriam never cried, *never*. But there she stood, Downie's arms around her, sobbing.

The world had turned upside down.

****

The world no longer made sense. No matter how hard she tried, Miriam could not find anything that made sense. How could anything make sense if she turned into an actual fucking dragon? Just by saying a few words. And just by chanting a few words, Mikhail Petrovsky could make people or things unseeable. And Rose had saved Downie by holding him in the air—

What made it worse was, a part of her loved being the dragon, strong and clawed—she hadn't needed to breathe fire, but she thought maybe she could. And then there was the flying. The flying was beyond words, beyond dreams. Flying was true freedom—

But she became a dragon, a fucking dragon, beyond explanation, beyond any rational thing anyone could think to say.

Downie's arms imitated safety, but it was an imitation.

"I'm sorry, Mir, but the sun is coming up," Downie murmured under the noise of her sobs. "We have to go."

He was right, she knew, but she couldn't go home to the condo. She would lie down on the bed and never move again.

Downie knew. "Come home with me, Mir. Let me be there for you."

She could only nod against his chest.

Chapter 43
Sunday Evening

This wasn't how she meant her life to turn out. Hannah Winkler Fried Levine was supposed to be happily married, happily teaching, happily cousining, if that was a word. Instead--Oh God, instead.

She'd told David to leave. He'd lied—the irony of it: He'd lied to the liar.

"To protect you, Hannah," he'd said. "I thought I could protect you from E.S.P. if I didn't tell you what I knew. If they thought you didn't use your ability, then they'd leave you alone."

At that point, she'd thrown his gym bag at him and told him she wouldn't listen anymore.

"If you need anything, call," he said as he left.

Hannah didn't know where he'd gone or where he was staying, and she didn't want to care. She didn't.

She cared about Miriam and Rose, too. But she'd seen Miriam's contempt and Rose's anger in the park.

She'd seen her daughter, too, and her fury. Because her daughter had believed the lies Hannah told too many years ago and forgotten, stories she never thought anyone would believe, never mind remember. Her daughter had tried to kill her with magic.

Rose and Miriam had stopped the magic using magic—a lot of magic. Miriam turned into a dragon! But they'd let those men take her daughter away, and they'd ignored her, walked away, leaving her sobbing alone.

So. Not happily married and not happily cousining. That left teaching, which would have to do. She liked teaching, she was good at teaching, and she wanted to teach.

She would teach. Not the life she expected, but she could live with it.

Hannah didn't laugh at her little joke.

****

This was not the life she wanted. Well, that wasn't quite true. Miriam wanted Downie, the best not-really-surprise she'd had since Isaac left and took their son with him. She'd always known Downie as reliable and steady and kind. They'd been partners for more than 20 years, after all.

Now he took care of her, had taken care of her since the park, feeding her, keeping her warm, holding her when she cried. He didn't tell her what to feel or how to behave. He simply took care of her.

But Miriam Winkler Fine didn't need someone to take care of her. She didn't cry, she didn't curl up and refuse to handle whatever was going on. She managed no matter what was going on. She always had—

Not quite true, she knew in those moments when she wasn't panicking. She'd relied on Downie as her partner, and she still did when they worked investigations. They'd relied on each other for ideas and protection, and they'd worked well together. Before they retired, their solve rate was consistently one of the highest in Robbery-Homicide, and now they cleared cold cases almost as well.

On the Downs-Fine team, Fine carried her weight.

But the dragon—that brilliant, terrifying dragon. She could fly, she could soar on beautiful wings, all the dreams of freedom come true.

It was magic.

Magic. The thing that terrified her because it meant the rational wall she'd built against her father's insistence on God's rules was a lie. God, the performer of magic miracles, did exist, and Miriam Fine, a mere woman fit only to make babies and serve her husband, didn't matter.

The rational structure she'd built for herself was gone, and she had to find a way to live with the new truth.

So she sat at Downie's kitchen table with a mug of tea and watched him stack dishes in the dishwasher. For a big man, he moved gracefully. He always had. When he finished, he joined her at the table with his own mug of tea and smiled.

"Are we going to work tomorrow?"

The question startled her. "Why wouldn't we?"

He tilted his head. "You've been…in rough shape these last couple of days, Mir."

Barely functional is what he had to mean. She knew. "That has to stop. I have to work. It's the only thing that'll keep me sane." Did she see hurt flash across his face? "I can't keep playing baby."

"Is that what you're doing?"

"Isn't it?"

"Am I allowed to say what I think?"

"Are you seriously asking me that question?"

"I don't think you'll like what I have to say."

Miriam had never been afraid of Downie's honesty. Till now. But she wanted his calm, steady presence. She might even be in love with him, and the only way to keep him in her life was to talk honestly.

She took a deep breath over the tea before she sipped and swallowed. "Tell me anyway."

He nodded. "You absolutely cannot explain that dragon except by absolutely irrational means."

"Magic. You mean magic." She heard the anger in her voice and winced.

His nod was bigger this time. "Okay, yeah. Magic. And you're worried that it means Izzy and your father are right about the universe."

So far, he hadn't said anything she hadn't figured out for herself. "I'm not worried about it. I'm terrified."

"Okay. But I don't think your equation, that magic equals God, is right. Or rather, we don't have enough data about either side of the equation. We just don't know enough about how magic works or why, and Misha Petrovsky, who was trained as a child in spell-casting by his aunt and her circle, says he's seen no demonstrations of the existence of God." He sipped tea and squinted at her through the steam. "In other words, you're theorizing too far ahead of your data."

That was a rational argument about the irrational. But she understood the argument. And she had to agree: She didn't have enough data to draw the conclusions she'd drawn. "You make sense. Okay." Miriam drew a long, shuddering breath and accepted the lifeline Downie had just handed her. "Okay. I'll defer judgment until I have more data."

He nodded firmly. "Good. We'll work on finding data for you. I do have another question for you."

"Okay."

"Don't go back to the condo. Stay here."

She didn't stop to think. "Okay. I want to."

He reached for her hand. "Thank you, Mir."

Miriam finally found a smile.

****

Life had surprised Rose. *No. Rephrase that, kiddo. Life has surprised you again, this time happily. There is a lovely man cooking for you in your kitchen, and you are going to take him to bed—again—after supper. So good.*

The first surprise in the latest bunch of surprises, the precognition that started with the hot flashes, made her think she was losing her mind. Everybody knows there's no such thing as precognition, telekinesis, clairvoyance, or ghosts, for that matter. No such thing.

Except there are such things, including ghosts. *Talk about surprises.* The proof was Nana Pearl, who had died almost 40 years ago, standing in the kitchen, the very same kitchen in which Misha currently crushed a garlic clove to add to his stew. Nana Pearl had warned Rose about Hannah's lies and vanished when the phone rang. Very woo-woo, also very emotional because Nana represented safety when Rose was a child. And she'd died too young.

That time, Rose thought she might be hallucinating. Except she smelled Nana's lavender sachets as certainly as she smelled Misha's stew. And she felt safe.

She wasn't hallucinating then or now.

Misha held the promise of good things in her life. He'd already done such good things. He'd brought her home and made sure she ate enough and had what she needed and was all right.

She didn't know whether she was all right or ever would be. The world was definitely not the way she'd thought it was, and it would never be "normal" again. But then, she'd never had a normal life.

Misha set a mug of tea in front of her, along with two slices of lemon on a plate. "I estimate one half hour until the *zharkoe* is ready. You are all right to wait?"

"Thanks. It smells delicious."

He grinned. "It is good to cook for someone who appreciates the food.

She could only agree and change the subject. "I'm going to work tomorrow."

"I was expecting so. You are all right."

Rose snorted. "All right isn't in it, but we did well, didn't we? And we're doing well, you and I, I mean." *So bold, kiddo, but it's good to know.*

"You and I do very well, I hope." He took her hand in his. "I must attend meetings tomorrow and Tuesday, but if you permit, I will return Tuesday evening.

She considered dancing around the kitchen. Instead, she squeezed Misha's hand. "I permit."

He nodded. "Together we are good. And you and your cousin are wonders, truly heroes.

Chuckling, Rose covered his hand with her free hand. "We're all Heroes of the middle ages.."

Misha laughed. "I like this. Heroes of the middle ages. Together."

Her heart threatened to pound out of her chest with joy. "Heroes of the middle ages together."

Chapter 44
Saturday, Two Weeks Later

The vampire sat alone at his preferred table in Song Hays, back to the wall, waiting for his bowl of egg drop soup, observing the various humans who had also chosen to spend their Saturday evening eating Chinese food in downtown Hartford. He had developed, over his centuries, a tolerance for the aroma of his natural prey, a forbearance, so he could indulge his enjoyment of the cuisine.

He enjoyed his surroundings as well. The dimly lit room, the crimson flocked wallpaper, the paintings of birds in heavy gilt frames, the small bouquets of spring flowers on each table, all pleased him, a refreshing change from his usual austerity.

The corner table where he sat, close to the kitchen, farthest from the customer entrance on Asylum Street, allowed him to smell everything in the kitchen, as well. The odors of raw beef and pork, the earthy vegetables, and the peanut oil helped him to ignore the humans.

What could not be ignored were the conversations all around him. His vampire ears heard everything, every breath, every clink of silverware against dishes, every sip of water, every rush of tea from pot into cup, everything. He could ignore all of that because he focused on the talking, so much talking.

At the table just up a few feet from him, two men in business suits read some sort of papers, eating almost absent-mindedly.

Lawyers, he suspected, working on a contract or some sort of filing. He'd seen Phillipe and Jean read papers and eat that way when they had an imminent deadline for a court filing.

The couple at the table next to the probable lawyers discussed which movie to see. She absolutely did *not* want to see *Fast Five*. He absolutely wanted to see it. Peter sniffed and knew she ate the vegetarian special, the Buddha's Delight, while her date ate dandan noodles. Either opposites attracted, or that couple would not last long.

The waiter bustled to his table then and set down the bowl of soup and a soup spoon. Peter nodded his thanks, picked up the spoon, and took a small amount of egg and broth into his mouth. He appreciated the heat, the salt and garlic, the texture of the egg. It made a good change from almost raw beef and blood, and for a few spoonfuls, he concentrated on his meal rather than the voices.

He gave in to the temptation to listen—he admitted to being tempted by all the lives around him, the talk about an elderly parent possibly in need of assistance, a child who wanted ballet lessons despite her two left feet, a bill that had surprised with its total. Those would not have been his problems. He would have faced problems, of course: his sons perhaps not wanting to learn to fish, his father growing too old to fish with him, trouble with the boat or the sails, weather, illnesses, all the appurtenances of an eleventh-century life, but it would have been a life, a genuine life with Junia beside him and death at the end.

Humans lusted after immortality, and he, quite probably immortal, envied humans their short lives.

But he maundered foolishly and to no point. He ought to pay attention to the food in front of him, which was quite good, after all. His beef and broccoli would be delivered soon, pork fried rice instead of white, and egg roll on a separate plate so it would not sit in the sauce and become soggy. All the waiters here knew.

So did the *curandera*, who sat up near the door with a man Peter did not know. The woman was an earth-caster, a hedge-witch—well, that was his prejudice speaking, that earth-casters are weak, not worth attention. He did not know how weak or strong her powers were, only that she did have real magic. She was no counterfeit preying on the fearful.

He also knew that she believed much of the lore surrounding Magicals, including that vampires like him were demon-ridden dead men. He smiled, remembering the first and only time he had walked into her *botanica* on Park Street. Where she obtained the liter bottle of holy water she emptied over him he had no idea, but he did understand her disappointment and confusion when he did not scream in agony or melt away.

There she sat, elegant as always, speaking intently in Spanish. Peter had given up that language centuries ago, using what he supposed would now be called proto-Ladino instead. He remembered some Spanish, but her rapid speech, her dinner companion's easy and quick responses, moved too fast for him.

His meal arrived as he considered relearning Spanish, and Peter decided the textures and tastes deserved all his attention. The *curandera* and her escort did not require anything from him. Nor did he require anything from her. She believed what she believed, and she could go her own way. He did perfectly well without her.

The crisp wrapper of the egg roll and the hot vegetable pieces it contained, however, were a wonderful departure from his usual diet. The crunchy broccoli, the sauce, even the rice all offered different textures and tastes, providing a sensual delight.

Inevitably, conversations broke into his concentration. The *Fast Five* argument had been replaced by a discussion of the Harry Potter books versus the movies. And a mother of a child who had been admitted to a private kindergarten, a quite good one as far as Peter knew, was concerned that it was the wrong school.

What made it the wrong school? Children who attended Avery, another private kindergarten in the area, were admitted to better elementary schools and, of course, better high schools. And one had to consider…

Peter frowned over a broccoli floret. He wondered whether the child in question—actually not in question, the child evidently being of no consideration except as the attendee of whichever school the woman chose—might not possess the particular academic bent that Mother expected. Kindergarten had never been part of his life, but he did know that Martin's pups, like humans, all had different abilities in their human camouflage. Choosing their paths based on what Martin decided for them seemed…short-sighted at best.

Not his business. What was his business was the last of the egg roll, so crispy and tangy from the onion—

Peter heard someone, a woman, speak in a deliberate hushed voice. "I'm sure I saw one of those fancy SUVs this morning."

Another woman responded in a strained whisper. "Fancy SU—you mean those Lincoln Navigators? The Men in Black? Are you sure?"

Peter shut out everything else as he waited for the first woman to answer. "I couldn't see who was in the car, but they slowed down when they passed the driveway."

"Damn it, Rose, you should have called me."

Men in Black. An apt description of the federal agents who used those Lincoln Navigators. The wolves had spotted neither those men nor their vehicles for two weeks when they inspected the pack boundaries, not since the episode of the rogues. That was why Peter had felt free to come into Hartford to indulge his enjoyment of Chinese food.

Peter could not be sure, of course, that the women were talking about the same men in the same vehicles. He thought it unlikely, however, that two different yet identical groups of men and SUVs would have infested the area. And the name Men in Black *was* an apt one for those *salauds* in their SUVs, who did not attempt to blend in at all, as if such attempts were beneath them..

The major question was, who were those women who had attracted the attention of the federal people? Why had they attracted the attention of the federal people? Those people, those Men in Black, had followed the rogue wolves because they were magicals. Were those two women magicals he did not know?

Food forgotten, he strained to hear more, but the women now debated whether Rose, whoever she was, should have called for help.

"You were at work," Rose said.

"I can always leave if you need help, especially with the...stuff we don't talk about in public."

"That's ridiculous. I'm a grown woman, and I'm perfectly capable of taking care of myself."

And so on. Suggestive, but he could not simply go to their table, introduce himself, and ask for information. "I am a vampire and you are..?" seemed unlikely to lead to a productive conversation.

His meal lay cooling, not forgotten but no longer of interest. Those two women, strangers to him, suggested that the rogue wolves were not the only reason those federal people had come to Hartford. Not definite, but the possibility existed.

The possibility also existed that there were more magicals in Hartford than the *phyle,* along with the three unaffiliated vampires, two vodousiantes, and the *curandera.* Perhaps Peter the Vampire did not know everything that went on in Hartford.

Interesting. Also concerning. He had to speak with Martin face to face.

Peter caught his waiter's attention, took care of the bill with the usual generous tip, slipped into his leather jacket, and stood. Now he could see the two women laughing over their fortunes.

Two curly-haired women in early middle age, he thought, attractive, trim, and not human. He knew that because he breathed deeply as he passed their table. Not human, but because of all the competing odors, he could not determine what they were. A wolf would have known, of course, despite the conditions, but vampires do not hunt by scent.

He therefore had to content himself with the knowledge that there were more magicals in Hartford. He did not know how he would identify them, but he now knew they existed. They hid themselves as well as he hid himself, but they existed. If they existed, they could be found. The wolves and their noses would find them.

As he reached the sidewalk, Peter smiled to himself and decided to go to Huntington's Bookstore two doors up from Song Hays. A dessert of sorts. The remote possibility of those federal people could wait an hour.

Before he reached the bookshop, the two women exited the restaurant behind him, still laughing together. Clearly, they were good friends.

Just as clearly, two men, crewcut hair, black suits and ties, white shirts, sunglasses though it was after sunset, walked slowly along the sidewalk across the street. When Peter glanced back, he saw that the two women had stopped to stare at those men across the street. And a Lincoln Navigator drove slowly up Asylum, so slowly it impeded traffic on the narrow one-way street.

"Oh, my God," Rosie said.

"Fuck," the other woman whispered urgently. "Back into the restaurant now, Rosie. They have a back door. *Now.*"

Peter was too far away from the restaurant to follow them, to take advantage of the rear door, which he knew well. Besides, he wanted to observe those two men. But they swung their heads toward him as he watched, so he just kept walking, hoping his casual gait convinced the *salauds* there was nothing worth their attention.

When he reached the alley on the other side of the bookstore, he turned in and walked several steps. He went invisible and rose up out of the reach of even the tallest human. There he waited, just to see whether anyone would follow.

Of course, one of the men trotted into the alley, carrying a stun gun. Why a stun gun? Did the *salaud* know bullets would not kill a vampire? Did he even know Peter was a vampire? Perhaps he worried that firing a regular gun in the city would bring unwanted attention. Such things did make noise, even with a silencer.

After a moment, Peter realized the *salaud* could not know anything about him. The human had come into the alley because he saw another man go into the alley. Had Peter simply kept walking, the Men in Black would quite possibly have ignored him as just another person out walking on a cool but pleasant late March evening. Peter had done something unexpected, and so he had been followed.

Peter had behaved foolishly. He had to hope there would be no consequences.

The human who had walked into the alley stopped and looked around before he swore loudly and hid the stun gun under his suit jacket. He did not look up.

Not that he would have seen Peter, but he might have caught the faint creak of the leather jacket as Peter breathed. However, this human, like nearly every human Peter had observed over centuries of watching and hunting, never looked up. Humans simply do not look up. How many excellent drinks had Peter enjoyed because humans do not look up?

Peter considered the blood on offer right there below him, but he knew that drinking that particular human would be a mistake. The other Men in Black—he did like the name—would come looking for the fool rather quickly. Besides, Peter had to return to the compound. He had to speak with Martin, then make sure everyone in the *phyle* and the rest of the magicals stayed alert to the possible danger and kept their magic out of sight.

Then he would have time to consider those two women. Already aware of the Men in Black, they might be allies in the drive to stay hidden.

Peter had no idea how to find them. His investigative skills ran to financial dealings. He knew good management from bad, could read a spreadsheet the way an English major read a novel, understood how to set up a blind trust, and knew at least two ways to break an irrevocable trust without the consent of all the beneficiaries—none of those skills would help him find Rosie and her friend. He had no idea how to proceed. But someone would know what to do.

So he alit in the alley well away from the street and walked to the narrow passageway that ran behind all the buildings along this long block of Asylum Street and that would take him quite near the parking lot where he'd left the car. The dark didn't bother him; vampires hunt in the dark, after all. In fact, he found the dark familiar and comforting. No one could see him.

Though he saw no fancy SUVs or Men in Black once he reached the parking lot, he felt oddly vulnerable becoming visible. He had to, in order to pay the attendant and drive the car, but he knew those men had seen him, however briefly.

He had not felt vulnerable in a very long time, nor did he care for that feeling. He knew that he would do whatever was necessary to end that feeling and protect himself, the *phyle*, and the unknown Magicals as well. *Whatever* was necessary. No mistake. *Whatever he had to do.*